Your Alluring Love
(The Bennett Family, Book 6)

LAYLA HAGEN

Dear Reader,

If you want to receive news about my upcoming books and sales, you can sign up for my newsletter HERE: http://laylahagen.com/mailing-list-sign-up/

Cover: RBA Designs
Cover Photography: Sara Eirew Photographer

Chapter One

Nate

"This family is larger every time I visit." Glancing around the room, I can barely believe my eyes. With nine siblings, the Bennett clan was always large, but now that half of them are engaged, or married with kids, the sheer number of people milling around this living room tonight is overwhelming.

"Never a dull moment with us," Sebastian says.

"Sorry I missed your wedding." Guilt gnaws at me because I missed most events in the Bennett family in the last few years. I first met Sebastian, the oldest of the Bennett siblings, when I was in high school, and we quickly became best friends. For years, I was a regular in the Bennett household; then my job as a TV executive producer required me to constantly travel. "Glad I could catch up with all of you before heading out again."

"Pity you're in town for only three weeks. We should—" Sebastian clasps my shoulder but stops midsentence, as his father asks for everyone's attention for a few moments. He gives a short speech, praising his wife of forty years. Her birthday is the reason for the gathering at their house this evening. I smile, imagining her reaction when she opens my present later. I wanted to do something special for her because I owe the Bennetts so much. My parents separated when I was thirteen, and they both started new families afterward. I didn't fit in with either. But the Bennetts treated me like I belonged in their family.

After the speech, Sebastian's wife, Ava, catches his eye from across the room, motioning to their ten-month-old son, Will, in her arms.

"I'll talk to you later," Sebastian says, heading toward his wife.

I walk to the makeshift bar area, planning to get myself a drink and then chat with each of the Bennetts. I've only spoken to a few of them since I arrived, but I want to check in with everyone. I think about them as my siblings… well, except for one. Alice. She's Sebastian's younger sister, and for the first few years, I saw her as one as well. An annoying, outspoken spitfire of a sister. But then she turned into this amazing woman, and I never could look at her like a sister again.

Speaking of her, Alice is at the bar as I approach it, pouring herself a drink.

"The prodigal son returns," she exclaims when she notices me, a smile lighting up her features. I stop right next to her. Compared to my six-foot-two, Alice is tiny. Her light brown hair is up in a bun, the curve of her slender neck looking more appealing than it should.

"In the flesh."

"What do you want to drink?"

"Bourbon on the rocks."

"Right away."

"I'll pour it myself."

She holds up a hand to stop me. "No, no. I need to practice my bartending skills."

"Why? I thought Blake was the one in the bar business," I say, referring to one of her younger brothers. Last I knew, she was in the restaurant business.

"Blake and I are opening a location together. Large bar area in the front, a restaurant in the back. I want to get my bartending skills up to par. You never know when they'll come in handy."

"You also want to make sure you can do your bartender's job better than he does, don't you?"

"Nate Becker! Don't you dare mock my perfectionist tendencies, or you'll pay for it."

Ah, how I missed Alice's fiery nature. She keeps me on my toes, and I never know what will come out of her mouth next.

"I apologize deeply."

She cocks a brow at my over-the-top apologetic tone. "Are you going to do a curtsy too?"

"If required, yes. If there's one person I believe could murder me and make it look like an accident, it's you."

"Not sure if I should be proud or offended." She adds a few ice cubes in a glass, pouring bourbon over them.

"Definitely proud. Now, tell me more about what you and Blake are up to." I drop in one of the chairs next to the bar and Alice sits next to me, rattling on about her plans. Color me impressed at how well she's doing. But then again, I always admired her. Though Sebastian and Logan are the founders of one of the biggest companies in the high-end jewelry market, Alice wanted to strike out on her own.

"You are amazing. I can't believe I missed so much," I say after she finishes.

"Then stick around. Are you here to stay this time?"

I shake my head, sipping my bourbon. "Moving to London in three weeks."

She casts her eyes toward her glass. "Moving?"

"Yeah. I got the job of executive producer for *The 300*."

The 300 is an internationally successful, long-running English show, and it's taken me years of hard work to finally have my shot at being at the helm.

"Congratulations."

I elbow her playfully. "Might want to sound a little more enthusiastic."

"I *am* happy for you. I know how much you love the show. But we're going to see even less of you from now on, huh? I always admired people who could just move wherever they found a job they loved. Won't you feel lonely? But then again, I suppose you're used to it, what with all your traveling."

Her question is legitimate, and I've asked myself the same thing. The truth is, all these years while I was traveling I imagined that whenever I would settle down, it would be in San Francisco. But then the opportunity of a lifetime came up, and I won't throw it away just because I have to start a new life overseas. But hell, I would have loved for this loud and boisterous clan to be a bigger part of my life again, like they used to.

"You can visit often," I assure her.

"I'd love to. Those Brits and their accents are so sexy."

I grip my glass tighter, the thought of Alice and another man not sitting well with me, which is ridiculous. She and I always had a dangerous dynamic, always danced a little too close to the flirting line, but she's not mine. *I have no claim on her.* I repeat the mantra in my mind a few times as Alice tugs at her lower lip with her teeth.

"You can stay with me when you visit."

"Thanks. I don't like hotels much. Always prefer a friend's couch over it."

I lean slightly toward her, my eyes still on her lower lip.

"You can even have my bed."

Alice exhales sharply, right before she bursts out laughing.

"That's not what I meant. I was saying you could have my bed, and I'd sleep on the couch."

"Such a gentleman."

"How else can I keep up with those sophisticated Brits?"

It takes her a few seconds to calm down, and then she flashes me a megawatt grin. "I was going to mock you for the worst pickup line in history. You sure you didn't mean it?"

Her cheeks are red and the flush is spreading down her beautiful neck, which tells me I'm not the only one who entertained thoughts of the two of us crossing the line of friendship, heading straight to full-blown flirting. The things I'd do to this woman between the sheets. Damn, I need to keep my head straight.

Alice deserves someone to take care of her, make sure she's always happy. All things I can't even attempt to give her, considering my imminent departure.

"I'd never dare to," I tease. "Your brothers would kick my ass."

She clutches her heart theatrically. "I'm wounded. After telling me you think me capable of the perfect murder, you think I need my brothers to do the ass kicking for me?"

Laughing, I shake my head. I always laugh way more when Alice is around. She raises her glass to her mouth, and on an impulse, I cuff her wrist midair, rubbing my thumb in little circles. I notice with satisfaction as goose bumps form on the skin of her arms.

"I missed your smart mouth, Alice."

She parts her lips, and I'd bet anything that she's about to serve me a sassy reply, but Blake joins us before she can utter a single word.

***

Alice

Nate lets go of my wrist the moment Blake pulls up a chair in front of us. My skin is still tingling where he touched me. This man is too potent, I swear. It doesn't help that I've had a crush on him for years. With dark hair, piercing green eyes, and a lean but muscle-laced body, he's pure temptation. Always has been, but like fine wine, Nathan Becker gets more irresistible as time goes by.

"Alice, don't monopolize Nate," Blake says. "He's a hard man to get a hold of."

"She was just telling me you're opening a new location together."

My brother talks about our plans eagerly, and hearing him talk with so much passion makes me smile. Over the years, I've opened two restaurants, but this third one is the first I will co-own, and I can't wait to work side by side with my brother. It'll be great running the business with someone I trust.

"Would you two like the location to be featured on the *Delicious Dining* show?" Nate asks.

"I'd give both my nuts for it," Blake answers.

"Fantastic visual, brother." Turning to Nate, I add, "It would be an extraordinary promotional opportunity. But they mostly feature celebrity restaurants or those with Michelin stars."

"It's not my area, but I can pitch it to the network. You have a good shot. We'll have to get together a few times to discuss some details, but it's doable in the three weeks I'm here."

"Thank you. I really appreciate it," I reply. My heart sinks at the reminder that he'll leave so soon. I've been carrying a torch for the man forever. In the beginning, he was just my older brother's friend, but over the years, he became my friend too. I have no idea when the friendship turned into something different, but here we are.

Damn, I'm buzzing with awareness just from being near him. It doesn't help that he's glancing up and down my neck and breasts every few minutes. I bet he believes he's really discreet about it too. I'm surprised Blake hasn't picked up on it yet, but then again, he is oblivious to these things. My oldest brothers are the ones who always flex their protective muscles.

"How about Alice and I meet you at Blue Moon, the new location, next week?" Blake suggests. "It's not open for business yet, but you can look around and we can discuss this in more detail."

"Great idea," Nate replies. The three of us chitchat for a few more minutes. Then Dad comes over, clearly wanting to talk to Nate, and Blake and I leave them to it.

I head to the opposite part of the room, where my sister Pippa is watching her twin daughters, Mia and Elena, building what looks like a tower from fist-sized Legos. The girls turned two last month, and I love them to bits. Just as I arrive, they start fussing, clearly losing interest in the Legos. Pippa scoops up Elena, and I scoop up Mia. She instantly calms once she's in my arms and cuddles against my chest. I kiss her hair, inhaling the scent of her sweet shampoo.

"Spill it," Pippa says, as we walk to the nearest couch with the girls in our arms.

"Spill what?" I ask with fake innocence. My sister is the family's matchmaker, and she's very good at it. She also knows about my crush on Nate, because well… she knows everything.

She flashes me a wicked smile.

"A certain family *friend* here couldn't keep his eyes off you."

"He's also moving to London in three weeks."

My sister's hand freezes in the act of rearranging her daughter's headband. Her smile drops. "Moving? As in permanently?"

"Yep. He's going to help Blake and me land a spot on his network's *Delicious Dining* show while he's in town, but I'd rather not talk about any of this tonight."

To my astonishment, Pippa doesn't insist. As Mia throws her little arms around my neck, clearly looking to cuddle, I happily oblige her, and I'm rewarded with sweet giggles. A few strands of hair fall from my bun. I love family gatherings, but lately, being surrounded by so many happy couples makes me wonder if there's a lottery out there. Some people find their half, some don't. With a history of dating running longer than a decade, I also wonder if there is something fundamentally wrong with me, something that makes me unlovable. The thought that I might never have a man I can shower with love, someone to share my life with, carves a hollow in my chest

Mia giggles loudly, grabbing one loose strand in her tiny fist.

"You love me, don't you?" I ask, rubbing my nose against hers. In response, she tugs at my hair, giggling louder. I decide it means 'I love you, Aunt Alice.' But then again, she loves anyone who spoils her.

"I need to be introduced to the younger Bennett generation." Nate's voice startles me. I was so wrapped up in my niece's antics I didn't see him approach. "Sebastian's son didn't seem too impressed with me. I'm hoping to have more success with the ladies here."

"Of course! So good to see you again, Nate," Pippa says. She rises from the couch, kissing his cheeks while holding her daughter on her hip.

"How can you tell them apart?" Nate asks with a frown, looking at the two girls. I chuckle because Pippa is always asked that since the girls are identical twins and they both have white dresses tonight.

"I usually dress them differently, but tonight, they only have different headbands. This is Elena. Alice is holding Mia."

Upon hearing her name, Mia unwraps her arms from around my neck and lifts them in Nate's direction. The little traitor.

"Can I?" he asks Pippa, motioning to Mia.

"Go ahead."

Nate takes Mia from me with grace and *holy hot bejeezus.*

Over the years, I've seen Nate in various poses that screamed sexy. Playing soccer—there's something incredibly hot about seeing a man score. Doing sit-ups in our backyard without a shirt—it was the first time I daydreamed about tracing those abs of his with my finger, possibly my mouth.

But seeing Nate with a baby in his arms speaks to me on a primal level. Especially when he kisses her tiny head, all loving and protective. I blame being thirty-one for this. My hormones are all over the place. When he reaches to my shoulder to grab the headband that slid off Mia's head, his fingers linger a little too long at the base of my neck, as if he can't help touching me. All my senses go into hyperalert, energy zipping through my veins. When he finally pulls his hand back, the spot he touched feels cold. Out of the corner of my eye, I see Pippa grinning as she looks between us.

"By the way, Blake suggested we could meet at Blue Moon tomorrow, talk some more about getting you on *Delicious Dining*. Do you have time?"

"Sounds good to me. Ten o'clock?"

"Perfect."

Mia starts fussing, reaching out for me again. Nate kisses the top of her head before lowering her in my arms.

"Where's your mom? I still have to chat with her. I've only wished her a happy birthday since I arrived." He surveys the room. "Ah, there she is." With a wink, he takes off.

Clutching the toddler in my arms, I sigh, looking after Nate.

"Don't forget to breathe when you're around him," Pippa says with a grin.

Damn it, I need to gather my wits about me. I'm being silly. This man will never be mine. It's time to pour a bucket of ice water over that torch I've been carrying.

Easier said than done… especially since I'll be seeing him tomorrow.

Chapter Two

Alice

The next morning I wake up too late, and then I'm in a frenzy, trying to get ready in time and choosing an outfit that is not too optimistic for early June. I love this time of year. The days are long and rain is rare, though the pesky fog takes hold of the coast too often for my taste, especially in the morning. Still, a contagious energy fills the entire city. Tourists pour in, festivals abound. I slip into a bright yellow dress, pairing it with tights and a warm coat.

Small secret: dresses usually make me look as if I've put effort into my appearance when I actually haven't. Low-maintenance is my middle name, so I own a stack of dresses. Before leaving my room, I put on earrings too. They're brightly colored, shaped like tiny fruits. Colorful and oddly shaped earrings are my guilty pleasure, along with high-heeled shoes.

To be honest, my love for them started by accident. What I lack in height, I make up for in personality and high heels. I realized early on that if I wanted to be heard in a family of eleven, I had to be loud and clear. Honing the skill turned out to be invaluable, especially when I ventured out into the business world. But being loud isn't always good, and everyone tends to overlook small people. Hence why high heels come in handy. Nude-colored pumps are a staple in my wardrobe. I can't help a smile as I remember when I wore my very first pair: to prom in senior year, thirteen years ago.

It was one of the worst, but also one of the best nights. Midway through the event, I ran into my date making out with another girl. For an eighteen-year-old, that ranked up high next to natural catastrophes, possibly even the end of the world. Slapping the crap out of my cheating date didn't help with the pain, even though it did calm me a bit. Then I realized I didn't want to stay there for the rest of the event and headed home. But when I arrived, I didn't want to go inside the house. I was torn between wanting to curl in my mother's lap and sob, and hearing everyone's pity. I ended up lying in a hammock outside which was hidden enough to not be viewed from the house.

"What are you doing here?"

Nate's voice startled me, and I wiped away my tears as best as I could. I hadn't known he was visiting.

"I live here," I replied with sass, scrambling out of the hammock. "What are you doing here?"

"Came to see the baseball game with your dad. Aren't you supposed to be at the prom?"

"Found my date kissing another girl in a dark hallway. Pretty sure his hand was under her skirt too."

"Show me a picture and I'll make sure he has a black eye tomorrow."

I grinned. It was something my brothers would have said, but hearing it from him, it felt different.

"He already does. My knuckles will be bruised too."

Nate eyed my tear-streaked cheeks. I was wearing waterproof mascara, so I hoped at least I didn't look like a raccoon.

"When are you supposed to be home?"

"In three hours."

He nodded in the direction of the gate. "Let's go. My car's outside."

Excitement coursed through me. "Where are you taking me?"

"Out. You need good memories from tonight. We're going to make some."

That was the first time I swooned in his presence. My crush had already been going strong for a few years, but this was different. It felt grown-up, and I thought it was incredibly sweet of him.

He took me to a hip, vibrant restaurant, where they had good food and even better music. After we finished eating, he took my hand and pulled me on the dance floor, and those were the hottest minutes of my life up until then.

Nate wasn't dancing like the guys at my school. There were no sloppy attempts to grab my ass or trying to grind against me. I realized it was because those guys were boys, but Nate was a man. I was eighteen, and he was twenty-three. He effortlessly led me across the dance floor, pulling me just close enough until our chests touched. His hands were on my hips when they needed to be, and only the firmness of his grip and the way his lips occasionally lingered on my cheek betrayed how much he'd love to touch me more.

That night was the first time I understood the meaning of a hot look. And I nearly melted at his feet. But he was a gentleman the entire evening. On the way out, we noticed the restaurant had a photo booth, which was cheesy, but I loved every minute we spent inside it. I've kept every single picture we took to this day.

When he brought me home, I was grinning ear to ear. He'd made me feel like I was on top of the world, and I adored him for it.

***

Half an hour later, I step inside Blue Moon and find Blake and Nate already seated at the small round table next to the bar. The bar area is the only complete part; the rest is still missing most of the furniture. But this place will be a knockout when it's ready.

"Hello, boys." I shrug out of my coat, leaving it on the back of the nearest chair, and then I stalk toward them with my chin held high, squaring my shoulders. They stop midsentence, rising to their feet.

"Alice, we were waiting for you before giving Nate the official tour. This is for you. Double espresso. When you texted to say you'd be late, I figured you wouldn't have time for coffee." He points to a Starbucks cup on the table. I hadn't noticed it before.

"Ohhh, you just saved me, thank you."

"Nah, I saved our asses." Blake gestures between him and Nate. "You're mean and cranky before you've had your two coffees in the morning."

What can I say… my brother knows me well. Blake kisses my cheek, and then I turn to Nate, only to find his eyes raking over my body. When he unleashes the full power of his gaze on me, my skin simmers with awareness, blood rushing to my cheeks. Right, so apparently deciding I must forget about my crush hasn't lessened my body's reaction to his proximity. It was silly to assume it would all go away just by sheer force of will, but one can only hope.

When he leans down, brushing my cheek with his lips, I swear my skin catches fire. This close, I can smell the faint scent of soap on him, and nothing else. He's not wearing cologne, but I swear his scent is pure sexiness. If someone could bottle it and sell it, they'd make a fortune.

I school my features when he pulls back, hoping I look like a professional business woman and not a girl with a crush. By the way one corner of his mouth lifts upward, my bet is I'm closer to the second option.

"Let's start with the tour," Blake says. For the next fifteen minutes, we explain our vision to Nate, describe how the restaurant area will look, even show him the kitchen, which is ready.

Once or twice I catch him looking at me with what can only be described as hunger, but I do my best to ignore it. *Come on, Alice. You just have to get through the day. Then you probably won't have to see him again while he's here, and then he'll be gone anyway.*

Once the tour is over, the three of us sit at the small round table next to the bar.

"What more do you need from us?" Blake asks.

"I have an entire report," I explain. "With financial stuff and—"

"Nah, I just need some catchy stuff so they'll pay attention. Hard facts too, like how many customers you have daily in your other restaurants, but essentially, I need a good story. What sells ideas is good storytelling. Not everything you tell me will make it on screen. In fact, most of it probably won't. But first, I need to convince the network to pick this place and not another one."

He's not just book smart but also street smart. Sure, he can work his charm in every conversation, but I'm willing to bet anything he didn't get to the top just relying on that. Since I met him, he never ventured into a conversation without having some strong arguments to dish out. I always admired his intelligence.

"What do you want to know?" I ask.

Nate takes out a notepad and a pen from the leather file in front of him—and glasses. I barely suppress a sigh when he slides them on square black frames around his green eyes. His sex appeal just shot through the roof. Normally I don't find glasses attractive, but they work on him.

"First, how did the two of you end up opening a location together? The family aspect works in your favor—viewers would love it."

As Blake and I rattle on, answering his questions, he jots down notes, and I can practically *hear* him spinning a story for the pitch in his mind.

"We should also include a funny story from your childhood. Those things work like a charm in pitches. How about the one where Blake tried to escape through the window and broke his leg?"

Nate is five years older than me, but he's also a little younger than Sebastian. As such, he sometimes got involved in the younger group's shenanigans.

"How about a story that actually makes me look good?" Blake deadpans. Ah, my brothers and their giant egos.

"Self-deprecation works great on camera," Nate explains, and my brother merely grimaces.

"If I have to potentially make an ass of myself on national television, then by all means, tell the story where I ended up with my ass hanging out because my jeans got torn in the fence."

I roar with laughter at the memory, and Nate chuckles.

"I still can't believe you got caught." There are two sets of twins in my family. Christopher and Max are younger than me but older than Blake and identical, and they used their likeness to pull pranks on us as often as they could. They also got away with it most of the time. Daniel and Blake are the younger set of twins, and while they look nothing alike, that didn't keep them from competing with Max and Christopher for the title of the best pranking duo. They got caught most of the time.

We continue to answer Nate's questions for about an hour when Blake's phone chimes. Picking it up, he frowns at the screen.

"Damn! I have to leave. My bar manager is sick, and someone has to be there for deliveries."

"I have a lot of info already," Nate replies, surveying his notes. The glasses slip a fraction of an inch down his nose, and my fingers itch to push them back up. Yeah… I'm not looking for every opportunity to touch him or anything.

"I can tell you anything more you need to know," I offer. To my dismay, I discover Blake is watching me with narrowed eyes. *Uh-oh.*

"Alice, can we quickly go over the to-dos for next week before I leave?" my brother asks. Clearly, this is an excuse, because we hammered those details yesterday before we went to Mom's party.

Nate rises to his feet, his notes still in hand. "I'll go outside for a few minutes, give you guys time to talk."

Blake wastes no time. The second Nate's out of my field of vision, he attacks.

"It's him, isn't it?" he asks in a low voice. "The family friend you've been holding a torch for?"

I groan, propping my elbows on the table and my chin in my palm. Apparently, my little brother is not as oblivious as I thought. And apparently, the Bennett rumor mill is working better than ever. In a moment of weakness, I once confessed to Max that I'm holding a torch for a family friend, without naming Nate. Blake using the exact same words proves the guys in this family gossip as much as the girls.

My brother interprets my silence as a yes.

"Do I need to threaten him? Tell him not to mess around with you? Give him the brother speech?"

"Hold your horses right there. This is none of your business, Blake."

"Barking up the wrong tree here."

"No, you don't need to flex your brotherly muscles. Nothing's happening."

Blake points his finger at me, but then his phone beeps again.

"Damn, this is my delivery guy. I have to go. If you change your mind about the brother speech, tell me." With those parting words, he strolls out of the restaurant.

Nate stalks back inside seconds later. The moment he drops in his chair at the table, the air between us charges. It's like the only thing that kept the usual sparks between us at bay was Blake's presence.

"So, what else do you want to know?" I ask, drumming my fingers on the wooden surface, racking my brain for ways to dissolve the tension. It seems to have seeped into my body, making me jittery.

Nate leans slightly across the table. "Tell me more about that torch."

It takes me a second to realize what he means, and then the round table suddenly feels far too small.

"How…?"

"I was barely out the door when Blake accosted you. So, you've had a crush on me for years, huh?"

My brain freezes for a brief second, embarrassment overwhelming me. Then, slowly, my fight-or-flight instinct kicks in. I've never been much of a coward, which only leaves fighting. I gather my wits around me, squaring my shoulders and looking him directly in the eyes.

"Answer something first. Have you been eye flirting with me for years or was it all in my head?" Yeah, I sound about a million times braver than I feel, but I don't see another way out of this besides grabbing the bull by its horns.

"None of it was in your head."

I swear my heart instantly doubles in size. For a split second, I understand the saying 'to see the world through rose-colored glasses.'

"But I'm moving, and even if I weren't, I'm not the man for you."

Yeah, that rose? Just turned into shades of shitty brown.

"Way to twist the knife, buddy." My voice is dry and flat, even though I was hoping I would sound humorous. I've always used humor as a shield. It's usually quite effective.

"It wasn't my intention to hurt you." Leaning across the table, he covers my hand with his. I think it was meant as a comforting gesture, but a bolt of heat singes me from the skin-on-skin contact. Judging by the sharp breath Nate exhales, he felt it too.

I pull my hand back quickly. "No touching."

"Right."

"Since we got that pesky detail out of the way, can we focus on your pitch?"

Nate flashes me a wicked grin, and I'm sure I'm in for some more teasing. He always did love to tease me. "Pesky details, huh?"

Luckily, I can hold my own, even though sitting across from his six feet of hotness and those bright green eyes doesn't help one bit. Add a sharp brain to the mix and I'm a goner.

"Hey, don't get your knickers in a twist," I say in an awful British accent. "You'll be gone soon. Until then, just try not to knock my socks off by being smarter, hotter, or funnier than usual."

Laughter bubbles out of him. "You're the most unpredictable woman I know, and I love that about you."

"See, you're not helping by saying nice things to me. It would really help if you turned broody and mean."

"Right. You don't dig broody guys, do you?"

"You have a great memory."

Nate was staying at our house during a Christmas vacation, and by then, I'd known him for enough years to be comfortable around him. We usually had a lot of fun together, typically at the expense of my younger siblings, but he spent that entire vacation frowning and being moody, and I wasn't having any of it. I wanted my laughing partner back.

I was still a kid, too young to really like him, but even then, my instincts were to comfort him. Mom had told me he had a big fight with his mother before Christmas. In my book, that wasn't a good enough reason to sulk all the time. I wanted to take all his sadness away but didn't know how. So in my typical fashion, I started picking on him.

"You'll get wrinkles from so much frowning," I informed him.

"No, I won't." His voice had been flat, and he didn't seem interested in carrying on a conversation. And it was exactly what bothered me. Nate would usually crack a joke, or at least toss a witty reply my way when I picked on him. I folded my arms against my chest and gave him a cold stare.

"For your information, broody guys are so passé. Girls don't dig them anymore. If you need someone to take that stick out of your ass, you'll find me outside."

Nate had watched me incredulously for a split second before bursting out laughing. It was the first time he'd laughed so wholeheartedly during his entire stay. I wasn't just proud, but also happy.

"You're right, let's focus on this." Nate looks down, reading through his notes. "I meant to ask, why do you work only with small, local farmers? Why the farm-to-table concept?"

Ah, I could talk about this all day.

"Farmers work hard. Remember, my parents used to do that work too."

A long time ago, before Sebastian founded Bennett Enterprises, our family was poor. Then our luck changed. Bennett Enterprises grew to become a mammoth, and our brother took care of the entire family. But before that, my parents owned a ranch. Cattle was their main occupation, but they also had fruit and vegetables. Growing them required dedication and care. Selling them was another matter altogether.

"Farmers put in long hours, work themselves to the bone. But when it comes to selling their products, it's hard for them to compete with the big guys. Supermarket chains often force them to sell far under the price to squeeze out a profit. Restaurants rarely choose to buy directly from small farmers because their prices aren't competitive. But if you're smart, you can make a profit without taking advantage of those hardworking people."

Nate nods but doesn't take notes.

"Why aren't you writing this down?"

"I'll remember it. I've never seen you talk so passionately about anything. You're brilliant."

"Why, thank you, mister. I suggest you lay off the compliments. Remember, you're not allowed to knock my socks off."

"Stop saying socks like that, Alice." The way my name rolls off his tongue should be outlawed. There is so much sensuality in those two syllables, it's giving me whiplash. The man isn't even trying to seduce me. I wonder what he'd sound like if he tried. *Damn.* It's this line of thinking that got me into trouble in the first place. I have to stop, or there is nothing good in store for me.

"How?"

"Like you mean panties instead." His eyes snap fire, and the intensity in them travels straight through me. I involuntarily press my thighs together, hoping to assuage the ache between them.

"You sure like getting ahead of yourself." I don't know if humor will get me out of this situation or sink me more, but I'm not one to abandon a project midway. Still, sticking to the topic of the TV show is probably a safer bet. Pointing to his notebook, I ask, "Do you have everything you need?"

"Yeah."

"Great. Can we wrap this up, then?"

"Afraid to be alone with me much longer?"

A witty reply begs to tumble from my lips, but I force the words back down and instead say, "No, but I need to get to one of my other restaurants. Saturday is our busiest day."

Nate nods, and I'm relieved I'm off the hook. He takes off his reading glasses, which is a pity. We rise from our chairs, and after I collect my coat, shrugging into it, we head out of the restaurant. I feel his gaze on me the entire time. Outside, I inhale a much-needed breath of fresh air.

"When will you pitch this to the network?"

"This week. It takes a long time to get from a pitch to actually filming the segment, so I want to get the ball rolling right away. I'll be in touch as soon as I have updates."

"Thank you. I really appreciate you doing this."

"Where did you park?" he asks once we're out on the street.

"Came by cab. My car is in the repair shop."

"You don't still own that old thing, do you?"

"Yes, I do, and I love it."

"There's a reason people change their cars once a decade. If I remember correctly, it was in the repair shop the last two times I was here."

"Coincidence. Do not mock my car."

I poke him, hoping to drive my point home. Big mistake. Poking implies touching, and feeling his granite abs under the pad of my finger is.... All I can think of is *yum*.

"We've gone from admitting our mutual crush to feeling one another up?"

Shit. It appears that while my brain was busy mentally undressing him, I splayed all my fingers on his abs. I take my hand away instantly.

"It's entirely your fault for being so hot."

"Don't forget funny and smart," he adds wickedly. "Come on, I'll drive you."

"No."

"It wasn't a question." Everything from the tone of his voice to his body language screams dominant, which turns my knees weak and makes my mouth water. And I can't have that.

"I don't like it when you go all caveman."

"Oh, but you do." Leaning forward, he brings his hand to my face, dragging his knuckles down my cheeks. "You're blushing, Alice. You love it."

Distance. I need distance to clear my mind. Stepping back, I cross my arms against my chest, trying to make sense of the situation.

"Don't overthink this. It's just a ride."

"Fine, let's go."

We've always had a push-and-pull dynamic, but this is something else entirely. And it feels dangerous. But then again, from carbs to sugar to Nate, I've always liked things that are bad for me.

Chapter Three

Nate

"Nate, can I talk to you for a few minutes?" my assistant Clara asks on Monday, knocking at my open door. We're in one of the network's studios on the outskirts of San Francisco. Until my job in London starts officially, I'm overseeing a local production here. As an executive producer, I'm in charge of everything from finances to operational implementation and logistics, casting, directing, overseeing shoots, and sometimes screenwriting too. Right now, my focus here is overseeing shoots.

"Sure." Sitting straight in my chair, I survey Clara closely. She's opening and closing her hands repeatedly. I've worked with her long enough to know this means she's stressed out. "What's wrong?"

"Well, I've worked for you for some time now."

"Three years." She started out as a back-office assistant but gradually took on more responsibilities. She could make a great producer one day.

She offers me the first smile for the day, albeit a weak one. "You're right."

"Clara, it's me. What's wrong? You can tell me to my face."

"I don't want to transfer to the London office," she blurts out. "I love working with you, but I can't see myself moving there."

"I understand."

I hadn't seen this one coming. She's stuck by my side, traveled the world with me. For the past few years, I was the executive producer of a show that required us to relocate every few months, sometimes weeks. I had eight people on my team, but Clara is the last one standing from the original group. People believe an international life is glamorous: the travel, the new people you meet, the new places you see. The truth is much less glamorous: planes to catch, hotels to check in and out of, adjusting to new time zones, food, language.

Traveling is great for a hobby, exhausting for a living. Whenever one of my team members decided to leave, I made sure to find them jobs if they wanted to stay within the network.

"You want to stay with the network?"

Clara nods eagerly. "I already looked at the internal job postings."

"I'm meeting Horowitz today. I can put in a good word for you." Horowitz is the head of several divisions of the network and has the ear of big bosses too.

"You'd do that?"

"Of course. I look after my people, Clara. You are one of my people." I think of her as a younger sister, who is usually very meddling—almost to the point of annoyance.

"Thank you." She bounces on her feet, clapping her hands together. "By the way, Sarah from editing stopped by earlier. She's single and seemed interested in having lunch with you. To catch up, of course."

I cut right to the chase. "Are you trying to set me up?"

"Who? Me? Not at all." Yeah, this is the Clara I deal with daily, not the shy version from a few seconds ago.

I cock an eyebrow.

"Nate, come on. Last time you went out on a date was in Paris. Two months ago."

Sometimes I can't believe the conversations I'm having with my assistant.

"How would you know when I go out on dates?"

"I have access to your calendar, remember?" she asks devilishly. "Your reputation as a lady's man is going down the drain."

"How's that a bad thing?"

It's fantastic how much bad reputations stick. True, in college and during the early years of my career, I wasn't a saint, but who is at that age? Later, as my work meant constant travel, I didn't even bother pursuing a long-term relationship. What was the point? I was going from country to country in a matter of months, sometimes weeks.

"It's not, but... You can't just work all the time."

"I do have a social life. I was at a party on Friday, and I met with old friends on Saturday."

"Are any of those old friends a sexy lady you'd like to take out for dinner and whisper dirty things in her ear?"

You have no idea. I'd like to do much more. I'd like to take Alice home and do every dirty thing to her I imagined over the years. Out loud I just say, "Mind your own business."

"But that's so boring."

I check the time on my phone, then stand up. "Luckily I have to leave to meet Horowitz. I'm going to put in a good word, even though you can be a pain in my ass."

She smiles. "Thank you. I'm going to miss you, boss."

***

"How do you like it?" Horowitz asks, waving an arm toward his office, welcoming me inside. "Was smaller last time you saw it."

"Was it?" Looks like any executive office to me. Large glass desk with a black leather chair behind it. To the side, a couch and a coffee table.

"Yeah. Since they wouldn't give me a bigger one, I took matters into my own hands and demolished the wall to the neighboring room."

"Where did the person working in that room move?"

Horowitz shrugs. I'll never understand why some people feel the need to measure their power in office size. The way I see it, it's the grown-up version of measuring dicks.

His assistant strolls in, smiling at me and dropping some papers on his desk. Horowitz eyes her ass the entire time. Nearing his fifties, and with more belly than hair, Horowitz is the very definition of a sleazeball. Most women in the network avoid being alone with him. He's not stupid enough to hit on them because he'd have a lawsuit on his hands, but he makes them uncomfortable.

"Why did you want to meet?" Horowitz asks after she leaves. He drops in his leather chair, prompting me to sit opposite him. I choose to stand. "Your contract for London hasn't come through yet. Unless you changed your mind?"

"I haven't changed my mind. I want to discuss two other things. One, my assistant, Clara, won't be coming with me to London. I want to make sure she gets a good job within the network. She's hardworking and an organizational talent. She took on a lot of producing responsibilities too, lately. She'll be an asset to anyone."

"Always looking out for your team, eh?"

"That's who I am."

"We'll find her something. What was the second thing?"

"I have a recommendation for the *Delicious Dining* show."

"I'm listening."

"It's a restaurant that will open in two weeks, run by a brother and sister who have experience in the industry. It's posh and focuses on local specialties."

"Name?"

"Blue Moon. Run by Alice and Blake Bennett."

"Any relation to Bennett Enterprises?"

"The founders' siblings."

"Isn't Blake Bennett the playboy the tabloids loved to pick on? Not sure he'd be such a draw in viewership."

I forgot how much of a pompous prick Horowitz could be.

"Do you have a severe case of memory loss, or are you trying to sweep under the rug that you were a trust fund playboy who only got his shit together when he was in his forties?" I ask. "Hypocritical much?"

Horowitz bursts out laughing, plunking his fist against the table. "Ah, you never pull punches, Nate. We need more people like you."

Early on in my career, people warned me that my big mouth and no-filter attitude would stand in my way, but I was never one for brownnosing. I call it like I see it, even with people who sign my paychecks.

"Alice Bennett owns two other restaurants. They've been listed in the Top 10 locations in San Francisco many times." I rattle off the names of the locations, and they get his attention.

"I've been to both. They are excellent."

"You could spotlight those on the show too." I launch my pitch, using all the information I got on Saturday. Whenever Horowitz raises an objection, I fight it. In my experience, when you want something, you have to push relentlessly. And I want this for Alice.

"This could turn out great." Horowitz crosses his fingers on top of his head, leaning back in the leather chair. "I even saw Alice Bennett when I ate there. She's one hot piece. How much does she want this feature? Enough to sleep with me?"

Just like that, I see red. "You so much as proposition her and you're going to have a problem with me."

Alice can hold her own against just about anything, but I'll be damned if I'll let her deal with this moron.

"Ah, you're tapping that."

"I'm not." Walking right in front of his desk, I push my knuckles on the glass surface. He pushes his chair farther from the desk as if fearing I might grab him by the collar. "The Bennetts are old family friends of mine."

"Your territory, got it." He's clearly intimidated. *Good.* He doesn't make any more unprofessional remarks about Alice for the rest of the meeting.

My thoughts, on the other hand, are not professional at all. For years I've kept my fantasy in check when it comes to her, but after Saturday, there's no going back. That wicked woman will be the death of me. Everything about her calls to me: her fire, her energy, her sassy and sinfully hot mouth. I almost kissed her on Saturday but stopped myself just in time. One kiss would never be enough, and seducing her is out of the question. She's practically family, and I'm leaving.

Anything except helping her land a spot on the show is out of the question. Scratch that. I'll add making her laugh to the list. And riling her up is just too much fun. It should be innocent enough. Unless it spirals out of control.

***

Alice

"Mark, table four is still waiting on their order. What's going on?" I inquire, heading directly toward the chef, who is currently bent over the stove, frantically stirring in multiple pans at the same time.

"Sorry, Alice! Someone sent their order back and I had to redo it, so now I'm behind."

I take one look at the sous-chefs around, and clearly not one of them is slacking. Tuesday is usually laid-back, but today, it's a madhouse. Bending, I search in one of the supply closets where we stack fresh aprons. Throwing one over me, I step beside Mark. "Tell me what to do. Anything except chopping stuff." I never could master the art of chopping anything at a reasonable speed, and after one too many incidents, which resulted in bloody fingers, I gave up.

Mark waves one hand in a dismissive gesture before stirring in a pan again. "Get out of here before your pretty dress starts stinking."

"Mark, I'm the boss. Tell me what to do. We have unhappy customers out there waiting for their food."

"Fine. Stir here continuously, and make sure you add cream in this one in four minutes."

"See? Easy. I'm on it."

"You're micromanaging."

"No, I'm taking care of the business."

Ever since I opened the first restaurant, I became a jack of all trades, doing whatever has to be done. I personally greet guests and help out in the kitchen when it's necessary. But I spend most of the time pursuing activities that bring us more customers, such as buying advertising and striking partnerships with tourist offices. Since opening the second restaurant, I rotate between locations. I'm not sure yet how I'll manage once the third one opens, but at least Blake will be co-owning it. I'll be able to rely on him.

***

At two o' clock sharp, I step in the small backyard of the restaurant and dial my baby sister's number. Summer is away in Italy, working at a museum. She's a painter, and they have an excellent program there for young artists. I miss her terribly, which is silly because she visits often and we speak every other day at designated hours.

"Hi, Alice." Just the sound of her voice makes me nostalgic. I swear, every time I speak to her I secretly hope she'll say that she'll cut her stay there short and return home.

"Hey, kid. How was the expo?"

As she launches into a detailed description, I can't help feeling very proud of my sister. As a kid and even a teenager, she used to be shy with people outside our family, but once she found her calling in painting, she slowly broke out of her shell. She's working hard, chasing opportunities and making the best out of them. I just wish I could see more of her.

I keep my ears peeled for any signs she might be in trouble. God, I'm such a pest, constantly worrying about her. When I think about my baby sister being in Rome, a million possible dangers spring to mind (not the least my sister falling for a hot Italian man and deciding to stay in Rome forever). I'm a closet mother hen.

"I still can't believe I missed Mom's birthday," Summer finishes, regret dripping from her voice. The museum had an expo over the weekend, and she couldn't take time off.

"Don't worry, kid. She'll have plenty more. You'll be here for them."

"Sooo… rumor has it Nate was at the party."

"News travels fast." I could try to brush the topic off because Summer isn't the type who insists—at least not as much as Pippa—but the truth is I need someone to talk to and get it off my chest. In a few short sentences, I tell her about the conversation he and I had on Saturday.

"I knew it!" Summer exclaims. "Every time I've been in the same room with the two of you, I swear I *saw* sparks."

"Well, the sparks aren't helping our case."

"Are you okay?"

"Of course, I'm a big girl. I'll go for a run later on. Helps me clear my head."

"Yuck! Sure you're a Bennett? Who goes for a run *voluntarily*?"

I burst out laughing. "Can I tell you a dirty secret? I'm thinking of training for the marathon this year."

"Ugh, stop right there or I'll file a petition to have your family name changed."

I'm the only girl in the family who runs, and I'm pretty sure I'm the only one in the clan who likes it. I love it, actually. The more demanding I am with my body in terms of training, the better I can concentrate. Alas, my love for working out was born out of the necessity to balance my love for sweets. I blame my sister Pippa for this. It's her legacy. Since I can remember, she instilled three values in me: always look after our family, don't be ashamed of loving steamy romance books, and never say no to a cupcake.

"I'm a running junkie and proud of it!"

"Well, I'm going to become a gelato junkie soon. I swear the ice cream in Rome is the best ever."

"Hey, we have great ice cream in San Francisco," I counter, knowing full well it's not as great as the gelato in Rome.

"Alice, your agenda to convince me to come home is becoming less subtle every time we talk." Summer lets out a small laugh.

"What can I say? I miss you, kid. I promise to learn to make gelato like the Italians."

"Oh, see? That's my sister. Not the weirdo who wants to run the marathon. Crap, I have to go."

"Sure. Take care, kid."

"Oh, last thing. Go on a date. It'll help getting Nate out of your system."

"I'm seriously considering buying cats instead. Dating is so exhausting. Going out with so many incompatible people while hoping to find *the one* is like a less violent version of *The Hunger Games*."

"Well, when you put it like that, cats sound like a better idea. Bye, Alice."

After she clicks off, I wonder when I turned into such a big pile of mush. I blame it on so many of my siblings being engaged, married, or parents. Must have triggered my mushy gene.

Heading back inside, I'm mentally preparing to throw myself into work when my phone beeps with a message from Nate. We exchanged numbers on Saturday.

Nate: Talked to the head of the division yesterday, and I just received a questionnaire for you

from the producing team. I'll forward you the e-mail. They want more info, but they're interested.

I jump up and down with joy, which garners curious looks from the crew. He e-mails me the questionnaire seconds later.

Alice: Got it, thank you. I really appreciate this, Nate.

Nate: You're welcome. Any plans tonight? Time for a drink?

I stare at the screen, trying to read through the lines, and also to decide if a drink would be a good idea. Sure, we used to go for drinks and chat for hours whenever he was in town, but that was *before*.

Alice: Working. It's very busy for a Tuesday.

Nate: Is this code for "Drinks aren't a good idea"?

Alice: Not at all.

Nate: Immune to my charms already?

Alice: I move fast. You snooze, you lose.

The great part about written communication? No one can see my facial expression. Right now, I'm positively beaming.

Nate: Drinks shouldn't be a problem, then. When do you have time?

Theoretically, owning my business means I can take time off whenever I want. Practically, I work nonstop. But Nate will leave in a few weeks, and who knows when I'll see him again. Yes, things have changed, but I won't allow that to overshadow the years of camaraderie and friendship.

Alice: Thursday in the evening sound good? The kitchen closes at ten o'clock.

Nate: Sure. I'll pick you up.

Alice: I can come by cab.

Nate: You could, but then I'd go all caveman again convincing you. Bad idea.

This man! What is he thinking?

Alice: You're a bad man, telling me things like this.

Nate: Hey, my ego's still recovering from finding out you're immune to my charms already.

Alice: Fine, pick me up. But you're not allowed to overstep friendship boundaries the entire evening.

Nate: Promise.

As I tuck my phone away in my bag, focusing on helping Mark, I try hard not to acknowledge that the chances of Nate sticking to his word are zero. I try even harder not to admit I'm looking forward to him breaking his promise.

Chapter Four

Nate

"Answer the phone, Mother." I glance at the digital time display on my car's dashboard: eight thirty in the morning, Thursday. I've messed up our call time on a few occasions while traveling—time zone differences are a pain in the ass. But I'm one hundred percent sure we scheduled a call for right now. Maybe she has a shift and forgot to tell me? Mom works as a nurse at the local hospital in the small town where she moved a few years ago. She lives three hours away from San Francisco and I rarely see her, though I'm determined to pay her a visit before moving to London.

"Nate, hi!" she answers at long last, her voice echoing through the car's speaker system. "Are you driving? It's not safe to talk while you're driving. You need both hands on the wheel."

"I'm using Bluetooth, Mother. Both hands are safely on the wheel."

"Hmm...." She sounds unconvinced. My mother is one of those who doesn't trust technology too much. I've tried to talk her into using Skype, or to let me buy her a phone with a camera so we could see each other while talking, but I've yet to win that fight.

"What have you been up to?"

"Same old, same old. Heading to the pet shop to start my first shift."

It takes me a second to put two and two together. "Wait, you got a second job?"

"Just part-time."

Worry nags at me. My mother's sixty-seven. Yes, she's full of energy, but a part-time job at a pet shop on top of her shifts as a nurse?

"I get bored between shifts at the hospital."

I'm not buying this explanation. "Are you having problems with the mortgage again? You know I can help. I can pay your entire debt, Mom."

"We're not having this conversation again," she says sternly, but damn if I'm backing down, even if this conversation will put her on edge.

During my childhood and teen years, she was always on edge. She and my father were constantly fighting. She remarried one year after divorcing my father, but she fought just as much with her new husband. She tried her best to be a good mother, but she was stretching herself thin. I chose to spend most of my time outside the house to avoid all the yelling. It's how I ended up spending so much time with the Bennetts.

Mom and I grew apart and never quite managed to repair that bridge, but we've both been trying, especially since she divorced her second husband five years ago. She's been much calmer since too, except when talking about my father or her financial issues.

"I'm not bringing in seven figures a year and letting you work two jobs just to afford your house. I can help. I want to help."

"It's not a child's duty to pay for their parents' mistakes."

Oh man, oh man, here she goes again. I once got to the bottom of why she doesn't want me buying her house. She said she wouldn't be having this problem if she still had a husband because the mortgage would be split in two. She keeps punishing herself for having not one but two failed marriages, and I have no idea how to help her. It frustrates me to no end.

"That's not what it is. But we're family. Family helps each other out."

"Do you give your father money?"

I groan. If I tell her yes, she'll just say Dad is a leper, which he's not. My father remarried too, finding a good woman who had kids from her previous marriage. I never really fit in his new family, but we have a cordial relationship. He never asked me for money though.

If I tell this to Mom, she'll flat-out refuse to be the family member who can't take care of herself. Even after all these years, my parents can't be in the same room without starting a fight. Two years ago, I received an award and invited both my parents to the fancy dinner party. Dad came with his family, and one hour into the dinner, all hell broke loose. Before leaving, Dad said that when I get married, I'd better throw two weddings and invite them separately.

"Not the point. I just want you to have a good life."

"I do. You take good care of me. The hose you bought me for Christmas is perfect. My flowers have never looked better."

Yeah, because a functioning hose improved her quality of life *so* much. It pisses me off that I can't reason with my own mother. I can't find the arguments to make her understand.

In an obvious attempt to switch topics, she starts talking about her friends at the book club and their antics, and I let the issue slide for now. I won't lie, I phase out sometime during her monologues, but despite the borderline ridiculous things her friends are up to (apparently holding pageant competitions among dogs is all the rage, because why not?), I'm glad she has a circle of people she can trust. For a long time after her second divorce, she was very lonely.

"So I'm going to get a dog," she finishes. "A pug!"

"You won't win any pageants with pugs, Mother. They look more like rats than dogs."

"Nate!"

"You already got your dog, didn't you?"

"Yes, and she's lovely. Found her in a shelter. I'm not too sure what her name is. The shelter owner said it's Becky, but she doesn't answer to that. I'm trying to get her to answer to Felicia. Isn't it a beautiful name?"

"It is."

"Now I'm fighting to get Clarissa Lawson to include her in the upcoming pageant. She says pugs aren't among the races admitted to the pageantry. I swear the woman's out to get me."

Or she agrees with me that pugs look a lot like rats, but volunteering this fact out loud would put me squarely in the enemy camp.

"Do you want me to pull some strings?"

"Really?" she asks hopefully.

"The network has a minor segment for canines. I can ask them to contact Clarissa and tell her they'd be interested in highlighting the competition, but only if she accepts pugs."

"Sounds wonderful. Thank you."

Yep, that's my mother. She won't let me lift a finger for her mortgage, but pulling strings for her pug? It's all fair game.

We chitchat until I arrive at the studio, focusing on me. All the while I rack my brain for any argument I could use so she'd let me take care of her mortgage. Right before we end the conversation, she asks me not to forget about Felicia. It takes me a few seconds to remember it's the pug's name.

"I'll see to it first thing today," I assure her, considering this a step in the right direction. A baby step, but it's better than nothing.

***

At ten sharp that evening, I'm in front of Alice's restaurant, but the woman in question is nowhere to be seen. Since she's not answering her phone, I head inside. The restaurant is chock-full, and servers are running around with plates. The kitchen might close at ten, but the restaurant remains open until twelve.

After explaining to one of the waiters that I'm here for Alice, he brings me to her. She's in one corner of the kitchen, placing lids on plastic containers with such force I'm surprised they don't break. The waiter scurries away, as if afraid Alice might see him.

The rest of her staff is at a considerable distance from her, tiptoeing around. Ah, I know what this means. Alice is mad, and her staff is trying not to cross her.

"Blowing me off already, Alice?"

She spins around, a plastic lid in her hand.

"It's ten already? I'm so sorry, Nate. I… lost track of time." She looks at the plastic containers on the counter with guilt.

"Need help finishing?"

She nods. "It'll be quicker. I should have started earlier, but I got caught up with… other things."

We work side by side for the next few minutes, and I can practically feel the anger radiating off her. She's wearing a cream-colored dress, and her skin is flushed. She only flushes when she's pissed, or embarrassed. Briefly, I wonder if her skin turns the same color when she's aroused. I think it would. The temptation to test my theory is stronger than ever. But she's off-limits, damn it.

"Tell me!"

"What?"

"Whatever has you so mad."

"I'm not mad."

Her head is bent as she focuses on the last container, so she doesn't see me lean in.

"Don't lie to me, Alice." Unable to keep my hands off her, I drag my knuckles down her cheek. Her dress is snug around her waist, with three buttons leading up to her breasts. "Or I'll have to *make you* tell me the truth."

She snaps her head in my direction, licking her lips. "You said you'd be on your best behavior."

"When we're out for drinks, yes. Right now we're filling plastic containers with food. We're off the clock."

"You're unbelievable."

"And you're mad, and I want to know why. If you don't tell me, I'll flirt the panties off you."

She pulls away quickly. "Damn, you're good with threats. Much better than keeping your promises, anyway." With a sigh, she adds, "I had to fight off a reporter earlier on the phone."

"Why? Press is good."

"Yeah, except this one was telling me about how he'll do an exclusive feature for my restaurants if I could get him a one-on-one interview with Sebastian."

"I had no idea that still happened."

"Not as often as it used to, but often enough to piss me off. I really don't want to keep talking about it."

Alice was in college when Bennett Enterprises became a star in America. As the CEO, Sebastian was sought after for interviews, but he rarely gave any. So reporters tried to get to him via alternative methods, such as pestering Alice. Knowing she still must fend off idiots has me seeing red. I'm about to ask her who the guy is because I can make sure he doesn't ever bother her again with a few phone calls, but I stop myself just in time. What she needs right now is for me to take her mind off the whole incident.

"Won't say another word about it. By the way, the *Delicious Dining* team e-mailed me today. They're going to decide next week if they go forward with you and Blake. My bet is they will." A smile instantly lights up her face, which is what I was going for. "What's with all these plastic containers?"

"They're for a nearby senior center. I bring them treats twice a week for their evening meetings. Someone from my staff will deliver them tonight for a party they're having." She looks with guilt at the boxes.

"We can bring them by, if you want, and then go for drinks."

"You don't mind?"

"Not at all."

"Thank you so much. Let me tell my staff I'm doing this myself, and then we can go."

"I'll wait. And Alice? Until we're having those drinks, we're still off the clock."

I relish the way her lips part slightly in surprise and the skin on her arms turns to goose bumps. When she dashes away, I tell myself I'm playing a dangerous game. I know there can't be anything between us, but this doesn't seem to keep me from breaking my promise over and over again. Being near Alice while being on my best behavior might be my definition of hell.

***

Fifteen minutes later, we enter the famed senior center. Call me clueless, but I imagined a senior center to be boring and quiet. I couldn't be more wrong. The distant sound of bad retro music assaults my ears the second we step inside. Alice leads the way, walking in the direction the lousy music is coming from.

We enter a room clearly decorated for a vintage disco, complete with a silver globe hanging from the ceiling. The place is absolutely buzzing with people.

"Alice, you made it after all, dear." An elderly woman with violet hair and a godawful pink lipstick hugs Alice. When she pulls back, she eyes me from head to foot. "And you brought a hunk with you." She wiggles her eyebrows at me. What the hell?

"Ms. Williams, this is Nate. He's a dear friend of mine. He's in town for a couple more days, so we're grabbing drinks after we leave."

Ms. Williams claps her hands. "But you must toast with us before you leave. I only turn eighty once."

"Happy birthday," I tell her, still stunned that an eighty-year-old is checking me out.

"Thank you, honey. Now let me relieve you both of those bags of goodies."

After Ms. Williams heads to the large buffet lining one wall, Alice pulls me to one side. "Could we stay for a drink? It would mean a lot to her."

"Depends. Will she give me more dubious looks if she drinks?"

Alice giggles. "Ms. Williams is harmless. She just likes to talk. Now Ms. Hannigan, she's a feisty one." She points to a white-haired, bubbly woman across the room, probably the same age as Ms. Williams.

"Define feisty."

"Don't let her rope you into playing poker. She'll beat you to a pulp and try to get you to agree to naked poker. Or she'll pretend she needs mouth-to-mouth."

"You're pulling my leg, aren't you?"

"Nah. Trust me, they might not have all their teeth intact, but their libido certainly is. Especially with eye candy such as yourself."

Ah, now this is an opportunity I just can't pass up.

"What's this eye candy doing for you, Alice?"

I enjoy immensely the way she drags her lower lip between her teeth. Her physical response is always strong when I speak her name. It makes me want to say it over and over until she succumbs to me.

"Don't do this. It's not fair and you know it." Her low voice is almost a whisper, but it slays me. She's right. I'm an ass. My lack of control around her is my problem, not hers, and it's my duty not to make it her problem.

"I'm sorry. I'll be on my best behavior."

She smiles. "Even if we're still off the clock?"

"Technically we're about to have the first drink."

Before Alice can respond, one of the seniors whisks her away, and I'm left watching her from a distance. That's when I see someone from the staff—judging by the uniform and name tag—approaching me.

"Who are you?" she asks sharply. "Where's your visitor badge?"

"I'm Nate Becker. I came with Alice."

That seems to instantly win her over. "How do you know her?"

"Old family friend. The seniors really seem to dig her treats."

They're all at the buffet, surrounding Alice.

"Yeah, they love her. She's been a blessing for this place. We would have been closed down if not for her."

"What do you mean?"

"This is a state-funded center. A couple of years ago, officials said there weren't enough funds. Alice made a generous donation. This place has survived off her donations ever since."

Well, I'll be damned. I thought I knew Alice well, but she just keeps surprising me.

***

Alice

One drink turns into… I've lost count. The seniors have mastered two arts: gossiping and living vicariously through others. Since most of them have alcohol restrictions due to their medication, they drink nonalcoholic cocktails. My drink definitely has alcohol in it. I'm hot and sweaty from it, and I tried going outside to cool off, but it's a terrible evening. It's not raining, but there is a thick and humid fog, and breathing in deeply feels like diving underwater.

So here I am between Ms. Williams and Ms. Hannigan, always with a glass in my hand. It doesn't seem to get empty, no matter how much I drink. I only realize it's more than I intended when my limbs relax. I was still wound up because of the reporter. I've been fighting this war for a long time, ever since college reporters would try to get information about my older brothers from me. But they were usually the least dangerous because they went straight for the kill. What really hurt were the people who approached me under the guise of friendship, while all they wanted was to get an internship or an interview, or were just looking for an introduction to my siblings. I used to be a trusting person, probably the effect of growing up in a large family where I could always count on someone to join me in any shenanigans, but also to have my back.

Since I'm no good at reading people outside of my family, it took me a while until I got a grip on weeding out the wrong crowd. I swallowed bitter disappointments but also sharpened my claws. No one will take advantage of my siblings if I have anything to say about it, and I typically have a lot to say about everything.

The ongoing joke in our family is that the older siblings protect the younger ones, but we youngsters have done our share of protecting the older trio, if only by serving as a wall, not letting moochers get to them. Sebastian, Logan, and Pippa had to fend off their own share of moochers without having to deal with the ones coming via our recommendations. Pippa's first husband was a jackass who only married her for money. The divorce scarred her deeply. She's happy now, but she was unhappy for a long time.

"Ms. Williams, stop giving me mojitos," I complain.

"Don't you like it? I can also make you a 'sex on the beach.'"

"No, I really should go find my friend. We were supposed to—"

"Go out for drinks?" Nate's voice sounds from my right. He's approaching us fast, nodding at my glass and then at his. "We're in the right place."

"Ah, smart and sexy. My kind of guy," Ms. Williams says. "I'll leave the two of you and chat with some of the other party animals here."

The second she leaves, I let out a sigh. "You always rescue me. Why? I don't need it."

"Yes, you do if you don't want to be drunk as a skunk."

"Hey! I'm just a little inebriated." When he stops right in front of me, I realize I'm just drunk enough to lose my head. Shit. I can barely resist his charms when I'm one hundred percent sober. How am I supposed to resist all this manliness? Steel pecs, strong arms, three-day beard. Scent so sexy it makes me want to lick him. Oh boy. I set my glass down.

Amusement dances in his eyes. "How many drinks did you have?"

"No clue. My glass is just always full."

"Looked like it to me from the other end of the room."

"You're drinking too."

"No alcohol. I'm driving, remember?"

"I'm perfectly capable of walking in a straight line."

"How about dancing?"

"With you?"

"Yes."

Oh boy.

"Sure."

Setting his glass on the table too, he takes my hand, pulling me on the dance floor, and I feel eighteen again. Thank heavens the music is slow, requiring nothing more than balancing from one leg to the other.

"This is just like prom night. You're my knight in shining armor again." He pulls me against him, and hot damn, those abs really are like armor. "Why do you always save me? I don't want to need saving."

"No, you need someone with whom you can make good memories. I'll always volunteer for that."

"Is it really okay that we're here? I didn't mean to stay so long—"

"But Ms. Williams kidnapped you. I saw."

"We can go out. It might be the last time we're together before you leave." At this, he pulls me even closer to him, and I was close enough already. But now our chests touch and my breath catches. His eyes are snapping fire, electrifying me too.

"I'm here for another two weeks. This isn't the last time." Bringing one hand to my face, he rubs his thumb along my jaw. His gaze pierces me with an intensity that turns my knees weak. We're so close that our noses almost touch. I can feel his breath on my lips. Luckily, the music ends, and he pulls back. Being on his best behavior, like I asked him to. He keeps being a gentleman for the rest of the night. We dance, we mingle with the seniors, and he quickly becomes the soul of the party, cracking jokes and sharing funny stories. He's always been very charismatic. Afterward, he talks to several of the seniors who are too shy to join the crowd, preferring to hang around the buffet or just sit and watch.

Nadja, the manager on shift tonight, looks around, leaning against the table with the buffet. I'm pouring water into a glass, intending to chat her up, when I see Nate crossing the room to her. He'd been talking to Ms. Everly, a lovely lady who has been morose the entire evening. She and her husband would have celebrated sixty years of marriage on Saturday, but unfortunately, he passed away six months ago.

"Nadja, can you do me a favor?" Nate asks. I try to focus on my glass, but I'm too close not to overhear.

"Sure."

"Can you take Ms. Everly to Alcatraz on Saturday? I'll pay for all your expenses and have a car and a private boat ready for you in the morning. She said she and her husband used to go there each time they celebrated another decade."

"Oh, the poor woman. Of course I can. Very generous of you."

"Here is my number. Let me know the schedule."

Yep, I'm not swooning or anything. As I watch him return to Ms. Everly, I sigh. This is what always called me to him. Not just his sinfully hot looks, though those also contribute.

But none of this matters. We've lived separate lives until now, and that won't change. I won't do anything to risk the friendship we have while he's here. Undressing him with my eyes doesn't count, right? Such a fine specimen of a male must be admired, often and with gusto. I volunteer for the task.

Chapter Five

Nate

"Earth to Nate. What's going on? You've been like a zombie the entire morning," Clara says the next day during the lunch break, tapping her foot against the hardwood floor of the studio while holding out two sandwiches. "Turkey or cheese?"

I grab the one with the turkey label. "Thanks."

It was four o' clock by the time I got into bed, waking up two hours later feeling almost hungover. Now it's lunchtime, and my head still throbs. Clara and I go out to the balcony overlooking the inner patio. It's become our designated lunch spot. Everyone else heads to the nearby restaurant, enjoying the hour off, but Clara and I typically only take half the allotted time.

"So? Any particular reason why you could barely keep your eyes open today?" She's practically bouncing up and down on her toes. I sit on the bench, unwrapping the foil from the sandwich.

"It's called a private life, Clara. Weren't you nagging me about having one?"

"Yes, but it interferes with your work. I've had to cover for you, saying you stayed up late to edit the last segment, and that's why you can't focus."

I stop midchew, standing straighter. "Who complained?" I pride myself on being able to do my job better than ninety-nine percent of my peers, even with my eyes closed and my hands tied behind my back. I don't want to give anyone reason to think I'm not giving my best just because I'll be leaving in two weeks.

Clara stares at me intently, right before bursting into laughter.

"You didn't have to cover, did you?" I ask, feeling sucker-punched.

When she eventually stops laughing, she shakes her head. "No one complained. Your work is great, as usual, but I just wanted to have leverage against you. To make you talk."

I don't have any siblings, but I always imagined if I had a little sister she'd be just like Clara, nosy and annoying.

"I went with Alice to a senior center last night. We were there until three o'clock in the morning."

Watching Clara's reaction is downright comical. I've talked to her about the Bennett family often, and she knows I'm pulling strings for Alice. When I mentioned Alice, her eyes went wide with surprise, but they narrowed to thin lines at the words *senior center*.

"Odd choice of a place for a date."

"It wasn't a date."

"Oh. So you were out until the early hours of the morning… why?"

While we eat our sandwiches, I explain everything, and Clara listens quietly, which is very unlike her. After I'm done, she remains quiet, which makes me nervous. A fact I've learned over the years: when a chatty woman is quiet, some major shit will go down.

"So, you have the hots for Alice."

"Well—"

"It wasn't a question. It's a fact." She holds her palm up, and all I can do is chuckle. "Why don't you ask her out?"

"I'm going to move in two weeks. What's the point?"

"The point is you glowed while talking about her."

I coil. "Clara, for God's sake. I'm a man. I don't glow."

"So if you weren't moving in two weeks, you would ask her out?" she continues undeterred.

"Good question."

"What's your answer?"

"Alice and I are different. She might not admit it, but she has stars in her eyes, believing in happy ever afters and all that jazz."

"True. Plus, her parents have been married for almost four decades. I suppose it contributed to her being a believer."

Usually I appreciate the fact that Clara remembers everything I tell her. Except when she's turning my words against me. I have a hunch this is what's about to happen.

"And your parents getting divorced when you were thirteen and still not standing to be in the same room with each other all these years later turned you into a nonbeliever."

I shake my head, not really in the mood to delve into this topic.

"Clara, no offense, but I don't believe in that crap. Justifying my choices by my parents' mistakes is a coward's way out. There's only so much one can blame on childhood stuff."

"It's not crap. It's scientifically proven. Our childhood years mark us." Clara's voice catches and she glances to her hands.

Way to put your foot in your mouth, Becker.

"Your story is different," I say gently. Her parents died when she was young, and Clara spent most of her childhood in foster homes. Of course that kind of background shapes you. "My parents just divorced. Half the marriages in this country fall apart."

She smiles weakly. "This is the last thing I will say about this, but there is a lot of research on the topic, concluding that people are afraid to perpetuate the same unhappy pattern they've seen in their family. So a child of divorce would not be a believer in marriage because he'd subconsciously fear that any marriage ends in divorce… and possibly kids going through the same thing he did."

I brush the theory off, even though it doesn't sound farfetched. In fact, it hits home surprisingly hard.

"How about I always choose work over relationships. There are only so many hours in a day."

"Suit yourself, but if you think about it more, you'll see I'm right."

We finish our sandwiches in silence afterward, and my mind slides to Alice and all the fun we had yesterday. If someone had told me that partying with a bunch of seniors would go down as one of the best nights of my life, I would've told them they're insane.

Then again, it wasn't the best night because of the seniors. It was because of a certain spitfire brunette who is monopolizing my thoughts.

After we head inside, Clara and I go over the schedule for my remaining days in San Francisco.

"We should squeeze in the meeting with the producer one day at dinner," Clara says. Dinner meetings are the last resort—something we do when every other option fails.

"Works for me. How about next Friday?"

She shakes her head, surveying her private calendar. "I can't. I have plans."

"Date?"

"Nah, I'm going out with Alice's sister Pippa and some other girls from the family."

"I didn't realize you knew them personally."

"I dropped by one of Alice's locations after the *Delicious Dining* team said they might be interested in featuring all three restaurants. Wanted to check it out for myself. Pippa was there and one thing led to another."

"Why am I suspecting I was the talk of the town?"

"Because you have great instincts. I like Pippa."

Clara becoming friends with the Bennett clan is an excellent thing. She doesn't have any family, and I like knowing she'll have someone to rely on after I move to London.

"Me too. But I'm also afraid of her."

Clara elbows me, chuckling. "You're a smart man. I haven't met all of them, but I think all the Bennett girls should be feared. Even those who married into the family."

I nod thoughtfully, imagining the women Sebastian and Logan married are fierce and determined too. It still boggles my mind that both are married, and the older set of twins, Christopher and Max, are engaged.

The image of Alice slightly off balance after one too many drinks pops in my mind. She turned into a lovely goof, but she also lowered her guard, leaned in too close, felt me up with no regrets. I knew it was time to stop dancing when I started imagining the front buttons of her dress popping open all on their own. I only have so much self-control, and Alice was testing it with dedication.

She was sober by the time I drove her home, and we agreed to meet again before I leave, even though I have a hunch things will escalate next time I see her.

Chapter Six

Alice

Go, Alice. You can do it. I repeat this over and over as I push myself to the limit, hoping to reach the six-mile mark today. I try to increase the limit each Monday. Training for a marathon requires as much mental discipline as it does physical strength.

Once I cross the mark, I slow to a walking pace, breathing in deeply. The afternoon air is cool and humid, and judging by the dark gray clouds hanging low in the sky, we're in for rain later on. I hate rainy evenings—people prefer to remain indoors and order in, which is bad for business.

I head into the restaurant through the back door. I keep training equipment at both my restaurants and often go for a run during downtime, which is usually between three and five. When Blue Moon opens, I'll keep equipment there too.

My office is equipped with a shower and I hop right in, mentally going through my to-do list, which is growing to epic proportions what with the opening of the third location—even though Blake is doing most of the work, bless him. I shudder thinking what my workload will look like once the location is open, but I'll have to learn to delegate better. Right now I suck at it. I have managers in each of the locations, but I double-check everything they do so thoroughly that I might as well do the job myself. I have no idea how Logan and Sebastian built Bennett Enterprises, or how they run that mammoth. Pippa, Christopher, and Max all work there too. They make quite the unstoppable team.

Once I'm dressed again and ready for work, I check my phone, which I didn't have with me while running. I have ten missed calls from various business partners, as well as messages from Nate. We haven't seen each other since Thursday.

Nate: I have some great news.

I check the time he sent me the message, ignoring my quickening pulse. Five minutes ago.

Alice: Do tell.

Nate: Nah, it has to be delivered in person. Can I come by for a quick snack? I'm in the neighborhood.

Alice: Sure. I can have lunch ready for you when you drop by if you tell me what you want.

Nate: Already had lunch, but I won't say no to a snack.

Alice: Done.

I try not to get ahead of myself imagining what the good news might be, so instead I focus on my to-do list. Thank God for downtime. Usually that means having about five to eight guests, but today there is just one, Colin. He works nearby and often has a late lunch here. Unfortunately, he's also asked me out, and I've turned him down often enough that it's almost embarrassing to meet his eye. We've chatted often enough for me to realize we have nothing in common. I'm not looking to date for the sake of dating or to have some action under the sheets. I simply don't have any more energy to pursue things I know will go nowhere. I greet him politely but then avoid further interaction while arranging the centerpieces on the rest of the tables. At the end, I bring him the bill, since all my servers are on break. And then he makes his move.

"Alice, do you have time to grab a drink tonight?" His voice is low, clearly intending to come off as seductive. Despite his best efforts and his English accent, he fails to incite an appropriate reaction in me. My pulse isn't quickening. There are no butterflies in my stomach. Still, I don't find it in myself to wipe the hopeful smile off his face. I might be known for my take-no-prisoners attitude, but I'm not heartless. On the other hand, how often am I supposed to tell him no before he stops insisting? I decide to go with an 'It's not you, it's me' explanation. Truthfully, it is me.

"Colin, I'm not looking to date right now. I can offer you friendship but nothing more."

His smile doesn't fade. "I'll wear you down. Have a nice day."

Great. Not what I was hoping for, but before I can come back with a firmer statement, he winks and takes off. It's only as I watch him walk out through the front door that I see Nate was inside already, sitting at a table. *Damn, did he listen to our conversation?*

"I didn't hear you come in."

"Saw you were busy, so I kept quiet. So, this Colin guy—"

"None of your business."

His shit-eating grin tells me he indeed listened to the conversation. "You could have been firmer. Now he'll keep pestering you."

"Maybe I'll change my mind," I tease.

His grin fades a tad. "So you'll go out with him?"

I give a noncommittal shrug, curious to see where he's going with this.

"What do you see in him?"

"He's a nice guy!"

"He's a wimp."

"You don't even know him."

"What else?"

"What else what?"

"What else do you like in him?"

"His British accent."

Nate snorts, shaking his head. "I'll never understand women's fascination with the British accent. Anyone can fake it. 'I'll have a bloody gin tonic, please.'"

I dismiss his impression of an accent with a wave of my hand. "Fake accents are like fake orgasms. All noise, no substance."

Nate's irises instantly darken and he rises from the table, stalking in my direction.

"If you had to fake orgasms, you've been dating the wrong men, *love*."

Damn. He says that typical British endearment word without any accent, but I'm tempted to double-check if my underwear is still in place or if it spontaneously vanished into thin air. I'm in such trouble. Shrugging one shoulder, I try not to let on how much his proximity affects me. I'm not sure I'm succeeding.

"That's why I'm still looking."

"A word of advice? Colin won't cut it."

"Because he's nice? Nice guys don't hurt women."

"Getting bored to death is also a form of pain. Should be officially considered an affliction."

"You know what's a pain? You!" I point my forefinger at him, following every word with a sharp tap on his chest. "You're a pain in my ass."

"Why, because I'm telling you the truth?"

"Yes," I admit, dropping my hand to the side, recognizing defeat. "I was just messing with you. I have no intentions of going out with Colin. Turned him down a couple of times, but he's persistent."

"Be firmer."

"I will next time. He weaseled out before I could today." Out of the corner of my eye, a movement at the entrance of the restaurant catches my eye. "Damn, he's coming back."

"You want him to stop asking you out?"

"Yes."

"You sure?"

"Yeah."

"I have an idea. Are you game for anything?"

Licking my lips, I avert my gaze from his mouth to a spot on his shirt. "Yeah. What do you have in mind?"

The bastard kisses me. The second his mouth covers mine, everything around us fades. Aligning his body with mine, he pushes me against the counter, lighting a match inside me, setting free all my pent-up desire. His lips are rough, scorching everything in their path. He kisses me like a man possessed, exploring my mouth, tasting and probing and demanding.

Somewhere at the back of my mind lurks the thought that this is all for show, but it sure as hell feels real. I become aware of all the points of contact between our bodies, of the slight tremor in his chest, as if he's fighting hard to control himself. My hands move along his chest of their own accord, shamelessly touching him. I start with the taut swell of his skin over his broad, strong shoulders, then lower my fingers to the defined squares of his abs. A smart woman with more self-restraint than me would stop there, but a haze of lust has befuddled my neurons. As such, I lower my hand even more until I reach the dent of his obliques. A groan reverberates from deep inside him. My fantasy supplies a terribly detailed mental image of the V formed by said oblique muscles. I imagine there is a dusting of hair starting under his navel and leading into his boxers.

Nate intensifies the kiss, his tongue inviting mine to dance in a maddening rhythm. One of his hands cups the side of my jaw, protective and possessive in equal measure. The other hand explores me. Feeling the slightly callused pads of his fingers trail along my exposed forearm is pure torture, lighting up all my nerve endings. When he reaches my shoulder, his thumb moves in small circles down to my clavicle, resting at the base of my neck. I legitimately fear I might spontaneously combust.

Desperately needing a mouthful of fresh air, I pull back. Nate rests his lips at the corner of my mouth. His hot breath caresses the skin on my cheeks, and the sharp rhythm of his inhales and exhales betrays how deeply this kiss affected him. I swear the air between us crackles. He steps back and I instantly move to the right, desperately needing to put some distance between us. Glancing toward the entrance, I notice Colin's gone. That's when it hits me how rude this was to Colin. I'd just told him I'm not interested in dating. It was also unprofessional. Granted, my servers are on their break, but someone could have still walked in.

"What was I thinking? Putting on a show?" I mutter on a groan.

Nate doesn't miss a beat. "I didn't give you a chance to think. As you can see, it worked out great." A satisfied grin spreads on his features as he steps in my direction.

I almost jump back, pointing a menacing finger at him. "Stay where you are. I haven't been kissed this good in a long while. My hormones can't be trusted."

And lo and behold, my legendary no-filter answers finally decided to make an appearance—at the most inappropriate of times, of course. Nate bursts out laughing, ignoring my warning and closing the distance between us.

"Always happy to be at your service." His voice is low and husky. With every word, a warm breath lands on my cheek. It feels like velvet against my skin. I want to wrap it around myself and sleep cocooned in that velvety warmth.

Breathing in and out, I try to gather my wits. It's a difficult task, given how everything about Nate is overwhelming. The mere memory of our kiss is enough to turn me on and, most dangerously, have me wanting a repeat.

"The news you mentioned?"

"Right. The *Delicious Dining* team wants to move forward. They want to include all your restaurants in the feature."

"Wow. I can't believe this. Thank you so much."

"As a next step, they'd like to meet with you in about two weeks."

"Blake too?"

"Their focus is on restaurants, so they specifically asked to see you."

"Got it. What do you want for a snack?"

"It's safest if I go now. Otherwise, I might do something crazy." He smiles at me, and I warm all over again. *Oh my.* I can still taste him on my lips and tell the exact places where he touched my waist and the back of my head.

"Okay." I won't lie; I was hoping he'd stick around a while longer, although for what purpose exactly, I'm not sure. Well, we could find plenty of purposes like kissing, ripping each other's clothes off. *Damn, I can't follow this line of thought. It's dangerous.*

I walk him to the restaurant entrance in silence, mulling over how one kiss can affect me so much. In my defense, it was a scorching-hot kiss. As he bids me goodbye in the doorway, he leans in.

"Alice?"

"Yeah?"

"That was one hell of a kiss."

Chapter Seven

Alice

My mind is reeling for the rest of the day, and more than once, I catch myself smiling for no reason. Well, that's not true. There is a reason. He's about six feet tall, candy on a stick, and his name is Nate. A small part of me still fears I might have imagined the kiss, or dreamed it. I want to call and ask him more details about the meeting with the *Delicious Dining* team, but I need a breather first.

I throw myself into work until late at night, and then reason it's too late to call him, so instead I do it first thing the next morning. Sitting cross-legged in my bed, still wearing pajamas, I dial his number. He answers right away.

"Took you an awfully long time to get those hormones back in check."

He effectively breaks the ice, and I find myself grinning.

"Yep. Whipped them good, gave them a lecture. Don't worry, you're safe now."

"You're not."

I lick my lips. "What?"

"You heard me."

Oh boy. His voice is low and seductive. *Bedroom voice.* Right, I can't let my mind go there. I called with a purpose.

"I wanted to ask for some tips. What will the meeting with the *Delicious Dining* people be like?"

"You should definitely have a pitch prepared."

"A sales pitch?"

"More than that. They'll want to know about you too, the story behind the restaurants. In a nutshell, they want a captivating story. Something to keep viewers glued to the TV. You should elaborate on the points we talked about when we met at Blue Moon."

My stomach sinks. I know my strengths, and captivating a group of strangers with my storytelling isn't one of them. I can efficiently prepare a sales pitch, and I can even confidently throw around marketing terms such as 'unique selling proposition' and 'competitive advantage,' but telling a story is another beast.

"Sounds complex."

"I'll help you prepare."

"I like how there's no question mark at the end of that sentence."

"Not giving you a chance to turn me down."

"You have time? I'm sure you have a million things to do before leaving." My throat almost closes up as I utter that last word.

"I have time. Does Friday evening work?" His tone is downright bossy now. A delicious twinkle of awareness travels through my limbs. I can't believe bossy is doing it for me. His alpha caveman tendencies were one thing, but this is different. Maybe it was just a mishap. I should test this some more, make sure I'm not imagining things.

"What if I say no?"

"I'll show up anyway."

"You don't even know where I'll be."

"Damn you, woman, stop fighting or I'll kiss you again when I do find you. And I'll kiss you good, hard, and long."

Oh my! There's definitely a twinkle, possibly even a sizzle. I don't recognize myself.

"You're a bad man." My voice is a raspy whisper—*my* bedroom voice. Pulling myself together, I smooth a wrinkle on my bedsheet with the back of my hand, forcing my trail of thoughts on a safe path again. "But thank you for wanting to help. I really appreciate it, Nate. Let's meet at Blake's bar so we can include him in the conversation. Even if he won't come to the meeting, I don't want him to feel left out."

"Sounds great."

"My car is out of the mechanic's shop," I add quickly before he can offer to pick me up.

"Afraid to be alone with me?"

"Yes."

"Good. You should be."

"See you on Friday."

"Looking forward to it. And Alice? Just because we won't be alone doesn't mean you're safe with me."

Oh God. This man is killing me.

***

Nate

I meet with both Logan and Sebastian the next evening for drinks, and while we're rehashing old memories, I feel like an ass because I kissed their sister. I owe these guys—the entire family. They kept me grounded in a time when I was lost, and how am I repaying them? I briefly consider coming clean about Alice, but what good would that do? It was a one-time thing, and even though she's been on my mind constantly since, there won't be a repeat, even if I have to fight myself every second on Friday evening.

Friday comes around quickly, and at four o'clock I receive an unexpected call from Horowitz, asking if I can meet him in his office. I assume he finally has the contract for London ready—the office in the United Kingdom took their sweet time sending it over—and I agree to meet him right away.

Horowitz is pacing in his office when I arrive. He gestures for me to sit in the chair in front of his desk, but I'm too wired to sit.

"No need. I can sign while standing too. I'm assuming this is about the London contract?"

Horowitz clears his throat, and I realize he looks uncomfortable. I've only seen him uncomfortable once before, when wife number two caught him banging someone. She came to surprise him at the office, and the surprise was on her. She raised hell, yelling at him loud enough for the entire floor to hear.

"There's been a change."

"A change?"

"The London office decided to go in another direction with the hire."

My body goes cold. I don't remember leaning in, but here I am, my knuckles resting on the desk.

"What?"

Horowitz throws his hands up in despair. "They decided to go with the good-for-nothing Abbott."

I finally sink in the seat, closing my hand into a fist. "Abbott? He doesn't have half the experience I do."

"No, but he has the right DNA."

"What's that supposed to mean?"

"He's David's nephew."

David is the head of the London headquarters. "I had no idea."

"Not many people do, only those at the top. What can I say, nepotism is alive and well in corporate America. Or corporate United Kingdom in this case."

"Screw this, Horowitz. David has seen what I can do."

"Yeah. My bet is the nephew won't last the year in the position. Ratings will go down."

My blood starts to boil with anger.

"I don't want the ratings to go down. I just want the job. I've earned it, and it was a done deal."

"Nothing's a done deal without a signed contract, I'm afraid. Look, there's nothing to do about London now." Horowitz leans forward, thumping his arms on the table. "But I have a good offer for you here at headquarters. We need a new executive producer for our star show."

That piques my interest, because the *star show*, as he put it, is the network's shining achievement in years. It's a local production, and it's killing it in national ratings. It's as far as it can be from *The 300*, but an interesting challenge. It also already has an executive producer. A damn good one. "Why do you need a new one? Teller is the best man."

"The poor chap has to retire early. He's too sick to continue working."

"I'm sorry. I didn't know."

"Yeah." He opens the drawer under his desk, taking out a stack of papers. "I have the contract ready for you to look over it."

"How long have you had this?"

"We've been searching for a while for someone to take over. When I heard the news from London, I thought, 'their loss, our gain.' Read this. The salary's seven figures, and you'd be running your own show." He pushes the stack of papers across the table toward me.

"I won't bother reading it unless you can assure me I have full creative control. It's the only thing that matters to me."

Horowitz laughs wholeheartedly. "You're a difficult bastard to work with. Read the contract. You'll like the terms, and everything is negotiable. A man of your talent is hard to come by."

"When do you need an answer?"

"As soon as possible."

"I'll read this over the weekend."

He claps as I take the contract off the desk. "Perfect. Be smart about this. It's a lot of money."

Rising from the chair, I shake his hand, and leave his office.

My mind is spinning until I pull the car in front of the studio. I have too much energy and I need to walk it off, so I take the stairs up to the studio instead of the elevator. Clara waves when she sees me. Her smile fades when she approaches—probably a direct effect of seeing my expression up close.

"I'm confused. You have a contract in your hand but look like someone pissed in your coffee. What's going on?"

"Let's head outside on the balcony."

"So, what went down with Horowitz?" Clara asks once we're outside.

In quick words, I tell her the London deal fell through, but I have a new offer here in San Francisco.

"Wow," she says after I finish. "What are you going to do?"

"I'm going to take the job." I run a frustrated hand through my hair. So many years of hard work just to see the opportunity I've busted my ass for disappear.

"Great! I don't have to find another boss. You don't have to find another assistant."

"There are many advantages to staying here." Alice being the most important one.

"Ah yes. Alice Bennett is one of them, right?"

"Clara, don't start."

She crosses her arms across her chest, giving me her trademark *Don't act like you don't know what I'm talking about* look.

"Would I be wrong to assume she's the reason why you haven't been out with anyone since you landed in San Francisco?"

"Why do I have the feeling that answering this will open a can of worms?"

Clara lets out a sound somewhere between a yelp and a cry of victory. "It's already open, but until now I've filled it with my imagination. I'm dying for some facts. Spill the beans."

"You've given this a lot of thought, huh?"

She nods eagerly. "My first thought was childhood sweethearts or something, but while I was having lunch with Pippa one day, Sebastian and Logan stopped by. They have big-brother behavior written all over them. They probably would've ripped you a new one if you'd gotten hot and heavy with their sister."

"Your confidence in me is astounding."

"Hey, you're a badass, but there's two of them. So, anyway, I discarded that idea. Now I'm going more for unrequited love? Love from afar? What is it?"

I mask my smile with a fist, watching her as she bounces on her toes, like she's preparing to take off.

"Come on, I'm dying here, Nate."

"I was rather enjoying your monologue."

She points a menacing finger in my direction. "Don't mess with the woman who buys your morning coffee."

"And I buy yours sometimes. How did we escalate to threats already?"

"That's how I roll. So?"

"It's a mix of everything you said—"

"So you did get hot and naughty when you were teenagers? And the brothers let you live? Or didn't find out? Huh… you're sneakier than I gave you credit for."

"Not what I meant."

Her shoulders sag in disappointment.

"We always had a thing for each other but didn't act on it. Part of that was Alice's age, and yeah, Sebastian and Logan did make it clear their sisters were off-limits. Later on, I was always traveling."

"And the other part?"

"You know my track record with dating and relationships. I always thought it was preferable to have Alice in my life as Sebastian's little sister, or as a friend as she grew up, rather than as an ex or not at all."

"Sounds like someone believes relationships, in general, are doomed."

"Not all, just mine. You think I'm not aware I keep women at arm's length?"

Clara chuckles. "Sounds like something a woman would throw in your face."

"I've heard it more than once. Can't say I disagree."

"Ah, ding, ding, ding. My theory about people afraid to perpetuate parents' unhappy patterns starting to ring more true?"

I scoff, then remember being thirteen when I first searched for divorce rates online. Before, I lived in the bubble all kids do, where they think all parents will be together forever. Seeing Mom unhappy in her second marriage didn't help. Sure, Alice's parents, Jenna and Richard, were a pleasant surprise, but I knew that for each Bennett family out there, there were ten times more families like mine: broken, patched up, dysfunctional. But I'm man enough to own up to my choices as an adult.

"No, it doesn't."

Clara groans. "You're a stubborn mule."

"I am. But I'm meeting Alice in one hour. And I plan to ask her out."

Chapter Eight

Alice

I'm about to head out the door for my meeting with Nate when my phone rings. As usual, I have so many random items in my bag that it takes me forever to find my phone. I really should clean it out more often. My fingers touch the hard case of the phone just as the ringing ceases. When I pull it out, I see Pippa was the one calling, and I dial right back.

"Hey, sis," I greet her as I hurry to my car.

"What are you up to? Want to stop by the house?"

"I can't." Guilt gnaws at me because I haven't seen my sister since my parents' party. Before the kids, she and I would go out on a whim to get a drink, or eat, or just catch up. But now going out requires more planning, which usually means I go to her house. Truth be told, I prefer the new arrangements because I use any chance I get to smother those angels with kisses.

"Oh shucks. I'll just tell you over the phone, then. Guess what words Elena said today? 'Aunt Alice.'"

I swear my heart grows twice in size. "She did?"

"Yeah, and now Mia is giving her the evil eye because she can't say it."

"She's two. She doesn't know how to give the evil eye yet."

"You'll believe it when you see it. Trust me, it's a little scary."

"Can you put her on the phone? I'd love to hear her say it."

"Nah, I haven't figured out how to make her say it. She sort of just blurts it out every now and again. Whenever I specifically ask her to say it, she just smiles at me and tries to poke my eye."

The twins have started speaking *very* late. Pippa was extremely worried for a while, even though the pediatrician assured her it's normal and some kids start talking later.

"Maybe I can stop by tomorrow," I say hopefully.

"Sure. So, what are you doing tonight?"

I clear my throat for no reason before saying, "I'm meeting with Nate at Blake's bar. He talked to the network about a feature on their *Delicious Dining* show, and the team wants to see me next week. He's going to give me some pointers."

"Oh!"

That one word tells with about ninety percent precision what's going on in her head. She's wondering if our meeting is strictly professional.

"I reached my car. Call you later?" Fingers crossed that she won't push for more info or I might crack under pressure and tell her about the kiss.

"Sure. By the way, Nadine just called to tell me she's pregnant."

"Wow. There's going to be a new baby in the family. How's Logan?"

"Haven't talked to him yet."

"Hmm, when you do talk to him, can you reassure him he'll be a good dad and all that?"

"Why?"

"When Sebastian found out Ava was pregnant, he was at the restaurant with Christopher and me, and he had a little freak-out. We tried to reassure him, and I'm not sure if Logan will follow in his footsteps, but just in case, talk to him. Since you have kids, your reassurances weigh more than mine."

"Of course. I love how our brothers are these big badasses, but when it comes to kids, they just transform."

"They do."

Someone starts to cry on my sister's end. "Shoot, I have to go. Good luck at your meeting. I can't wait for details."

***

Twenty minutes later, I elbow my way through Blake's bar, hoping to make it to the counter in one piece. The place is not just packed—it's *packed* packed. My brother is behind the counter, even though there are two other bartenders on shift. He seems to have as much a grip on delegating as I do. We'll make quite a pair running the new location together.

"Hey! Don't stay here, these nutheads will squish you," Blake says when I finally make it to the counter, gesturing with his head to the right. "I kept the table next to the bar empty. I'll join you there when Nate gets here."

Nate arrives exactly ten minutes later. From where I sit at the high and sleek bar table, I have a perfect vantage point.

Where I had to elbow my way through the crowd, Nate has no problems getting through. People *make* room for him, moving out of his way. Men are intimidated, women fascinated. He exudes confidence, power, and masculinity.

For the next hour or so, Nate, Blake, and I talk about the upcoming meeting. Nate informs me he'll be attending too, since he was the one who put in the recommendation. I could hug him with joy. He knows this stuff inside out, and I'm hanging onto his every word, taking notes. After Blake apologetically says he should return to the bar before it all goes up in flames, Nate suggests we do a Q&A, a meeting simulation of sorts. When we're done, I have a great feeling about the whole thing. With some of the pressure lifting off my shoulders, I drum my palms against the edge of the table, excitement coursing through me.

"Do you want a drink?" Nate asks. We haven't had anything while working.

"Yes, please. A glass of chardonnay."

"Be right back."

While I wait for Nate, a tall man with neatly trimmed blond hair and a smile that's easy on the eyes approaches the table.

"Can I buy you a drink?" he asks.

"I'm already waiting on one, but thank you."

"Later, perhaps?"

"Already getting a drink is code for she's here with someone." Nate appears from behind him with my drink. The guy practically winces.

"Hey, man, no harm no foul. She could have been here with girlfriends."

Nate glares at him. The guy scurries away immediately.

"Hey, why did you scare him away?"

"Wimp."

"Him too?" I ask with amusement, remembering he called Colin one too.

"He winced. Wimp behavior."

I take the glass of wine from him, sipping. Nate brought a beer for himself.

"I haven't been out with a man in months. Almost forgot what it feels like."

Nate climbs on the barstool next to me. "That's an outrage and must be rectified immediately. I can help."

"How, by scaring away the next man who asks me out? Or shoving your tongue down my throat in front of him?"

His eyes sparkle as if I just had the most brilliant idea.

"Is that your way of telling me you want me to kiss you again?" His tone is playful, but it throws me off balance. Where is he going with this? I feel like I'm trapped in a cat-and-mouse game, only I'm not sure if I'm the cat or the mouse. I don't mind, but I want to know where I'm standing.

"Is there a point you're trying to make?"

"You deserve someone who can sweep you off your feet, Alice."

I blink, momentarily speechless. This isn't where I thought this conversation was going.

"Meaning?"

"Someone who's man enough for you. Who'd make you say yes to a date in a heartbeat, and when he does take you out, you'll enjoy it so much you'll practically beg for another date."

"How would he do that?"

"He'd take you somewhere fancy and order your favorite dessert."

"How would he know my favorite?"

"If he doesn't do the legwork to find out, he doesn't deserve the date."

"Never used it as cutoff criteria. I'll put it on my list. Any other things I should add?"

"By the end of the date, he'd kiss you on a table or against a wall."

"Kissing on tables or against a wall is inappropriate for a first date," I say reasonably, but a shiver of excitement travels down my spine and heat pools in intimate places. Damn Nate and his effect on me.

"You've really been dating the wrong men."

"Know any right candidate?" I challenge.

"Me."

My heart rate picks up so fast I'm afraid it might leap out of my chest.

"What?" I have to ask because I don't want to risk even the slightest possibility I've misheard him.

"I know what your favorite dessert is. I'm excellent at kissing on tables or against walls, or anywhere, really. Date me."

Oh my. Every cell in my body wants to sing with joy, but the reasonable part of my brain is still confused, needs more explanations.

"A date?" I repeat clumsily. The word bounces back and forth in my mind, not quite making sense yet. But even though my mind can't fully process this, my body does. Hope surges in my chest as my pulse spikes. Adrenaline and heat course through my veins, resulting in a mix so powerful I'm nearly giddy. Dating Nate would mean holding hands and finally, *finally* being able to lose myself in those big arms of his. It would mean I'd finally have carte blanche to openly admire that fine body of his instead of just sneaking glances. It would mean carte blanche to do more than admiring: to touch and taste him, to kiss every inch of his body, to please him.

I lick my lips, mentally berating myself for already picturing the two of us in bed. But I'm so high on anticipation and giddiness that I can't help riding the wave. Dating him would mean I'd get to take care of him, making him laugh every day, making sure he has someone to turn to when stress at work is putting too much pressure on him. I'd get a chance to make him fall in love with me.

Woooooooow, I'm not getting ahead of myself or anything.

"But you're leaving," I say finally, remembering that particular detail.

He shakes his head. "The London deal fell through."

Despite all the ramifications this might have, right now all I can think about is how terrible this is for him. He wanted it so much.

"I'm so sorry. What happened? You said the job was practically yours."

"Turns out it wasn't. They decided to go with someone who's related to the big boss over there."

"Ouch."

"So instead, I was offered a permanent job here."

"Oh?"

"Yeah. I haven't officially accepted it yet, told them I'll think it through over the weekend, but I'm going to take it. It's not what I was going after, but there's a lot I can do with it. A new challenge."

I always loved Nate's determination to see the positive side of everything, to take what's thrown at him and turn it into something beautiful. But beneath his bravado, his voice is tinged with disappointment and hurt. I want to make it go away, make him smile again.

"So, how about that date?" He slides to the edge of his seat, inching even closer as if determined to overpower me.

I clear my throat. "Sounds great. But I'll have you know, I have a five-date rule."

"What do you mean?"

The corners of my lips twitch. "I don't put out until after the fifth date."

"You don't put out what… the trash, the light, fires?"

Flashing him a grin, I take a sip of my wine. Torturing him feels far too good. I make a mental note to do it more often. *Don't look into his eyes more than five seconds at a time.* My willpower weakens the longer his gaze traps me, and I want to stick to my guns.

"Don't mess with me. You know what I'm talking about."

He straightens in his chair, a look of intense concentration on his face. "How about three dates?"

"This is nonnegotiable, you brute."

"Okay, but why five? I've heard of the three-date rule, but five is just cruel."

He looks positively crestfallen now, and it occurs to me that no woman has ever said no to him before. By the way he referred to the three-date rule, it's clearly something he only heard of as an urban myth, not something he experienced himself. I bet women succumb to his charms from the first date, and if I let him cage me in with his gaze again, I might join their ranks.

"Well, the first one is to make sure we really want to date, if there is a spark. The second is to confirm we didn't just imagine the spark, and to get to know each other better. The third is to discover what more we have in common." Since I completely made up the rule of five, here's where it gets tricky. All I want is to make sure he really wants this. The chances of getting my heart broken will be lower then, I hope.

A few seconds into brainstorming, inspiration strikes. "The fourth is for testing whether we're still interested in each other. The fifth is a prelude for sealing the deal."

Part of me had hoped Nate's expression would become even more crestfallen by my explanation (yep, I can be a little witch), but instead, he's grinning like the Cheshire cat. I feel like I've walked into a trap, only I don't understand how. With this also comes a realization: I'm definitely the mouse in our game.

"I've known you for a long time, Alice. That covers about four of your dates."

"It does not," I insist. "The spark—"

"We nearly set fire to your restaurant with one kiss." He slides two fingers under my chin, lifting it up. I have no choice but to look directly at him. "We have spark."

Damn, what can I say? My skin instantly reacts to his words and touch. Goose bumps form on my arms, and blood rushes to my cheeks and neck.

"Look at you," he murmurs. "Your skin is all flushed already."

"You're distracting me." Pushing his hand away, I square my shoulders, gathering my wits. My skin prickles with heat where he touched me moments ago.

"So knowing you for years doesn't count at all?"

"Nope. You don't know me romantically. I might be into stuff you don't like."

"Like what?"

"I might be into kinky stuff."

Throwing his head back, Nate laughs throatily. I love his laughter so much, I don't even feel embarrassed that it's at my expense.

"What kind? Bondage? Whips? Kinkier? I'm not turning you on with all this kink talk, am I?"

Sure enough, I burn everywhere. Truthfully, I'm not into any of it, but just hearing him talk about it messes with me. Also, my five-date rule requires me to volunteer more information. "I just want both of us to be sure this is a good idea, that we won't regret any of it."

Nate brings his chair closer, resting his legs on the outside of mine, trapping me inside. For a split second, I'm convinced he's about to seal his mouth over mine, but then he does the oddest thing. He lifts my hand to his mouth, feathering his lips on the back of my hand. He lingers there for several long seconds.

"I'm going to wait for as long as you need me to, Alice. This isn't about getting you into bed. This is about giving us a shot. I've wanted this for a long time, and I think you've wanted it for even longer. We deserve a chance."

I nod enthusiastically. "We do. But tonight, we're focusing on you."

"First date?"

"Nope. This is just two friends getting together. One had a shitty day, the other is lightening him up. A date would require me to at least take a trip to the beauty salon first."

"Killing me here."

"Counting on it."

Chapter Nine

Alice

Who am I, and what have I done with Alice Bennett?

The question pops in my mind more than once as I inspect my appearance in the mirror the morning of the meeting with the *Delicious Dining* team. I'm wearing a sleeveless dark blue dress that falls all the way to my knees. It hugs my waist tightly, flowing down in a straight line. I've styled my hair in an asymmetric ponytail to the right and put on more makeup than usual. I want to impress them, and looks matter, especially when it comes to people working in television.

Grabbing my coat, I rush out the door. There is a thick layer of fog all around me, but it doesn't dampen my mood in the slightest. It does, however, make me shiver and pull my coat around me tighter right until I climb in my car. Damn San Francisco mornings. It's mid-June; why can't it be warmer, clearer?

Half an hour later, I step inside a lush office building. It takes a few minutes to check in at the reception desk and receive a visitor badge.

"You look gorgeous," a deep, manly voice says from behind me, nearly making me jump. Turning around, I inhale sharply, taking in the vision before me. Nate Becker is wearing a suit, and he's looking *damn fine*. He so rarely wears a suit that he knocks me off my feet every time he does. The first time I saw him in one was at one of Bennett Enterprises' collection shows. I was young and impressionable, and he was gorgeous. Now I'm not so young anymore, and I'd like to think I'm less impressionable, but he's still as gorgeous as he can be.

The black color of the suit jacket and the white shirt underneath are clearly meant to send the message that he means business.

"Thank you," I reply. "You clean up well yourself."

Nate scrutinizes me, his gaze traveling down my body and then upward again, resting a split second longer on my waist and chest than on my other parts. My mouth and lips instantly feel dry, and I involuntarily wet my lower lip with the tip of my tongue just as Nate focuses on my face again. He catches the gesture, and his irises darken a notch. Damn. No matter how hard I try to stay at the top of my game with this man, he's always one step ahead of me. It's probably part of what pulls me to him like a magnet. He has a kind of power over me no other man has ever had.

Just as I mentally whip my thoughts back into line, promising myself not to let myself be affected by his presence, he adjusts one hem of his suit jacket, revealing he's wearing cuff links. *Well, hell.*

Nate in a suit is my weakness.

Nate in a suit and cuff links is my kryptonite.

To my surprise, he asks for a visitor badge himself.

"Why do you need one?" I ask as we head to the elevator.

"Anyone who doesn't work in this building needs one, even if they work within the network." He walks a step behind me, so close I can practically feel his breath on my neck.

"You did something with your hair," he comments as we come to a halt in front of the elevators and I press the button to summon one. "I love that it gives me easy access to your neck." As if to prove the point, he brings his mouth to my ear, adding, "I've always loved your neck."

Every nerve ending on my neck and face snaps to life, buzzing with his proximity.

Damn it, this won't do. We're about to go into a business meeting, and I don't want to appear anything less than a hundred percent professional.

"Nate," I admonish, stepping to one side and turning to face him. He looks amused. "Please behave during the meeting. I don't want anyone thinking you only agreed to this because we're…."

"Yes?"

"Dating."

His smirk grows more pronounced. "Might I remind you that we haven't been on a single date yet. You're playing hard to get, Alice." His green eyes scrutinize me with an intensity that nearly has my knees buckling. As if knowing the exact effect his words have on me, he steps closer, leaning slightly forward. Without breaking eye contact, he adds in a low, gruff voice, "It'll be my immense pleasure to *chase* you."

With a ping, the elevator doors open and half a dozen suits step out. Nate and I move out of their way, and I'm careful to keep my distance from him because *holy hell.* This man has a dangerous way with words. Several other people join us in the elevator ride, and they serve as an effective buffer between Nate and me.

Our stop, the third floor, arrives all too soon. As we step out of the elevator, he whispers in my ear, "I never play by the rules, Alice. You should know that by now."

I don't get the chance to admonish him because a blonde bombshell—for lack of better word—welcomes us.

"Welcome, Ms. Bennett. Welcome, Mr. Becker. I'm Sarah, Mr. Andrew's assistant." She shakes hands with both of us, and she all but drools over Nate. Irrational jealousy rears its head almost instantly, and I barely bite back a snappy reply. I remind myself we haven't even been on a date yet, as Nate correctly pointed out. Theoretically, he's a free agent. I discreetly observe him as Sarah leads us down a maze of corridors to the meeting room. He makes polite conversation with her, and his body language is perfectly professional. Or maybe I'm just reading into it what I want.

Five men and three women are already in the meeting room when we enter. I recognize one of the women because she regularly appears in front of the camera on *Delicious Dining.* They all sit on one side of the long table, and Nate and I are asked to sit on the opposite side. I feel like we're in front of a jury.

The moment Mr. Andrews, the head of the team, asks me if I can tell him why I'm a good fit for them, I begin with my pitch. Shoulders squared, chin held high, I speak with confidence, knowing my numbers are good, my food even better. The most efficient way to become confident in an area is to be the best at it. I've done this before when I talked to partners such as tourism agencies and local attractions, and I roped them in to recommend my restaurants to their customers.

But a few minutes into my pitch, I notice some of their expressions turn skeptical, and my confidence wavers. Drawing in a sharp breath, I try not to panic. Truth is, I've never been good with first impressions. Or rather, I make the wrong impression. More than once, people have told me they thought I was a stiff, unapproachable ice queen when they first met me. I refused to believe it at first, outright dismissed it. But after receiving the same feedback multiple times, I knew there must be some truth to it. I can usually shake off that impression as I get to know people better, but here I only have this one shot.

Casting a glance in Nate's direction, I notice a crease on his forehead as he looks around the table. My stomach sinks. This isn't all in my mind. When I finish my pitch, Nate steps in, retelling a small anecdote from our childhood. It only loosely ties to my restaurant business and what I was saying moments before, but the atmosphere at the table instantly changes. Several of them chuckle, and the others openly laugh. I'd worked in three funny lines in my pitch, and I didn't get nearly the same reaction.

Then again, Nate always had this incredible charisma. It takes me some time to realize what he's doing: he's projecting his own charisma on me, and damn if it isn't working.

The winning moment is when Nate tells them he was the first tester for my now-famous casserole, and I nearly poisoned him, it was that bad. He adds how proud he is that I've come this far. Everyone at the table bursts out laughing, and I smile sheepishly.

"Ms. Bennett, your restaurants will be a wonderful fit for our show," the head of the team exclaims, with a few others nodding in agreement. A weight lifts from my shoulders, a knot unfurls in my chest, and I cast a glance full of gratitude at Nate, who winks at me and then offers one of his trademark Cheshire cat smiles. Confused, I cock a brow at him. In response, he merely glances downward to my legs. *Oh no!* My dress inched waaaay up my thighs, probably because I nervously crossed and uncrossed my legs too many times during the pitch. As inconspicuously as possible, I rearrange my dress, and Nate *accidentally on purpose* touches my outer thigh with his knee. He's done being on his best behavior.

***

Nate

Alice is smiling from ear to ear when we leave the building. I love seeing her happy, and it gives me pleasure that I played a part in putting that smile on her face.

"It went fantastic," she exclaims.

"They absolutely loved you."

"Only after you cast some of your magic charisma over me. They were starting to look right through me two minutes into my pitch. Thank you."

We walk side by side toward the coffee shop three blocks down where Blake is meeting us so we can report how the meeting went. Even though the *Delicious Dining* show focuses mostly on the food, the bar is an added bonus, and they'll showcase it properly.

"Yeah, you sometimes come off as…."

"Ice queen? Stiff? Don't spare punches. I've heard it all before. No idea how to fix it."

"It's a matter of trust. When you first meet people, you're not comfortable enough being yourself. After you warm up to them, they fall under your charm."

I invited myself to this meeting precisely for this reason. It doesn't always happen, but I figured if it does, I'd rather be next to her and help out. She's not exaggerating about my charisma. It has helped my career a lot. No one likes someone who has no problem calling them out on their shit, but they might accept him if he makes them laugh too.

"What was your first impression about me?"

"Are you kidding? I was shell-shocked when I saw the lot of you. I mean, Sebastian did tell me he had eight siblings, but hearing about it still didn't prepare me for seeing all of you."

"So I didn't stand out?" she asks with a pout, and damn if I don't want to kiss it away from her pretty face.

"I remember thinking you were the most annoying."

"Wow, talk about a low blow. And I thought the sun shone out of your butthole from the moment I saw you."

I come to a halt as we turn right into the narrow side street leading to the cafe and she stops too, half turning to me. "Really?"

"Yeah, but I used to get a kick out of making you smile. Took it as a personal victory. My affliction only got worse with time, especially after the hormones kicked in."

"So much appreciation for me and you're still torturing me with the rule of five?"

She shrugs. "That was puppy love. It faded. Now we're adults. Totally different game. I'm older now, and wiser."

I know what she's doing: protecting herself. But she shouldn't bother because I will not hurt her. I'll make mistakes because I'm out of my depth when it comes to seriously pursuing a woman, but I'll make an honest effort to not screw up often. But if there is one thing I know, it's that trust must be earned.

"And I like busting your balls."

Alice is one hell of a woman! I never know what might come out of her pretty mouth, but right now, her words travel straight to my groin, and we're out on a street.

Lifting one hand to her face, I place the pad of my thumb on the center of her lower lip. "Careful, Alice. I don't want to hear that word from your pretty mouth unless we're alone, and you're about to do something other than 'busting' them."

She exhales sharply, and I have a crystal-clear vision of us getting down and dirty. She licks her lower lip, but since I haven't lowered my hand, she inadvertently licks the tip of my thumb too.

My control snaps. The next seconds pass in a blur. I hook an arm around her waist, lifting her off her feet. Blindly, I back her up against the nearest wall, crushing my mouth to hers. Nothing else matters in this moment except Alice. I slide my hand to the back of her head, my thumb resting at the base of her hairline. I slip my other fingers under the fabric of her dress, splaying them on her back. She moans like I've touched her intimately. And the thought of her sweet, wet pussy is enough to make me groan too.

"You drive me crazy," I inform her after I pull back, resting my forehead against hers.

Something feels off, and it takes me a few seconds to realize why. She's barefoot, standing on her toes on top of my shoes. We seem to realize this at the same time. She bursts out laughing, and the sound is so contagious that I join her instantly. Her shoes lie a few feet to our right, in the spot where I lifted her minutes ago. We attract stares as we clumsily make our way to her shoes. She stands on her toes on top of my feet the entire way. A few passersby snicker as I help her into her heels again.

"Well, I'll give you this. No one's made me forget my shoes before." Just then, Blake turns onto the side street too, waving at us. "Let's give my brother the news and tell him what a great team we made during the meeting."

While Blake is still out of earshot, I whisper, "We'll make a good team somewhere else too, Alice."

"Oh yeah? Where?"

"In a bed. Against a wall. On the hood of my car. I promise I can make you forget more than your shoes anywhere. When I'm deep inside you, when you're full of me, you'll even forget your name."

Chapter Ten

Alice

Next Monday, Blake and I are preparing a prelaunch party for Blue Moon. Only the family is invited, and they give feedback on anything they believe can be improved. I've done this ever since opening my first restaurant, and it's served me well. I can count on them to give me honest feedback before opening the doors to guests and reviewers. I invited Nate too, but he's swamped at work. Since he officially accepted the job here last week, his schedule has become even nuttier than mine. We're finally having our first date next week. After being kissed out of my shoes, saying that I'm looking forward to it is an understatement.

"This is going to be perfect," I exclaim, drumming my fingers on the bar. Excitement courses through my veins. "Do you need help?"

"The bar is my domain." Blake's behind it, crushing some ice for drinks. "You're not allowed to touch anything."

Smiling lazily, I lean across the bar, grasping one of Blake's squeaky clean glasses and then promptly removing my hand, leaving my fingerprints on it. He points a menacing finger my way.

"Stop."

"Come on, you're the fun brother. Why so serious?"

"Just want things to work out perfectly."

***

At six o'clock sharp, the family starts arriving. Ava and Sebastian arrive first with baby Will. My big brother pulls me into a bear hug while Ava sniffs the air, rubbing her son's head.

"Oh, this is going to be a feast," she exclaims.

Logan and Nadine arrive next, closely followed by Max and Christopher and their fiancées. I've always had trouble telling the identical twins apart, but it became significantly easier ever since they each have a fiancée on their arms. Neither pair has set their wedding date yet, but we're expecting it any second now. Max confided in me that he and Emilia wanted to throw the wedding this year, but then Emilia's grandmother died, and no one was in the mood to celebrate anymore. The poor woman had Alzheimer's, and her last months were very hard.

My parents, Daniel, and Pippa with her family close the convoy. The only one missing is my baby sister Summer. I invited her, but she had a ton of work at her gallery in Rome. She would've caved if I'd pressed more, but I would've felt like an idiot making her fly over just for this.

Blake and I give the family the grand tour, starting with the bar area. I'm so proud of our work it's ridiculous. Finding the perfect location for Blue Moon took a while. My other two restaurants are high in the hills, with scenic views of the city, but I really wanted one on the waterfront. So when the opportunity came up to buy an old restaurant in Fisherman's Wharf and refurbish it, Blake and I bought it immediately. The view of San Francisco Bay and the Golden Gate Bridge in the distance is fabulous, and we made sure to build in large panoramic windows so guests can enjoy all this beauty. The interior is sleek and elegant, but also warm. The walls are the color of champagne, and the furniture is a deep, dark brown with tints of red. Victoria Hensley, Christopher's fiancée, was the decorator, and she did an excellent job.

During the tour, I let my brother do most of the talking while I focus on everyone's reactions—what catches their attention, what has them wrinkling their nose, and so on. A lot can be learned from body language. Sometimes people can't pinpoint exactly what they dislike about something, so they don't mention it at all.

Afterward, Blake starts preparing cocktails for everyone. Soon he becomes overwhelmed, so I join him.

"Alice—"

"Yes, this is your man cave, but you're going to give yourself carpal tunnel if I don't help you."

My brother elbows me playfully but doesn't reject my help.

"They weren't so excited for my bar opening," he comments.

"Because the ultimate payoff here is a feast. Food will always be a bigger attraction than booze in our family. Keep that in mind, little brother."

Once everyone has emptied their cocktails, we invite them over to the restaurant area.

Over dinner, everyone shares their impressions, and I jot everything down. Blake listens intently, following up any criticism with smart questions.

"You're so much better than me at asking for feedback," I murmur to him. "Love your questions."

Blake winks at me. "Thank fuck you're writing everything down. I never bother and then forget half the feedback. We make a great team."

"We do."

When Blake and I first decided to work together, I wasn't sure how this would pan out. My relationship in the past with him can be summed up as follows: I covered up his and Daniel's wrongdoings whenever necessary, and by way of thanking me, both my darling brothers teased me incessantly. But we're working together beautifully. I love having someone I can trust completely by my side, running things. I don't trust people outside the family easily, and it takes me a while to warm up to anyone new on the staff. Probably why I have such a hard time relinquishing control to my restaurant managers.

Logan raises his glass. "Alice and Blake, you've outdone yourself."

"Say, Logan," Daniel interjects from across the table, "what's it gonna take for you to give me some compliments? Now that you're freely handing them out even to Blake, I feel like a second-class citizen."

Half the table bursts out laughing, including me. Logan shakes his head, running his thumb and forefinger over his jaw, a look of fake concentration on his face.

"Don't get on my bad side, Daniel," Logan warns, but his tone is playful. Daniel and Blake used to spend most of their time partying until a few years ago, and Logan was always riding their asses because of it, edging them on to become more responsible. Now that Blake and Daniel both own businesses, Logan backed off, but the twins still love to pick on our older brother for fun.

"Well, I have an invitation for all of you. It's short notice, but I hope you'll be able to make it. I want to add some of the more interesting climbing routes at Joshua Tree to my company's offerings. Would anyone like to help me test them? I'm heading out there in two weeks."

My brother Daniel owns an outdoor sports and extreme adventure business. His question is met with an awkward silence, and I can practically hear everyone's mind spinning, searching for an excuse. Yep, that's where the Bennett clan draws the line at family loyalty: extreme adventures. I'm brave, but when Daniel says interesting, he actually means dangerous. After all, they're meant to offer an adrenaline spike. Several of us, myself included, have been on such climbing trips before, which is why I understand the silence. I have a few gray hairs, and I swear they sprung up after every trip.

"Daniel," Logan says, "I hate to break it to you, but we're not exactly your target market."

"We all know your idea of wild means an outfit that doesn't require you to wear cuff links," Daniel deadpans. "I was referring to the younger crowd." His eyes travel over to Max, Christopher, Blake, and rest on me. *Damn, damn, damn.*

Christopher and Max immediately say they already have plans.

Even though I'll regret it, and quite possibly end up with more gray hairs from the experience, I say, "Sure, why not? I'll do it."

Under the table, I stomp on Blake's foot lightly. He winces, setting his jaw.

"Can you guarantee I won't die?" Blake asks. A pit forms in my stomach. That even Blake has such fears gives me heartburn.

"Don't be so dramatic," Daniel volleys back. "Where's your spirit of adventure?"

"There's a difference between adventure and danger," Mom comments. She and Dad have tried to be supportive about Daniel's venture, but every now and then their worry for him comes through. I don't blame them. I get heartburn every time he tells us what he's up to.

"Who's ready for dessert?" I ask loudly, wanting to switch topics. After a unanimous "me," I let the kitchen know we're ready for the sugar overload. After the last bite of dessert is gone, we all return to the bar area where Blake and I prepare some much-needed digestives. Drink in hand, everyone scatters to the seats in the room, except for Sebastian, who is still waiting for his.

"Great job, you two," Sebastian says. "We're really proud of you—"

"Hold it," Blake cuts in, finishing our oldest brother's drink. "When it comes to praise, I don't want to miss one word."

Seconds later Blake places Sebastian's mojito in front of him, watching with rapt attention.

"I'm listening now, and wouldn't mind if you lay it on thick," Blake says. "At the very least I'm expecting praise for investing the income from my dividends so well." Back when Sebastian started Bennett Enterprises, he made everyone in the family a shareholder. I don't think it's fair because it's his work, and Logan's and Pippa's. Christopher and Max also work there but the rest of us don't. Changing my brother's mind is like trying to move a mountain though, so I've given up.

"You both have," Sebastian says.

Blake frowns, holding up one finger. "Correction. Alice hasn't. Her share of the investment came from profits of her two other locations and a loan."

Damn Blake and his big mouth. Granted, I never specifically told him not to share this piece of information with our oldest brother, but….

"Why aren't you using the shares money for expansion?" Sebastian asks.

"Because I didn't need it. I've been donating that money for years."

"All of it?"

"Yeah."

Sebastian seems too stunned to speak for a moment. Blake correctly weighs the situation and moves a few steps away, giving us privacy.

"It's not that I don't appreciate what you did for all of us," I say quickly. "What you're still doing, as a matter of fact. But you never wanted to accept the shares back—"

"I didn't give them to you expecting you to return them," he says gently.

"So you're not upset?"

Sebastian has known for years that I'm donating a big chunk of the money I receive as a shareholder of Bennett Enterprises, but I never owned up to giving away all of it.

"Of course not. It's your money, and you can do with it whatever you want to. It's very commendable on your part."

I let out a relieved breath.

"Alice," he says gently, "you don't have to prove anything to me, or to any of us. You've always wanted to do things on your own, and you succeeded."

"Only because I had a safety net. I'm not a hypocrite. I wouldn't have ventured out to do all of this if I didn't know I'd be okay even if I failed. It's a fantastic certainty to live with, and I will always be thankful for it." Pressing my lips together, I search for the right words. "I'm not trying to prove anything to anyone other than myself."

"I understand." Sebastian nods thoughtfully, and the twinkle of pride in his eyes makes my heart double in size.

***

When I step inside the lobby of my building many hours later, Sam, the doorman, smiles, eyeing the small take-out box in my hand.

"I have your favorite bagels here, Sam."

"Your food is bad for my figure, Ms. Bennett." Despite the protest, he opens the box, immediately digging in.

"I know, but it's so good for the soul."

"Have a nice evening."

"You too."

Yawning, I head to the elevators. I'm bone-tired but also happy that tonight went so well. When I reach the door to my apartment, I stumble over something. Glancing down, I notice a small gift bag. Energy zips through me, instantly pushing thoughts of sleep away. Like a kid on Christmas morning, I lift it up, barely making it inside my apartment before opening it. Inside is a delicate flask of lavender essential oil and a card.

Sorry I couldn't be there for you tonight. Sleep tight.

Nate

Oh, sweet heavens. This man is turning on the charm all right.

I'm typically still so wound up in my thoughts at night I lie awake for hours, thinking. I keep a bowl of water in my room, where I pour a few drops of lavender essential oil in the evenings because it helps me relax and sleep. I ran out of oil last week and didn't have time to buy a new one. Which I mentioned in passing to Nate, and he remembered.

Clutching the flask against my chest like it's a prized diamond, I stroll to my living room, grinning from ear to ear.

I want to call him, but maybe he's gone to bed. It's very late. A text message shouldn't wake him though, right? Gah, if I don't do anything, I'll just burst from so much energy and excitement.

Alice: Thank you so much for the lavender oil. Hope I'm not waking you up.

Yeah, sending the message didn't really do anything to dampen my energy. Smothering Nate with kisses might. Just remembering the way he kissed me in that alley is enough to send my senses into overdrive. I startle when my phone starts ringing. *Nate.*

"You're not sleeping," I say by way of greeting.

"Nah, I'm just now heading home. How did it go?"

"Great. We got helpful feedback." I rattle on about my evening, finishing with Daniel's invitation for our family to test out rock climbing trails at Joshua Tree National Park, and how only Blake and I are brave—or stupid—enough to try it out with him.

"Hey! That's something I could do with my new team. Not extreme rock climbing, don't think anyone's into that, but some other team-building activity, like maybe hiking. I'll give Daniel a call."

"He'll try to rope you into rock climbing too."

"I'll try it. I'm no coward."

"Are you implying the rest of my family is?" I tease, curling into my favorite armchair in the living room. "Watch it or I'll cook up a revenge plan for our date."

Nate chuckles, but despite his good humor, he *sounds* tired. I wish I could go over to his place and take care of him, make sure he relaxes and puts the stressful day behind him. Yeah, that wouldn't send him running for the hills or anything, considering we're just going on our first date next week. I've known him for a long time, and he likes to have his space.

"I buy you lavender oil and offer to put my life on the line for your brother, and all I get is threats?"

"Well, when you put it like that, I sound terrible. Thank you for the lavender oil. Very thoughtful of you. How did you get it on my doorstep? Did the doorman bring it up?"

"No man worth his salt reveals his secrets."

"Do you have anything secret planned for our date?"

"Ah, that's no secret. I plan to drive you crazy. You might even forget about your rule of five."

"You sound a bit too self-assured."

"I kissed you out of your shoes when we weren't on a date. I like my chances, Alice."

Holy hotness and sweet mercy. My name rolls off his tongue in a lower octave than the rest of the sentence, sounding seductive and forbidden. *Damn it, he shouldn't use his bedroom voice on the phone. There should be some rule against it. Does this man have no mercy?* I ignore the way my pulse spikes, chastising myself for being so overresponsive to him. Instead, I clasp the lavender flask tighter.

"Game on, Becker."

Chapter Eleven

Alice

Two evenings before my date with Nate, I rope the girls into a trip to the spa. It's become our designated activity for a girls' night out. A few years ago, we usually went to a bar, downed cocktails, and talked about everything under the sun. But since Pippa and then Ava gave birth and breastfed, and now Nadine is pregnant, bars have lost the appeal. And honestly, a few hours of getting pampered at a spa are infinitely more relaxing than cocktails.

Pippa, Ava, and Nadine are already there when I arrive. Victoria and Emilia, Christopher's and Max's fiancées, usually join us too, but they're all gone on a trip.

This place has an incredible vibe. From the moment I step through the front doors, I already feel like I've left any stress behind me. Whether this is because of the relaxing music playing in the background, or the sound of water dropping coming from the small waterfall built into the wall behind the reception, I can't tell, but I love coming here.

"Hi, girls," I greet Pippa, Ava, and Nadine. We're in for a few hours of treats: sauna, swimming in the heated pool, and we'll also take turns going in for our mani-pedi, massage, and facial appointments.

The deck has a nice view, with the Golden Gate Bridge looming in the distance. The heated pool is half outside, half inside, perfect for when it's chilly outside as you can just relax in the indoor area.

As I said, I love this place. Whenever I feel like I'm about to burst from stress, I drop by, even if it's just for a mani-pedi or massage if I need a quick fix.

"Oh, this is so great," Ava comments. The four of us are in the juice bar adjacent to the pool, relaxing. We're alone in this space, which I prefer.

"So, who starts sharing news?" Pippa asks, clapping her hands excitedly. She looks at each of us in quick succession, then lingers on me. "Alice, you look like someone who has big news."

"I agree," Ava adds. Nadine merely smiles.

Oh yeah. I have no doubt they heard through the Bennett rumor mill about Nate's permanent job in San Francisco, but I haven't updated Pippa on the rest. Heck, I haven't even told her about the kiss, but it was mostly because I wanted to put it out of my mind. Thinking about it got my hopes up. But now things have changed. Now I can hope and dream.

"You agreed so quickly to this spa day just so you could quiz me," I accuse my sister.

She shakes her head with vehemence.

"That's not the only reason. But I agree, it was a great incentive."

"Fine, here's the short version. Nate asked me out on a date."

The girls erupt in cheers, with Pippa saying under her breath, "I knew it."

"We really want the long version though," Nadine chimes in.

"Don't leave out any detail," Ava adds.

They listen with rapt attention while I tell them everything.

"Five dates?" Pippa says, awestruck. "Sister, you have great self-restraint if you can resist him for so long."

"I'll do my best," I assure her. Almost unwillingly, my mind flies to my conversation with Nate about what kind of kissing is proper for a first date.

"Did any of you ever have good wall sex?" I blurt out.

Pippa jerks her head back, and Ava and Nadine seem too stunned or embarrassed for a split second before we all burst out laughing. We talk about *mostly* anything but carefully avoid the sex topic, since half the girls in the group are actually dating or married to our brothers, and neither Pippa nor I want too many details. I'm sure Nadine and Ava talk about it, but I hope such details never reach my ears. Some conversations you can't unhear.

Well, now the cat is out of the bag. Anyone else would balk down and switch topics, but not me. The way I see it, I've already put my foot in my mouth, so I want my answer. "A yes or no is enough, no need for details."

A chorus of "yes" greets me, followed by chuckles.

Damn it, Nate.

"So, I predict you won't make it through three dates," Pippa says.

"Make that two," Ava says.

"Thanks for the vote of confidence."

"He's already got you thinking about wall sex," Nadine says wisely. "By the way, not to volunteer too much information, but the most important part in wall sex is for the man to be strong enough. I took a good look at Nate. The man is a mountain. He'll have his way with you any way you can imagine, and do it exceptionally well."

"True," my sister adds. "He looks like someone who'll know how to love you up good."

I swallow hard, blood rushing to my cheeks. These girls are crazy, but they're my brand of crazy, and I love them to bits.

"Right, how about switching topics? Who else has news?" My imagination is running amok already.

"Well, mine is less interesting, but my morning sickness finally subsided," Nadine says. "But I'm still sleepy all the time."

"Do take advantage of that," Pippa says. "Sleep is the one thing you won't get back for a while. Oh, how I miss it."

"Me too," Ava says wistfully. She looks as tired as Pippa was in the first year after giving birth, but the dopey grin she has when talking about Will is adorable.

"Oh, I have some fun news," Pippa says. "Julie has been asked out on a date, and Eric completely freaked out. It was fascinating to watch him in full overprotective dad mode. I managed to reason with him about two days later."

Her husband, Eric, was a widower with a twelve-year-old daughter when Pippa met him. Julie's a teenager now though, so I predict Eric will go into overprotective dad mode on a regular basis. It'll be good practice for when their twin girls grow up.

Though judging by the way our dad and brothers react when Summer and I speak about dates, that overprotective gene is deep in their DNA. Once activated, it never dims.

Our chat turns to us reminiscing over the crazy bachelorette parties we threw for Ava, Nadine, and Pippa. I swear to God, each one was crazier than the one before. We didn't even plan it, but things got out of hand, fast.

My mind flies to Nate too, to the way he kissed me after the meeting with the *Delicious Dining* team, how he was championing me during the meeting. Just knowing he believes in me so much warms my chest, and *that* is dangerous in more ways than one.

He just asked me out on a date. I need to pace myself, keep my hopes at a reasonable level. Just because I've been carrying a torch for him for years doesn't mean we're meant to be together, or that we'll work out. Maybe we'll discover we're not compatible after all and this is all just *crazy* chemistry we need to get out of our systems. My heart stings as I consider that thought, but I have to be prepared for any outcome, keep an open mind and heart.

Even so, my grin grows wider.

***

On the evening of my date with Nate, I stop by Blue Moon just before, bringing in the last of the supplies needed for the official opening tomorrow. The *Delicious Dining* team called earlier, informing me that the network green-lighted the project, and they'll film the segment next month. As a result, I'm feeling on top of the world tonight.

Right until I step inside the kitchen, slip on the tiles, and nearly face-plant. Luckily, I grab the nearby counter in time, steadying myself.

Turning on the lights, I inspect the slippery floor. The tiles are wet, as if someone just wiped them. The cleaning crew finished two hours ago though, so they should be dry by now. This can only mean one thing: water is coming from somewhere. Within thirty seconds, I locate the problem. The pipe from under one of the sinks is leaking.

I call the maintenance company but get the answering machine, stating I'm calling outside office hours and the earliest I can contact them is tomorrow morning. Fantastic. Desperate, I start to search online for emergency plumbers when my screen lights up with an incoming call from Nate.

"Hey! Sorry, I'll be late. A pipe is leaking at Blue Moon, and I'm trying to find a plumber who'll come right away."

"No need. I'll come and fix it."

"Are you sure?"

"Yes. Is there a toolbox there?"

"Yeah."

"I'm on my way."

***

Fifteen minutes later, I'm desperate because the water isn't leaking anymore—it's coming in a heavy stream. I place a bucket underneath the pipe, but unable to just stare at the water and do nothing, I sit on my haunches and inspect the pipe closer, hoping the water won't come anywhere near my dress. I swear loudly.

"Sailors have nothing on you, Bennett."

I bang my head against the sink as I flinch.

"Jesus," I exclaim, pulling back and putting my hands on the painful spot above my eye. Nate is just a few steps behind me. "Announce yourself next time."

"I did."

"Try knocking at the door first, then saying something like 'Hot plumber here. At your service, ma'am.'"

"I love how you don't lose your sense of humor even when you nearly poke your eye out."

Chuckling, he motions me to step aside. He glances at the toolbox, then lowers himself to his haunches like I did minutes before. While he busies himself under the sink, I call the restaurant where we're going for our date, informing them we'll be late. Afterward, I hop on a counter, ogling Nate's ass. Damn, from this position his backside looks even more perfect than usual. A naughty voice at the back of my mind tells me there are plenty more pipes I could *accidentally* break around the kitchen.

"Are you ever gonna offer to help?"

"I'd rather stay here and enjoy the view," I tell him.

A few short minutes later, Nate pulls back, rising to his feet. He turns the sink on, which nearly gives me a panic attack, but what do you know? Not one drop leaks from the pipe.

"All done."

Hopping off the counter, I check his work for myself, even though it's not necessary.

"Thank you, Nate."

"At your service, ma'am," he says, repeating my earlier words.

"Can I give you a tip? Take your shirt off next time."

He pulls his head back. Up close, I can see a thin sheet of sweat dotting his upper lip. I barely hold back the impulse of lifting on my toes and licking him.

"To fix a pipe?"

I shrug one shoulder, offering a grin. "They do that sometimes in movies."

"What kind of movies have you been watching, Alice?"

"Naughty ones."

I haven't been watching any movies other the ones in my head, but seeing his look of shock was totally worth stretching the truth a tad.

"Since we're exchanging information, I was half hoping you'd be waiting here for me wearing just an apron."

Damn, damn, damn. The air between us instantly charges, firing up my synapses. As if sensing it too, Nate cradles my face with both hands. I cuff his wrists with my hands, loving the feel of his pulse under the pads of my fingers. It races frantically. As he kisses my forehead, the smell of him overpowers everything else. This feels so impossibly good; I wish we could stay like this the entire evening. But the strong smell of soap and *man* serves as an aphrodisiac, clouding my brain and awaking all my senses. My body responds to his proximity by humming incessantly, pure energy coursing through me, jolting every cell to life. I clamor for him, needing him to touch more than my face. I initially went to the spa for a mani-pedi, but then thought I'd better get a Brazilian wax too. I'm oversensitive after waxing. When Nate kisses the spot above my eye where I hit myself earlier, my center becomes slick. With a low sigh, I press my thighs together. Gathering my wits, I step to the side, needing to gain some distance.

"You're handy to have around," I say once I'm out of his grasp. "How would you know how to fix a pipe?"

"When you're constantly on the move, it's easier to learn to fix things than to find people to do it for you."

"Makes sense. Guess you don't seem the fixing type."

He winks at me, and my intimate spot tingles dangerously.

"Lots of things you don't know about me. There's more to me than my pretty face."

Oh, why yes there is, Mr. Becker. You have strong arms to go with it, and I don't want to get ahead of myself, but I'm pretty sure the package in your jeans is just as alluring. Can't wait to discover what you're hiding in there.

"What just went through that dirty mind of yours?"

"Nothing," I say a little too quickly. His eyes zero in on my mouth, and I become aware I've been gnawing at my lower lip.

Nate steps in front of me again, placing either hand at my sides, propping his fingers on the counter. He's caging me in.

"Liar." He brings his lips to my cheek, peppering the side of my face with kisses, trailing to my ear. "You're a naughty woman, and it's a fucking turn-on."

Oh no. Not the dirty talk. If he starts with the dirty talk, I'm a goner.

"I didn't mean to. But I got a Brazilian wax two days ago, and I'm very sensitive there. Even the friction with my panties is too much. When I'm thinking about you, I go up in flames in minutes. When you're with me it's even worse."

"You got a Brazilian?" His mouth is still at my ear, so I feel every hot exhale against my skin. It isn't helping my cause at all.

"Yes. I went to the spa in the evening and thought, 'What the heck. If I'm here, I'd better be practical and take care—'" I stop when he pulls back a notch, and I take in the expression on his face, wanton and desperate.

I realize I've been rattling off like a madwoman, which is very unlike me. Something happens to me when I'm around Nate. I can never find my balance when he's near. I'm in a continuous freefall.

"Too much information?" I ask weakly.

"Way too much," he says on a groan. "You tell me that and expect me to behave? I'm not a weak man, Alice, but I'm weak for you. And right now, I'm dying to taste you. I need to taste you."

I fist his shirt, a jolt of pleasure rippling through me at his words. Not "I *want* to taste you" but "I *need* to taste you."

Sweet heavens, I need it too.

"How turned on are you now?" One of his hands moves across my collarbone, up my neck, and to the back of my head. He threads his fingers in my hair with barely restrained passion. When he presses his forehead against mine, I can feel his breath against my upper lip, hot and heavy. A soft moan is the only answer I manage to give him. His fingers tighten their grip on my hair.

"Are your panties wet?"

Nodding, I fist his shirt even stronger.

"Do you want me to touch you?"

"Yes, I need it so much, Nate." My words come out in a rush. "So much."

He moves the hand that was still propped on the counter to my waist, then drops it south, letting it slide down my thigh a few inches before gathering up the fabric of my dress. When his warm fingers touch my bare skin, I shudder. When his hand inches closer to the apex of my inner thighs, I grip one of his arms tightly, needing to steady myself.

"Open your legs, Alice." His voice is a little hoarse, a lot commanding. Licking my lips, I do as he says. The very next second, he slides his fingers over my panties, rubbing my slick spot. My knees almost buckle as pleasure spears me.

"Ah!" Exhaling sharply, I pinch my eyelids closed, seeking to ground myself.

He presses the heel of his palm against my clit while his fingers move up and down my seam, drawing small circles over the soaked fabric. I nearly break out of my skin from the pleasure. "Fuck, I love having you so hot and bothered. You could come just like this, couldn't you?"

"Yes. Yes, I—"

I don't manage to finish the sentence because Nate seals his mouth over mine in a kiss that is the perfect mix of sweetness and passion, of tenderness and heat. When he pulls back, I groan in protest.

"I want my mouth here"—his fingers press right into my opening—"when you finish."

Holy hotness. I think I had a mini-orgasm just from hearing him say it.

Taking his hands off me, he steps back.

"Strip for me, Alice."

"Here?"

"Yes. Now."

Biting the inside of my cheek, I look around nervously. "I've never done anything like this here."

"Then let me be your first."

My breath catches as I nod because I don't want him to just be my first. I want him to be my last. The heat in his gaze is so powerful it melts away all my questions and insecurities. Nate kisses my shoulder, then slowly inches toward my neck. He stops time and again along the way, breathing in deeply, occasionally teasing me with a dip of his tongue.

"I don't want to rush this," he whispers against my skin, the shot of hot breath turning my knees to rubber. "I want to worship you, lick every inch of your skin, commit every part of you to memory."

I'd be completely on board with his plan if I didn't have years of pent-up desire threatening to spill out. But when Nate snaps his head up, his gaze holds more than heat. There is so much tenderness in his beautiful green eyes that my chest fills with warmth. The warmth travels all over my body, making my toes curl.

With one swift move, he undoes the zipper of my dress. Strapless, the fabric falls to the ground within seconds. His gaze rakes over me, hunger flashing on his features as he zeroes in on my panties. Feeling bold, I push them down to my ankles, stepping out of them as seductively as I can. Next I unclasp my bra, which lands with a soft thump at my feet.

"You're beautiful."

His voice is a low baritone, rich like caramel, and it turns me on to no end. Lifting his hand to my face, he traces the hinge of my jaw with the back of his fingers before resting his hand at the side of my neck right about where my hairline begins.

After undoing the button of his jeans, I push the zipper down. Licking my lips, I lower my hands in his boxers and *hot damn*. To say the man is well endowed would be an understatement. Judging by the way his mouth curls into a smirk, he's well aware of this. Wrapping my hand around his impressive erection, I move up and down in a rhythmic stroke. He slowly comes undone, his Adam's apple dipping low as he swallows hard. When I drag my thumb over his tip, he rewards me by rasping out my name on a low, almost primal groan.

"Alice!"

Desire roars inside of me, singeing the tips of my breasts like a lightning bolt. Greedy to touch more of him, I undo the buttons of his shirt with my free hand, kissing every inch of skin I reveal. God, the taste of him is pure bliss, and his grunts of pleasure are music to my ears. When I undo the button just below his navel, Nate abruptly says, "Stop."

Pulling back both hands, I straighten up, looking at him questioningly. He tilts his head to one side, sizing me up and down.

"What are you doing?" Suddenly, a prickle of shyness gnaws at me. I've never paraded buck naked in my kitchen.

"Trying to decide which part of you to worship first."

Without warning, Nate loops an arm around my waist, lifting me onto the counter.

"Oh!" Damn, I wasn't expecting it to be so cold.

Nate pulls his brows together. "Everything okay?"

"Yep. Counter is a little cold."

The corners of his lips twitch. Stepping between my legs, he lifts them, placing my feet on the counter. I momentarily lose my balance, falling back on my elbows.

"Don't worry, I'll warm up your nice little ass right away."

A white-hot current races through me at his words, and I'm soaked between my legs as he leans lightly over me.

"Your breasts are beautiful," he murmurs. "Every part of you is."

He circles the edge of one of my nipples with his thumb, lowering his head and suckling on the other. My head falls back as I enjoy the sinful sensations he spurs inside me. The heat intensifies, the ache between my thighs becoming almost unbearable.

A loud moan escapes my lips when he lowers one hand, dragging his fingers along the edge of my opening in one swift move. I spread my legs farther apart to give him better access, wanting to take anything and everything this man has to offer. His mouth moves to my other nipple while he presses his thumb on my bundle of nerves.

Lifting his mouth from the tip of my breast, he blows a hot breath on the sensitive skin there. My entire body seems to be made of pure sensation and need. Every part of me responds to his expert lips and fingers.

"Fuck, I love seeing you this wet and wild for me." Keeping his thumb firmly pressed on my sensitive spot, he slides one finger inside me, and my breath catches. While his fingers torture me, he places his mouth on the hollow of my neck, licking me there before descending between my breasts, lavishing my torso with kisses.

When he abruptly removes his hand from between my legs, I'm left feeling cold and empty. I'm about to complain when Nate leans back, lifting my ass, taking each cheek in his large hands, bringing my core level with his face.

"This ass of yours is so sweet. I bet you'll taste even sweeter."

Nate Becker's between my legs. Heavens, I might come just from this sight alone. The first stroke of his tongue against my slick sex appeases my ache. The second intensifies it. This will be both bliss and torture until the very end.

When I feel the roots of my orgasm pulling at me, I cry out his name. His mouth on me is delicious, every second bringing me closer to my release. My fingers desperately gnaw at the counter, seeking to ground me, but the hard surface offers no reprieve, just as his lips and tongue offer me no mercy. Nate squeezes one ass cheek tighter as he brings his other hand to my belly, resting it there with his fingers splayed before inching downward and pressing his thumb on my clit.

"Nate, oh I'm going to—ah!"

I come hard, a million tiny beads of pleasure exploding inside me, clouding my vision for a split second, my body giving in with an almost violent arch. Nate holds me tight until my body calms down and I descend from cloud nine.

He helps me hop down from the counter and caresses my cheek, his eyes still hooded with desire. I wrap my palm around his erection again. He needs his release. I want to give him pleasure, to make him happy.

He inhales sharply as I move my hand up and down, dragging my hand across the thick crown. There are drops of clear liquid already on his tip, and I know he won't last long. I squeeze him tight and good, increasing my rhythm, seeing him slowly come apart. Seconds later, he fists my hair, a primal groan reverberating from his throat. Liquid squirts on my belly, hot and sticky. After he calms down, he turns on the water, cleaning us both.

"As far as first dates, this one's going great," I tease as I shimmy back into my dress. "But we missed our reservation. When I called, they told me if we don't make it in half an hour, we lose our spot. Where do you want to go?"

"Anywhere you want."

"A few nearby places have an intimate atmosphere."

Nate smiles wistfully, caging me in again against the counter. "Not a good idea."

"Hmm?"

He presses himself against me and I feel the bulge in his pants—hard again. "I didn't get my fill of you, and if we're going to be alone, or somewhere intimate, I might try to seduce you. So we should go somewhere where there are many people and I can't get away with making you forget about your five-date rule. Remember?"

"Oh."

The corners of his mouth tilt up. "I do, and I don't want us to do something you might regret tomorrow."

Even through the post-climax haze, I realize he's looking out for me, and I all but melt.

"Let's go to Blake's bar. It'll be full, and my brother will be keeping an eye on us. Seductive maneuvers will be out of question."

"Great idea."

***

Several hours later, I'm in my bedroom, sliding under my covers, a satisfied smile on my lips. As I predicted, the bar was full, and we both behaved. Completely unaware that we were on a date, Blake spent most of the evening with us. It was a lot of fun. I'm nearly asleep when my phone beeps.

Groaning, I'm tempted to just ignore it, but it will beep periodically if I don't read the message. So even though all I want is sleep, I push myself out of the bed. I never put my phone on the nightstand, because in the morning I'd just hit the snooze button on the alarm. Instead, I place it on the vanity across the room, which forces me to get out of bed in the morning.

When I see who sent me the message, I instantly light up.

Nate: Home safe?

We left the bar separately.

Alice: Yeah. Was just about to fall asleep.

The little dots indicating he's writing appear on screen. Then they disappear, but no message arrives. *Hmm… someone can't find the right words?*

Alice: Was checking in on me just an excuse? You can talk to me about anything.

His reply hits my inbox in a matter of seconds.

Nate: I really did want to make sure you got home okay. But I also wanted to talk to you.

A pause follows, in which my heart seems to double in weight as my mouth suddenly goes dry. I rest my ass against the vanity, trying hard not to imagine scenarios of doom. God, I'm ridiculous. Instead of writing back, he calls, and I answer right away.

"You had me panicking for a moment there, waiting for you to write," I say into the phone.

"Yeah, I thought calling would be better."

The tone of his voice has a slight edge to it, which does nothing to soothe me.

"Okay."

"Tonight was amazing, and I want to be honest. I don't know how to let people in, Alice."

I breathe out slowly, carefully choosing my words. "I know."

"You do?"

"Yeah. I've been watching you closely since I was a kid. Sure, there's been a gap in which we haven't seen each other, but some things don't change. So yeah, I'm aware you have some solid walls around you."

"What do you plan to do about them?" There's a playful note in his tone, and a lump in my throat dissolves. I hadn't been aware of its existence. I also realize he's giving me an opening, which I take with both hands.

"Depends. I need more information. What are those walls made of? Ice? Stone? Concrete?"

Nate laughs, and I make myself a promise. I will make him laugh often. You can never go wrong with that. The way I see it, people don't laugh nearly as much as they could.

"Those are some pretty specific questions."

"I need to know what tools I'm gonna need."

"You won't need any. You're a force of nature, Alice."

"Best compliment I ever got." I fight to stifle a yawn, but it gets the better of me.

"Go to sleep," Nate says immediately.

"Nooo, I love talking to you. Especially when you're complimenting me. And especially after you've given me an orgasm. I'm still a little high."

"So, good, huh?"

"Oh yeah. Wait, why do you have to ask?"

"My ego needs it."

"Men," I mutter. "Don't worry, I'll be louder next time."

"Next time, you'll be underneath me, and I'm going to be deep inside you. The only thing you'll be doing is begging me for more."

"Oh my. That's a promise right there." I intended for my reply to come off as playful, but my voice is breathy and needy.

"It is. Now go to bed."

"Good night."

After ending the call, I place the phone back on the vanity table and crawl under the covers. Nate might think this is new territory for him, but he sure is sweet and attentive. His message to ask if I'm home is proof.

My last thought before falling asleep is that I'm going to tear down those walls, take care of him, and also try to guard my heart in the process.

Chapter Twelve

Alice

The next week flies by in a blink of an eye, the official opening of Blue Moon taking up most of my time. When Saturday rolls around, I'm on pins and needles. We're driving out to Joshua Tree National Park today to try out Daniel's newest idea of a good time, or a death trap. Blake and Daniel are already there, together with Summer, who announced at the beginning of the week that she was coming in for a visit. Like a good sister, she said she'd fly out there and join us, then drive back with us to see the rest of the family. Nate and his team are joining us too. He and Daniel agreed on hiking as a team activity, with Nate alone trying out rock climbing.

I'm driving with Nate, since it didn't make sense to go separately. At four o'clock in the morning, I roll my suitcase to the foyer with less than a few minutes to spare until Nate is supposed to pick me up. The sun hasn't even come up yet. I had one cup of coffee, but I can still barely keep my eyes open. My stomach flutters at the thought that we're going to spend about eight hours alone, confined in a car. Almost involuntarily, my mind flies to the way he pleasured me the last time I saw him, and I nearly sway remembering the sheer force of his passion.

I'm so lost in the memory that I jump when my doorbell rings. I check my appearance one last time in the mirror hanging next to the entrance. My hair is pulled in a messy bun, and I have minimal makeup on. I'm wearing jeans and a tank top, which doesn't scream sexy or trying too hard. The top might be too thin for four o'clock in the morning in San Francisco, but it'll be hot and sunny in Joshua Tree.

When I open the door, Nate greets me with a wink and a bright smile, and my breath catches.

"Speechless already Bennett?" he teases. "I like how this is going."

I shrug, scrunching my nose. "Was merely taking a moment to enjoy the view. Can't blame a girl."

"Since blatant ogling is on the table, allow me to do the same." Stepping inside, he takes my hand, twirling me around once. He stops when I'm facing him again, and we're so close I can feel the heat of his skin.

"So you weren't going to ogle anyway?" I whisper.

Nate shakes his head, cupping my face with one hand. I love when he does this. There's something incredibly intimate about the gesture. It's protective and speaks to me on a primal level.

"I'd planned to be a perfect gentleman today, to make up for last time."

In an involuntary gesture, I press my thighs together, leaning more into his touch like a kitten. "Hey, I'll never complain about orgasms."

"Oh, I see. So you torture me with five dates but won't complain when you benefit from my weakness for you?"

"I have a dark side."

I barely have time to take note of the corner of his mouth lifting in a smirk before he tips his head down. Every nerve ending in my body zips to life as he seals his lips over mine. He starts out gently, but the kiss spirals into a passionate tangle of limbs before long. When I feel a hard surface against my ass, I realize he backed me against the door.

"Whoa!" Nate breathes in deeply when we pull apart.

"That escalated quickly," I murmur, and then we're both laughing. Stepping back, he glances around the foyer, then heads to my suitcase, grabbing the handle and rolling it after him. "Back to your gentleman ways?"

"Trying to."

"Okay, let's go."

"Aren't you taking a jacket with you?"

"I have one in my suitcase."

"Take it out. It's chilly outside. I don't want you to get sick."

I cock a brow. "It's a short walk to the car, and I don't feel like rummaging through my bag for it."

Letting go of my suitcase, he glances around the foyer, finding my coatrack. He stomps toward it, takes one of the coats—a black one with silver buttons—and returns, holding it out for me.

"Come on, put it on." His eyes are hard and focused. That bossy alpha streak is my downfall, I swear. I can't help wanting to rile him up more, because this man is downright delicious when he's in persuasion mode.

"I'm not a kid. Nate—"

"Alice!"

Oh, I love it when he says my name in that tone. But if I don't put a stop to this, we won't make it to the car.

"Stop it. I can't handle bossy before I had my second cup of coffee. It might make me do crazy things, like asking you to back me up against the door some more."

He blinks. "Were you messing with me on purpose?"

"Maybe." I slip into the coat he's still holding out, fastening my buttons. "Turns out it's a bad idea before

I've had my second coffee. Just can't handle all the testosterone."

I'm half turned to him when he tips my chin upward with his thumb.

"Careful, Alice. I remember how you felt coming on my tongue, and I can't wait to do it again. You keep egging me on and we'll never even make it to the car."

Oh man, man, man! A gasp tumbles from my lips as heat strums through me like a lightning bolt. I'm unable to form a comeback, neither witty nor seductive. How can he talk to me like this and expect me not to spontaneously combust? He should come with a warning label, or I should always have a glass of ice water when he's around.

Letting go of me, he takes my suitcase again, gesturing for me to lead the way.

Once outside, I have to admit, the coat is a good idea. It's very chilly for July.

Five minutes later, we're all set to go. He guns the engine, and as the car lurches forward, a loud ringtone echoes around us. Nate reaches in the holder between the seats, glancing at the screen once before swiping to answer. A female voice fills the space, and I realize his phone is connected to the sound system of the car.

"I've checked with the hotel, and they promised they'll have the meeting room ready one hour earlier," she says. Her voice is nasally, as if she's fighting a bad cold.

"Thanks, Clara."

Her name rings a bell, and I remember Pippa telling me she had lunch with her a few times.

"Really sorry I can't make it. When I woke up, I realized I'm too much of a mess to go anywhere."

"Don't worry. And take care of yourself," Nate replies with a smile.

"I will. By the way, a request came through from the London office. They asked if you have time to look over the script changes Abbott suggested for this season."

"Why?"

"My guess is they're not happy with what they have. I still can't believe they put Abbott in charge."

I take a furtive look at Nate, my heart in my throat. It's been there ever since Clara mentioned London. His smile is gone now, and his jaw ticks. "Sure, e-mail it to me. I'll look over it this weekend and send my comments."

"Good, I'll forward it right away. I'm going to have the phone next to me, but at the rate I'm going, I'll probably be asleep most of the time. Damn fever."

"Forget about the phone. In fact, if I get a call or an e-mail from you, we're going to have a problem. Just rest."

"Sure, boss. Have fun."

She hangs up and Nate drums his fingers on the wheel, lost in thought. I turn in my seat so I can see him better. A frown clouds his expression, and I don't like it one bit. This whole situation is unfair, and remembering with how much enthusiasm he talked about the job in London when he thought that was his future makes my gut clench. Of course, I'm over the moon that he's here, but having to shelve his dream is a huge thing to live with. I resolve to bring back his smile, put him in a good mood.

***

When we stop at a gas station on the highway about two hours later, I have my chance. There is a small shop at the station, and besides the usual sandwiches and coffee, they also sell CDs and books. One in particular catches my attention. It's a mix of hits from the decade

Nate was in college and I was in high school. Nostalgia overwhelms me, and some of the singles were Nate's favorites at the time.

Wanting to surprise him, I linger at the back of the shop, pretending to look through some books while Nate pays for the gas and buys us coffee. He tells me to take my time, that he'll pull the car in a parking space behind the gas station.

After he leaves, I pay for the CD and whistle happily on the way to the car. I find Nate pacing the parking lot, his phone plastered to his ear. He's gesturing agitatedly with his free hand. The coffee cups are on the hood of the car and I sit next to them, watching him in silence, trying to gauge who he might be talking to. Eventually he notices me and hangs up a few seconds later.

"That seemed to be an intense conversation," I remark, sitting with my feet crossed in a yoga position and holding the CD behind my back. Nate stops just in front of the car, surveying me as if he's considering joining me on the hood.

"My mother."

"Oh, how is she?" I always did like his mother. She was a tad hot-tempered, but all in all a good person and a determined woman who was dealt a shitty hand when it came to her love life.

"Stubborn, as usual. She's having some trouble with her mortgage payments, and I'm trying to convince her to let me buy the damn house for her. Emphasis on trying."

"Parent pride," I say. "It took a while for my parents to accept Sebastian's help. But then again, he always insisted it was because they risked everything for him when they sold the ranch and gave him the money to start Bennett Enterprises."

"He had a good argument."

"Yeah, but he would have worn them down anyway. You'll do that with your mom too."

"Working on it."

He doesn't offer more of an explanation, and I don't push. He'll share more with me if he feels like it. In the meantime, I can be here for him, help him relax. Perfect time to show him my finding.

"Look what I have." I slide down the hood closer to him, holding the CD with the back cover toward him so he can read the songs on it.

"Nice find," he says appreciatively. "I was a big fan of most of these."

"It's why I bought it. Thought it would cheer you up."

He looks at me in surprise. "You're amazing."

Wrapping his fingers around one of my ankles, he pulls me even farther down, until my ass slides almost completely off the hood. When he kisses me, the feel of his mouth on mine is different than it's been before. He's exploring me with hunger and curiosity, like he's discovering a different meaning to kissing, and I'm discovering it with him. Being kissed out of my shoes after that meeting was thrilling. Being kissed on the hood of his car, slowly and deeply, is making my stomach flutter and my toes curl.

Until a gust of wind sweeps through, chilling me to my bones. I'm wearing the coat Nate insisted I take with me, but it's not helping much. The fabric, while soft and elegant, isn't too thick. Instantly, Nate wraps his arms around me, unhitching his lips from mine and peppering my neck with kisses instead. Like the opportunist I am, I cocoon against him, soaking in his warmth.

"And you wanted to go out without a coat."

"Ah, but this was my secret plan all along. To get you to warm me up."

"If you want me to hold you, Alice, all you have to do is ask."

Ah, but he doesn't understand. Snuggling under the pretense of needing warmth is safe. There's no danger of demanding or giving too much too soon. "Give me the CD. I'll plug it in the sound system. You go inside the car with the coffees."

"Where are you going?"

"You can only put in CDs from the trunk."

Grabbing our coffees, I head inside the car, and he joins me a few minutes later.

"Why does my trunk smell like coconut?" he asks.

"Oh. I baked Summer her favorite coconut cookies, but they're in a Tupperware container. They shouldn't smell."

I show my love by stuffing people with their favorite food. The way I see it, nothing spells love better than that.

"I can sniff out goodies from miles away. You think she'd mind if we stole some? They'd go perfectly with the coffee."

I stare down at him. "They're for my sister. Don't you dare touch them."

"Didn't know you'd draw such a hard line at this."

"I'm a closet mother hen. Can't help it."

He gets the car moving, smiling silently as we head back out on the highway.

"You know what else you are? A closet romantic."

"Why would you say that?" I ask in a small voice.

By way of answering, he starts the sound system, and the first track on the CD starts playing. Okay, so buying the CD might count as a romantic gesture.

"I wasn't always one," I admit. "I must have caught it from Pippa."

Nate surveys me. "Nah, you always were. You just didn't know it."

"But you did?"

He nods with determination, and I imagine this is how a judge acts when declaring a case closed.

"You're not the only one who was watching closely for years, Alice. I've watched you too."

"Yeah?" I'm ridiculously pleased, so I lift my coffee cup to my lips, hiding my grin behind it.

"Yep."

"Then why did you act so surprised at my five-date rule?"

He gives a fake and exaggerated shudder, as if the words alone frighten him. "Because it's cruel! But I'm so glad you mentioned the topic."

"Really?"

"Yeah. This should count as our second date."

"That's your comeback after telling me I'm a romantic?"

"I'm being practical. We're going to spend the next few hours alone in this car. Better make them count."

"Don't expect me to swoon over your offer anytime soon." Sipping from my coffee, I brainstorm ways to punish him for the next three hours. Luckily, the caffeine boost is kicking in, and my neurons are really starting to wake up. It's a few seconds before I realize he's unnaturally quiet.

"What's with the silence?" I ask suspiciously.

"I'm waiting for that second coffee to kick in so you can feel the full effect of my charms. I *can* make you swoon." He leans slightly toward me but keeps his eyes on the road. I have a hunch he plans on whispering the next part, and I want to hear him over the music blaring from the sound system, so I lean into him too until our shoulders touch.

"I can also make you writhe, and scream."

Oh. I press my thighs together.

"I can make you *come.*" The word tumbles out of his mouth with too much sensuality. "Take your pick."

Licking my lips, I decide to stick to my guns. "You still have some work to do on the swooning part, Becker. I suggest you start by making me laugh."

Chapter Thirteen

Alice

By the time we pull up in front of the hotel, my abdominal muscles hurt from so much laughing. We talked about every single shenanigan we pulled as kids, and damn it felt good. Our hotel is conveniently located about fifteen minutes away from the Joshua Tree National Park. It's four stories, painted in shades of dark orange and warm brown. The temperature is sinfully hot. Not the best for rock climbing, or anything other than lying in the sun.

"Can you have my luggage taken upstairs?" Nate asks the receptionist after we check in. "I'm meeting my team in a few minutes, and I don't have time to do it."

"Of course," she assures him. "Ms. Bennett, we can take your bag to your room as well."

"Thanks, but it's small, and I'm heading there anyway." I try not to think very hard about both our rooms being on the fourth floor.

Turning to me, Nate says, "The hiking tour Daniel planned for my team starts in two hours."

I nod. "Yeah." Blake, Summer, and I are going with Daniel on our climbing adventure before. Daniel said he chose one of the shorter routes. Short but *exactly* what he's looking for. Nate and his team will meet us there, and Nate will try his hand at climbing before the hike with his team.

"Can't wait to see you climbing," he says with a smirk.

"Hey! I am very sporty. I run three times a week." On straight ground, solid concrete, or the treadmill.

Nate opens his mouth, no doubt with a witty reply, but someone—one of his team members, I presume—calls him from the other end of the lobby. Nate takes off with a wink and I look wistfully after him, wishing he could spend the entire day with us.

Fastening the grip on my suitcase's handle, I admire the rustic design, heading toward the elevators.

"Alice," Summer exclaims, stepping out of one of the elevators. My smile turns into a megawatt grin as I hurry toward my sister. With light brown hair and at one head taller than me, she looks nothing like me and more like a younger version of Pippa, but with darker hair. She's already wearing her climbing gear. I throw my arms around her waist when I reach her, pulling her into a hug.

"I missed you so much," I tell her unnecessarily.

"Back at you." Her arms are around my shoulders, and I'm pretty sure we look a little—or a lot—silly, but I don't care in the least. When we finally pull away, she says, "You should change into climbing gear soon."

"Where are the boys?"

"Blake's in his room, and Daniel is meeting us inside the park."

"Oh?"

"Yeah, he went to do some scouting by himself hours ago. Said he'd be back in time."

"I'll go change quickly. Wanna join me? I have coconut cookies for you."

That's all it takes to convince Summer to go up with me. While I change, she happily munches on the cookies while talking my ear off about Rome.

After I'm done, I look like a pro, which I am definitely not. I love running and working out, but rock climbing is a different beast.

"I almost don't recognize us," Summer says, looking at me with fake horror. When she and I get together, our favorite pastime is watching movies and doing each other's nails. If we're in the mood to go outdoors, we hit the shops. "The things we do for our brother."

"Remember the time we bailed him out of that masquerade party?" I elbow her playfully.

"God, don't remind me. I'm trying to block out the memory."

"Hey, look at the bright side. This all means we have leverage against him." Whenever our brothers ask some ungodly favor from us, we hang it over their heads forever because Summer and I are sweet little devils.

We find Blake pacing outside the hotel. He stops, shaking his head as he inspects us.

"You're gonna make Daniel pay for this, won't you?" he asks with fake concern.

"We've taught you well." Wiggling my eyebrows, I hook one of my hands around his arm. Summer does the same with his other arm, and together we head in the direction of the park. It's a glorious day out here, hot and sunny, quite different from the chilly morning in San Francisco. The sky is devoid of any clouds, just blue as far as I can see.

Blake dishes out useful information we can use against Daniel the entire way to the park, which makes the journey seem considerably shorter. It's remarkable how easily Summer lures out information from my brother.

Pippa and I usually have to do some serious legwork to get them to loosen their tongues, but Summer has them wrapped around her little finger. I listen intently to Blake's stories, filing the information carefully for later use.

When we finally arrive at the visitor center where we're meeting Daniel, he's nowhere to be seen. There are several exhibits inside, as well as a shop. It's buzzing with people, so we wait outside at the picnic tables.

"If he dragged us out to the middle of nowhere just to make us wait," Blake comments, "I'll dish even more dirt."

"I'm sure he'll be here soon," Summer says brightly. "But we won't say no to more blackmail material."

Ten minutes pass, then fifteen, and there's no sign of Daniel. Groups of tourists pass by, popping in and out of the center.

I call Daniel a few times, but his phone has no coverage.

"Maybe he's waiting for us at another visitor center?" Summer suggests.

"Nah, I specifically asked him," Blake explains.

"He would've sent a message anyway," I add. "Unless his battery is dead." I hadn't thought of that before. "I'll head inside to the information desk. Maybe he left a message for us with them."

Inside, the man behind the information desk looks like a kind grandpa, down to the round belly and white hair.

"Hello, Tom!" I greet, reading his name tag.

"Hi, miss. What can I do for you?"

"We were supposed to meet my brother here twenty minutes ago. I was wondering if he left a message with you, if he's expecting us somewhere else, maybe."

"What's his name?" he asks good-naturedly.

"Daniel Bennett."

The smile he had since I walked in fades. A lump settles in my throat, a sense of foreboding creeping up the back of my neck.

"And he's related to you, you said?"

"Yeah. He's my brother."

"Right. Mr. Bennett went on a trail this morning, and we received an alarm that he fell into one of the deeper cracks. A rescue team is already there."

"A rescue team?" I repeat dumbly. Possibly my brain hasn't processed the meaning of the sentence.

"Yes."

"But he's all right?" I grip the edge of the desk, bracing myself.

"We don't know yet, miss. We'll know more once the rescue team arrives and gets a hold of him."

"Are you not in contact with him?"

"No, the alarm was raised by some travelers who saw him fall."

"If they saw him, why didn't they go after him?" I ask angrily.

"It's dangerous, which is why a rescue team is necessary."

"Oh my God." Now the words sink in, and my chest tightens with panic. "Is he…?" I can't bring myself to ask the words, but I have to. "Is he alive?"

"Yes."

"Is he injured?"

"Yes, but I don't know the extent."

Gripping the edges of the desk tighter, I swallow hard, attempting to calm my racing pulse. "How can I help? We? Two other siblings of mine are outside. Can we join the search team?"

"No, only trained professionals are part of the rescue team. I suggest you and your siblings wait inside the restaurant. I'll let you know as soon as we have news."

"Wait? That's all we can do?"

"I'm afraid so. Please don't worry. Our rescue team is very efficient."

If he thinks that statement calms me down, he's completely wrong. Realizing there's nothing more I can do in here, I head back outside. The sight of Summer and Blake sitting at one of the tables and laughing stops me in my tracks. Tension accumulates in my shoulder blades as I consider how to best break the news to them. Briefly I ponder if there is any way I can keep this to myself, avoid worrying them. But before I can come up with any sharp idea, they notice me. My expression must give me away, because both their smiles freeze on their faces.

"What's wrong?" Blake asks.

Steeling myself, I sit next to Summer and relay the information the man gave me as calmly as possible. The second I'm done, Blake springs to his feet, storming inside the building.

"Poor Daniel," Summer murmurs, her voice trembling. I hug her tightly, insisting they'll find him in no time, hoping I sound more confident than I feel.

Blake is livid when he returns. "I can't believe they don't have more information."

"Should we tell the rest of the family?" Summer asks.

"No," I answer firmly. "Let's wait a while longer, at least until we know more."

They reluctantly agree, and we immediately launch into a debate over what could have happened and how all this could play out. I do my best to calm Blake and Summer every time they veer too deeply into negative scenarios, but my bravado begins to fade as no news reaches us.

"We should tell the others," Blake insists after an hour during which we have no further news.

"I'll do it in a few minutes." I massage a spot on my temple where a piercing pain pulses every few seconds.

"We can do it together," Blake offers. "Each of us call part of the clan."

"Nah, I'll do it."

Next to me, Summer's eyes are glassy, and by the way she keeps chewing on her lower lip, I can tell she's really fighting to keep it together. This was her telltale sign when we were kids.

I could tell when she was about to cry by the way her lower lip would move, and I typically had just enough time to distract her with a joke or a change of subject. Now neither of those options will cut it. I don't have an inkling what would. With an encouraging clasp on her shoulder, I rise from the table, moving farther away from the picnic tables to make the calls.

My fingers tremble over the screen of my phone as I decide whom to call first. In the end, I decide to start with Sebastian.

"What's taking them so long to find him?" Sebastian exclaims the second I finish telling him everything. "I'll make some calls to the local mayor and—"

"Sebastian," I say gently, "their rescue team is already on it."

"I'll get on a plane right away."

"Please don't. It won't make a difference. It's frustrating, but all we're doing here is waiting. I promise they'll find him soon."

"Okay. Please call me as soon as they tell you more."

"Of course."

My palms are sweating as I click off, my heart rate more frantic than before. Damn, I'm used to having to calm down my younger siblings, but usually when there's a crisis, I can count on Logan, Pippa, and Sebastian most of all to be a calming presence. I won't lie; a part of me was hoping Sebastian would impart some of his usual calmness over the phone, reassuring *me* that Daniel will be safe. A girl can hope.

I call Logan next, and he's with Max and Christopher, so he switches to speakerphone and my younger brothers hear the news at the same time. I barely convince them to stay put, their reaction almost identical to Sebastian's.

Telling Pippa and then my parents almost breaks my heart. They've always been the pillars and the glue of the family, keeping everything afloat in crisis situations. I only ever saw my mother look completely lost a few years back, when my father had an accident. While he was in surgery, Mom seemed completely out of it. Pippa stepped up to the plate and calmed Mother down.

Right now, they are both distressed, and schooling my voice to sound reassuring and optimistic becomes more taxing by the second. By the time I head back inside to Summer and Blake, I'm on the verge on tears, but I stubbornly withhold them.

"Drink water," Blake says the second I return to the picnic tables. "We'll dehydrate in this heat if we don't drink." And I can't help worrying about Daniel, and if he has enough water.

Sometime later Tom comes out to us. Summer locks her eyes on him, and Blake's shoulders go rigid. At one point Tom all but begged us not to bust into his office again, assuring us he'd tell us when there is news.

"The rescue team got a hold of him, but his right ankle is blocked between two boulders. They're working on getting him out."

"Oh!" Summer drops her head between her hands.

"Is he injured otherwise?" I ask.

"There were no apparent life-threatening injuries at first sight."

"At first sight," Blake repeats, his jaw set.

"They have a paramedic with them."

"How can this take so long?" I bellow, rising to my feet.

"I assure you everyone's doing their best." His jaw ticks. His patience is wearing thin, but I couldn't care less. This is my brother we're talking about.

I swear loudly after he leaves.

"I'll call everyone and tell them about the update," Blake says, and all I can do is give him a grateful smile. I couldn't make it through another round of calls.

Just as Blake puts his phone to his ear, the sound of my own ringing startles me. Fully expecting the caller to be someone in my family, I steel myself mentally. Glancing at the screen, an unexpected name pops up: *Nate*. For the first time in hours, a smile tugs at the corners of my lips.

"Hey," I greet him, placing the phone to my ear, and hurry away from the tables.

"How's the climb? Did you murder Daniel yet?"

At the sound of my brother's name, I inhale sharply, the knot in my stomach twisting.

"What's wrong?" Nate asks at once, his voice devoid of humor.

"How could you tell something is wrong?"

"Don't know. Something tipped me off. What happened?"

I tell him quickly.

"Shit, I'm sorry, Alice! But I'm sure everything will be okay."

"Can you please repeat that at least a hundred times?" My voice is pleading, even as the muscles in my body unwind a tad. God, how I needed someone to tell me everything will be okay.

"I'll do it as soon as I'm there."

"You're coming here?"

"Damn right, I am."

"Oh shit, I forgot you had plans with Daniel afterward. Your team—"

"Will be fine on their own. I need to be with you," he says simply, and I all but melt.

"I'd really like that. If it's not too much trouble."

"I'll be there right away, baby."

Despite my general state of anxiety, my stomach flutters at the word *baby*. He's never called me that before. As I hang up, the muscles in my body relax a tad at the mere idea of him here.

Nate arrives shortly afterward. "Any news?"

Blake, who is lying on one of the picnic benches, merely groans. Summer shakes her head.

"Not since we spoke on the phone."

"I'll go talk to the information desk," he offers.

"I'm coming with you." It's pointless, because Tom would have told us if there was any news, but it gives me an excuse to feel like I'm doing something productive.

The second we're inside the center, Nate places his hand at the small of my back, which has the surprising effect of liquefying my bones. I lean into his touch, hungry for more. I could really use a bear hug right now, or any kind of hug, really. Together, we step inside the information office.

Tom snaps his head up, smiling at Nate. His smile morphs into a grimace when he notices me. "I don't have any news, miss. As I said, I'll pop outside as soon as the rescue team contacts me."

"When does the center close?" Nate asks.

"In three hours, but I'll stay here to update you."

"Thank you," I say.

Tom disappears into a side room before Nate and I have time to open our mouths again.

"Why did he look terrified when he saw you?" Nate asks once we're back outside.

"I might have lashed out at him earlier."

"Of course you did." His hand is still at the small of my back, moving in a small motion.

"Are you sure you can be here? You said being with your team during this kickoff time is important."

"Alice," he says softly, bringing his hand to my chin, his thumb rubbing small circles at one corner of my lips. "This is important. You are important."

His words travel straight through me, and my heart gives a little squeeze.

"Let's walk around a bit." I guide him in the opposite direction from the picnic tables because I need a breather. Putting up the bravado in front of my siblings has completely depleted me.

"Do you need anything?"

I bite the inside of my cheeks, remembering what he said to me this morning on the hood of his car—that if I want him to hold me, all I have to do is ask. So I go out on a limb.

"Can you hold me? Really tight?" Damn, I didn't mean to sound needy.

By way of answering, Nate pulls me in for a hug. I lose myself in his strong, warm arms, resting my head against his chest, breathing in deeply. It's the first deep breath—the first *real* breath—I've taken in hours.

"I'm so scared for my baby brother," I whisper after a while, pulling away. My voice is so low, I'm not sure if Nate heard me at all. "I read online about all the things that can go wrong in a situation like this. It's awful."

"Why? Avoid the Internet. It'll always bring out the worst-case scenarios. Years ago, I made the mistake of looking up my symptoms when I had the flu. I was convinced I was going to die after *researching*."

Shrugging, I pull the phone out of my pocket, holding it up. "I wanted to feel productive, so I searched online on my phone."

Nate snatches the phone, shoving it in his pocket.

"Hey!"

"No more phone for you."

"But what if my parents call, or any of my siblings?"

"I'll talk to them." There's no room for negotiation in his voice and I don't argue, grateful there's someone here to take charge.

Nate wraps his strong arms around me again. "Everything will be all right."

In this moment, I allow myself to believe it will be.

***

Eventually we return to the picnic tables, and hours pass. After the sun sets, my anxiety skyrockets again. I exchange glances with my siblings and Nate, but none of us speak, which I think helps. I once read that verbalizing a fear increases its power.

I run my palms up and down my thighs, pressing the tongue to the roof of my mouth. On the other side of the table, Blake massages his temples and Summer chews on her lower lip so aggressively I'm afraid she'll draw blood. Sitting next to me, Nate touches my outer thigh with his knee.

When I can't stand sitting around waiting anymore, I spring to my feet, intending to head inside to Tom. The door swings open at precisely the same moment, and Tom himself walks to us.

"Good news! I just spoke to the rescue team. Your brother is safe and sound and—"

We erupt in cheering, drowning Tom's voice. My body feels as light as a feather.

"Since it's dark and late, and the park is officially closed, he'll stay at one of the camping stations tonight," Tom continues, instantly dampening everyone's mood. I was hoping to see my brother tonight, check for myself that he's all right.

"Did the paramedics check him?" Summer asks.

"Yes, and they confirmed he's in good shape. He just needs to rest."

"Is there any way we can get to him?" I add.

"No, as I said, the park is closed. You'll see him tomorrow."

With no other choice, we head back to the hotel, right after Nate returns my phone and I call everyone in the family to share the good news.

Chapter Fourteen

Nate

Once we enter the hotel, I bring up the subject of dinner, but all three of them shake their heads, insisting they just want to sleep. Alice's phone beeps again. I tell Summer and Blake that they can go to their rooms, and I'll wait for Alice. I pace the lobby while she talks in a low and soothing voice. I catch a few sentences, enough to learn she's talking to Jenna.

"Everything okay?" I ask once she hangs up.

"Yeah. Mom was just checking in again."

"Let's go upstairs, then. Both our rooms are on the fourth floor."

"Elevator's this way." She throws her thumb over her shoulder.

"After you."

Turning around, she walks in front of me. Without heels on, Alice is tiny. But it's not just her height that has my protective instincts on high alert. It's the way she hunches her shoulders. When Alice is hurt or afraid, she has a way of curling up, like she's trying to shrink inside of herself. She rarely allows her hurt to show. This is one of those times. The other one I remember vividly was when Pippa's first husband turned out to be a complete douche, and Pippa was devastated. That time Alice's hurt was short-lived, quickly replaced by anger. Now she's just exhausted from so much worrying, and I don't want to leave her alone because I know her. She'll worry herself sick right until the morning.

When we reach our floor, she leads the way again, sashaying down the narrow corridor before coming to a halt in front her door.

"This is me," she announces, jingling her key between her fingers. She's not ready to say good night either. I step right behind her, swiping her hair to one side, bringing my mouth to her ear. "Some schools of seduction consider playing with keys as a sign that you want to be kissed."

I exhale sharply as goose bumps form on the skin of her arms instantly.

"The Nate Becker school of seduction?"

"Nah." I run my fingers up and down her exposed forearm. "It's a thoroughly researched theory."

"I don't want to say good night yet."

"I can come in with you and keep you company for a while."

Wordlessly, she unlocks her door, pushes it open, and steps inside.

"Sit down." I point to the couch in the center of the room. "I'll make you some tea. Was your mother still worried on the phone?" At the four corners of the room are lamps, casting a yellow glow in their corner, yet leaving the center where we are in a pleasant dimness, which is both smooth and inviting.

"Yes. She'll only really believe he's okay when she sees him."

"That's true for you as well, isn't it?"

"Yeah."

When I hand her the tea minutes later, she's reading something on her phone, a look of intense concentration—and worry—on her face.

"What are you doing?"

"Just reading through my e-mails."

I snatch her phone.

"Come on."

I glance down at the screen. "I knew you'd be reading something like 'Top 10 dangerous injuries not immediately apparent to paramedics.' Shitty title."

Pointing a menacing finger at me, she says, "If you don't return my phone, I'll tickle you, Nate Becker."

"If I were you, I wouldn't."

"Why not?"

I lean over her. "Because I'd wrestle you away from me, which might lead to very inappropriate things."

She licks her lips, looking away.

"You'll get your phone back tomorrow. I don't want you to worry yourself sick overnight. You need a good night's sleep, and I'm going to make sure you get it even if I have to stand next to your bed and watch you all night."

"Please morph back into your cavemanish and arrogant self."

"What?"

"I can go toe-to-toe with that version of you. It's hard to say no to this caring version."

"Then say yes."

***

Alice

His voice is low, husky. This is Nate's bedroom voice and I love it. He fixes me with his gaze, and I stubbornly hold it right until I feel the rush of heat in my cheeks, then look away. A prickle of pain stabs me at the spot right where my neck meets my back. I run my palm over it, attempting to assuage the ache.

"Damn, I hate it when this happens."

"What's wrong?" Nate asks.

"Whenever I'm stressed, it seems all the tension accumulates at the back of my neck."

"Turn around," Nate says unexpectedly.

"Hmm?"

"I'll take care of you." Wiggling his eyebrows, he adds in a lower tone. "I'm good with my hands."

His words travel straight between my thighs, and I have to press my tongue against the roof of my mouth to keep a sigh from escaping me. Not trusting myself to speak, I simply turn around. Nate places the teacup on the coffee table in front of me, then sits next to me on the couch. I'm half turned to him and Nate pushes my hair to one side, baring my neck to him.

"Show me the painful points."

I gesture to my neck, running my fingers over the specific spots. No sooner do I place my hand on my lap than Nate presses his thumb exactly on those points.

It relieves the pressure somewhat, and also turns me on. I can feel every rough patch on the pad of his fingers, and I remember how it felt when he had me up on the counter, one hand supporting my ass, the other bringing me over the edge. I remember it all so clearly, the pleasure and the ache. I ache now too.

Belatedly I realize why—Nate hasn't stuck to the points I showed him. Instead, his wandering fingers reached the spot at the edge of my hairline. Those damn fingers are not to be trusted at all.

"Sweet spot?" he asks.

Instinct probably tipped him off, and the explosion of goose bumps was a dead giveaway.

"Yes."

He places his other hand on my waist, splaying his fingers wide. My breath catches, as if someone sucked the air out of here. Then he pulls away.

"What are you doing?" I complain.

"You had a rule. Five dates, remember? I respect you and I respect your choices, even if I want you so badly it hurts. But respecting that means keeping my hands away from you or I'll die from frustration."

Licking my lips, I say in a low voice, "The rule wasn't as set in stone as I made it out to be. I just needed to be sure you wanted me. Us."

I hear him move on the couch, feel the leather cave in with his weight as he's right behind me again.

"I've always wanted you. That was never the question. It's always been yes." Only our heavy breaths fill the silence for the next seconds. "Alice, do you want me to go to my room tonight?"

The implication in his question is clear, and it sends all my senses into a tailspin. I answer without a morsel of hesitation.

"No."

That one syllable is enough for the tension between us to explode. Taking his thumb away from the sweet spot on my neck, he tilts my head slightly, placing his mouth on the exact same spot. His gorgeous, hot mouth. The sensation travels straight to my sex, and I can't stop a shudder. He reaches to the lower hem of my shirt, pushing it up, barely a fraction of an inch. The gesture is a silent question: He's seeking my permission. By way of answering, I push the fabric further up. My breath catches at the same time he exhales sharply.

"Nate." Licking my lips, I dig my nails into the leathery surface of the couch, seeking to ground myself. "I want you too. So much."

Before long, we're both completely naked. I drink in the sight of him, all hard and hot, ready to love me and be with me in all ways. His hand on my chest, he pushes me onto my back on the couch until I'm lying with my head on the armrest. His gaze rakes over me and my nipples turn to pebbles under his scrutiny. When he leans over me, placing a chaste kiss right on my abdomen, I shudder. He trails upward to my neck, and finally my mouth. With every kiss, he steals more of me until he owns me so utterly and completely that it frightens me. This man has a power over me that I haven't given anyone else. No matter where his lips touch me, I feel his kisses everywhere.

"I like seeing you like this, trembling with anticipation," he whispers.

"Better make all this anticipation worth my time," I tease, pointing to his hard length between us.

"Ah, sweet Alice, don't you know that pleasure is best savored only after yearning for it?" He grips his erection at the base, placing the tip right under my navel, sliding it down a few inches on my belly. "Anticipating it until it's almost painful?" He slides farther down until his tip is on my clit, and I go up in flames. A tremor shakes through me, the ache low in my body so real and deep I can't stand it one second longer. "Fuck, I want you so badly."

"I'm clean and on the pill," I tell him. He blinks, as if not quite understanding. And then his nostrils flare as he exhales sharply, the meaning of my words clearly reaching him.

"I'm clean too, but are you sure?"

"Yes," I say confidently.

"Because I want nothing more than to be inside you with nothing between us, nothing at all. Just your pussy squeezing me—"

His words detonate a million tiny explosions across my skin, deep in my body, unleashing a rabid desire.

"Yes."

He tilts my head back for better access, kissing my neck. The tip of his erection slides up and down my folds, coating himself in my slickness.

"So wet and ready," he murmurs in my ear, right before sliding inside me. He does it slowly, giving me his erection inch by inch, stretching me. I love that he's careful and considerate. And I love that he's shaking, which means it's taking every ounce of his control not to unleash all his passion.

"So good. You're so tight."

"You're just big," I whisper. "Don't hold back, Nate."

"Oh fuck. I'll be a brute."

"I want it. I can take it."

He slams against me, pulling out and slamming back again, not holding back. I drink up his passion, reveling in it, basking in every sensation he awakens in me. He owns me right now, every single cell in my body.

Digging my nails in the back of his neck, I drag them down the expanse of his back, feeling every ridge, line, and muscle under my fingers, slipping lower still until I reach his ass. Yummm… those sculpted muscles are a work of art. Planting my feet firmly on the couch, I push against him, meeting his desperate thrusts, moan after moan tumbling from my lips. Realizing how loud I am, I attempt to muffle the sounds by burrowing into one of his strong, muscle-laced arms.

"No!" he commands. "I want to hear you."

"The neighbors will hear," I tell him just before yet another moan—a cry, really.

"Let them hear."

He slams into me deeper still, and the friction at the base applies pressure on my clit, sending an electrifying jolt through me.

"So close," I murmur, digging my nails deeper in his skin. When I feel him widening inside me, I know I'll tumble over the edge in seconds. "I'm gonna—oh!"

Blinking my eyes open, I want to focus on his beautiful face. I want to see what he looks like when he's on the cusp of pleasure, but his edges blur, the room behind him a mass of indistinguishable colors. As pleasure ripples across my skin, he covers my mouth, claiming my cry of pleasure while giving me his.

We stay entwined for what feels like hours, regaining our breath and our composure.

Chapter Fifteen

Alice

The next morning I wake up with a jolt and instinctively cross an arm over my face. Drawing in a deep breath, I can't detect one single whiff of lavender in the air. Seconds later, I remember I'm not in my bedroom. I'm in a hotel with Nate. With my eyes still closed, I pat the bed beside me. It's empty and cold. Maybe Nate's sleeping at the edge of the bed. I blink, peering to my right. Nope, he's not here. My heart rate picks up as I push myself into a sitting position, glancing around the room. There's no sign of him. My clothes are in a messy pile by the couch, but his are nowhere to be seen. Still, I'm persistent.

"Nate?" I call loudly, then add in a smaller voice that sounds like a whimper, "Are you in the bathroom?"

I receive no answer, and there is no sound of water running from the bathroom. My throat closes up and I bite into my bottom lip. Then I shake my head, pushing a hand through my hair. I'm being very unreasonable. Maybe he had to meet with his team again and he left early. I don't remember him saying anything yesterday, but that's not saying much since I was out of sorts over Daniel. It's possible I just tuned out that particular bit of information.

Pushing myself out of the bed, I head to my bag, which is next to the couch. My phone is in it, and I need to check the time. It must be before eight thirty, because I set the alarm for then. Daniel will arrive at nine.

It's eight fifteen. I play with my phone for a few seconds, looking over the message icon, which isn't showing any new messages. Then I shove it back in the bag and walk straight into the shower, leaping under the warm spray and spreading soap on my body with vigorous moves.

Even as I try to keep calm and reasonable, a small voice at the back of my mind teases me. *Stupid, stupid Alice. Why do you keep hoping?*

Well, if he thinks he can hurt me and get away with it, he has another think coming. I'll hide my heartbreak under vengeful tactics.

By the time I turn off the water and step outside the shower, I've brainstormed about ten different ways to get back at him. That's when I hear someone singing in the other room, then abruptly stopping.

"If you don't hurry, your coffee will be cold," Nate calls.

My heart soars and I slap my forehead. Oh my God. I have to dial down the crazy a notch… or a thousand.

Wrapping the towel around me, I tiptoe back into the room, hoping he can't guess all my previous thoughts of revenge and whatnot. I shouldn't have worried because my relief that he didn't take off manifests in a grin so out of control, I suspect he might think I'm nuts. Which, in all honesty, I am.

"I bought turkey sandwiches, hummus and falafel wraps, a salmon wrap, and a salad. Didn't know what you like in the morning." He points to a plastic bag on the table full of sandwiches. Sitting on the couch, he takes a hearty bite from his wrap.

"What's in yours?" I ask.

"Beef."

"Then that's what I want."

He sets his jaw, shaking his head and muttering "Women." With one regretful look at his wrap, he stretches his hand out. "Take it before I change my mind."

Aaaand butterflies explode in my stomach, making my heart soar even more. "You don't like to share food. You've never liked it."

"I'll have to learn if I want to coexist with you. I forgot your favorite pastime is stealing people's food."

"Not anyone's food. I just steal food from people I like."

"That's supposed to make me feel better?"

I nod with conviction, then let him off the hook.

"Keep it. Next time buy me whatever you're having. I'll eat the turkey sandwich."

Filled with too much energy to sit down, I double-check if my towel is safely fastened over my boobs, then grab the wrap with one hand, the coffee cup with the other. I realize I'm drinking from a plastic take-out cup. And the sandwiches were in a plastic bag. I'm really slow this morning.

"This isn't the hotel's breakfast, right?"

"Nah. Woke up at seven and went down with my team to eat before the day started."

"Oh. Are they waiting for you now?"

"No, the joint program for today starts at ten. They all have free time until then."

"Okay. So, you were saying about breakfast…."

"The food and coffee was so appalling I knew you'd have an aneurysm if you saw it. Clara did warn me about online reviews slashing their breakfast, but I figured the reviewers were jerks. Turns out I was wrong."

"So where did these come from?"

"Drove around town until I found a decent-looking place."

"Wow, how thoughtful."

Thoughtful is an understatement. It was kind and sweet, and it fills me with an infectious joy. I nearly want to pinch myself to make sure I'm not dreaming, and I might have done it if Nate wasn't watching me. Grinning, he pats the empty space next to him on the couch and I sit, munching on my delicious sandwich.

"Just doing my part in saving the world from a hungry Alice Bennett."

"Uh-huh… and you were accusing *me* of being a closet romantic."

"What can I say? You're rubbing off on me." Having finished his wrap, he sips from his coffee cup, eyeing the rest of the food on the table.

"Why did you buy so much food?"

"Thought Summer and your brothers would appreciate a good breakfast too."

I put two and two together. "Are you trying to bribe my siblings with food? They'll sniff this out"—I point with my finger between us—"right away."

"Are you calling me a coward?"

"Hey, I was going to say you're smart." I place my now-empty coffee cup on the table and lift both hands in mock defense. "But if you want to go with coward, your choice, not mine."

"You're too sassy for your own good. The only time you're not sassy is in your sleep."

"Fair assessment. I didn't hear you get up this morning."

Something in my expression must betray me, because Nate asks, "You thought I took off?"

I clear my throat, trying to downplay it because I feel like more of an idiot with every passing second.

"Alice?" he insists.

"Well, I woke up alone. The bed was cold and all your clothes were gone. I hadn't had coffee, so my neurons weren't up yet."

"So you jumped to planning my early death?" he supplies, a corner of his mouth lifting in a half smile.

"I love your confidence in me, but I was merely contemplating painful torture methods. I'm far more innocent than you give me credit for."

"Bet you are," he murmurs. "You do know my entire team is here, and my bag with fresh clothes is in my room? Even if that weren't the case, I'd never just leave."

I lick my lips, nodding. "I see that now. It's all about the coffee. Breakfast helps with thinking too. Basically the only thing I'm good at on an empty stomach is being neurotic."

I'm rambling now. Nate plunks his coffee cup next to mine on the table, surveying me closely. I'm sitting with my feet tucked to one side, and I barely have time to register that Nate is up to something before he grabs both my ankles, pulling me toward him. As if anticipating I'll try pushing my ass against the couch to stop from sliding right into his lap, he reaches under the towel, grabbing my ass firmly and lifting it.

When he drops me in his lap, I desperately check my towel, but of course it's come undone. I'm flashing him my tits and my hooha. I thought he'd take advantage of this, but to my astonishment, he meticulously covers me with the towel.

"What are you doing?" I ask suspiciously.

"We're having a conversation. Having your nipples in my face is distracting me."

"Okay, then. Get to it."

"You're not gonna help?" he asks as he tries to fasten the towel above my right boob. By the way his fingers linger on my skin, it's obvious he'd prefer to yank the fabric away altogether.

"No, I'm quite enjoying watching you struggle."

His eyes flash, and I'm certain I'm going to pay for this. What does it say about me that I'm looking forward to it?

After successfully fastening my towel, he rests his hand on my inner thighs, very close to my intimate spot. I cock a brow at him.

"If you're distracted, I have the advantage," he explains, and I know this is my payback. Right up my alley. I open my thighs a tad, wiggling my eyebrows at him.

"If you're gonna distract me, do it properly."

Nate chuckles. "I was saying I'd never just leave. I might not have any 'boyfriend of the year' trophies, but I know a thing or two. Since I'm a lucky bastard and have you, I'm going to do nice things for you. Take care of you."

"Well look at that," I say in a rough voice. "You *can* make me swoon."

"Told you. Doesn't mean I won't screw up, but"—he holds up one finger, as if saying, pay extra attention to this—"you have good instincts. If you feel a screw-up coming, don't be afraid to do something about it. But in the meantime, I'm gonna do the right thing by you." He kisses the tip of my nose and, despite his warning, I sigh happily. It's all we can do, really. Do our best and see where this takes us.

Next thing I know, Nate kisses down my neck, undoing my towel, which falls around me, leaving me naked and exposed.

"What are you doing?"

"Rewarding myself for being on such good behavior." He circles a nipple with his thumb. "I made eye contact the entire time, despite these beauties pressing against the towel."

"How would you know that if you looked into my eyes the entire time?"

Nate doesn't miss a beat. "I have distributive attention."

Palming one breast, he pushes me gently off his lap until my ass is on the couch. He lowers his head over my stomach, then trails his lips up and down my skin.

"Lie back, Alice."

His voice has dropped an octave, and *damn* his bedroom voice is sexy. As I do what he says, he spreads my thighs, his hand inching closer to my center.

"We don't have time," I protest weakly. "Daniel will be here at nine."

"We still have plenty of time. I want to make you come, baby. You're so beautiful when you come apart." He turns his head slightly, focusing on me. "It's my favorite sight."

Still holding me captive with his sinful gaze, he runs two fingers from my clit to my opening, and my hips buck off the couch. He coats his fingers in my arousal before sliding them in, arching them in a come-here motion that drives me crazy. The heel of his palm presses against my clit, and I become a bundle of sensations.

Nate peppers kisses all over my torso, moving from my stomach up to my breast while keeping his hand between my legs. I don't know how much time passes before my orgasm builds inside me, but I feel like I'm burning up from the inside.

"I love seeing you like this, Alice," he murmurs. His voice is all it takes to send me over the edge. I'm only vaguely aware of my fingers tugging at his hair as I cry out, holding on to him, hoping I'll never have to let go.

Chapter Sixteen

Alice

I grin like a lunatic as Nate and I leave the room some twenty minutes later, taking the bag with sandwiches and salad with us. There are three other guests in the elevator car with us, and they give us suspicious looks. Nate has mussed-up, disheveled hair which could raise questions about his morning activities, but I check my appearance in the metal doors of the elevator and confirm I look perfectly composed. Except for the damn grin. I can't rein it in, hard as I try.

We find Summer and Blake in the sitting area next to the reception desk. They stop talking upon seeing us. Summer chuckles, while Blake whistles loudly.

"What?" I challenge.

"Anything to share?" Summer asks boldly, her gaze wandering between Nate and me.

"Haven't heard from Daniel, no," I reply, knowing full well that's not what she meant. I wasn't expecting an ambush first thing in the morning.

"Alice, your evasive maneuvers suck when you haven't slept much," Summer continues. Next to me, Nate presses his lips tightly together in an obvious attempt to keep a straight face and not laugh. He's not helping my case at all, the bastard.

"I slept well, thank you very much."

"That smug grin can only mean you had a great night… but no sleep," Blake says helpfully. Turning to Nate, he adds, "You hurt my sister, you're a dead man, family friend or not. Just so we're clear."

"Crystal clear," Nate answers with a smile and a wink.

"Can't wait until Sebastian and Logan hear about this," Blake continues, and Nate's smile fades a tad. "Sebastian will be calm, but Logan? Man, oh man." My brother rubs his palms together like a cartoon character. "I'll ask for a front-row seat to the show."

"I used to like this one," Nate tells me, jerking his thumb toward my little brother. "Don't remember him being such a dickhead."

"I'm like red wine," Blake retaliates. "I grow more intense with age."

"I bought breakfast for everyone," Nate announces, though now that he's in the lion den already, food isn't likely to help his case much.

"Oooh, you're a lifesaver." Summer reaches for the bag with grabby hands, reminding me of her toddler days when she'd sit on the floor of the kitchen while Mom cooked, reaching up toward her with both hands when Mom was tasting the food.

"Just make sure Blake doesn't get anything," Nate tells her.

"So, what are your intentions?" Blake asks him.

"Blake, come on," I complain.

"What? It's good for him to rehearse this. I'll give him honest feedback if his answer isn't good enough. Our dear brothers might punch him."

Summer holds her salmon wrap with one hand, patting our brother's chest with the other. "Since when do you actually like it when Logan is in alpha-ninja-brother mode?" she asks Blake.

"Hey, I like when he's riding other people's asses. Come to think of it, I like when he picks on me too, just because I have a reason to give him shit. It's good for Logan too. Constructive. No one outside the family dares to give him shit. He'd start buying his own hype without me."

Ah yes, if there's one thing you can count on in my family it's that they'll keep you grounded.

"Fantastic logic," Nate deadpans. "You'd be an excellent salesman, Blake. You could sell ice to an Eskimo."

"What did I miss?" Daniel's voice booms from behind us. I turn around, and Summer immediately hurries to him. I inspect his appearance, cataloguing the long scratch running from one corner of his mouth up his cheek, the purple spot under the other eye. The rest of his body is covered by clothing, but he limps slightly on the left side.

"Summer, you're strangling me," Daniel says after a few minutes pass and our sister still doesn't let go. Reluctantly, she steps away from him. I want nothing more than to hug the living daylights out of him too, but if I do, I'll get emotional.

"Are you okay? Did the paramedics check you again in the morning?" Summer inquires.

"Yes, they did. They even walked with me right to the hotel entrance."

"What happened?" I ask.

"Wanted to try one of the more challenging climbing routes." He shrugs and something in the forced casualness of the gesture tips me off that he's trying to downplay everything.

"And what happened?"

"Well, part of the thrill is completing the route without part of the equipment."

"What? Why?"

"Adrenaline," he says simply. "Some customers pushed for a more extreme variation of climbing, and I wanted to try it out before—"

Blake swears and Summer covers her cheeks with her fingers, pressing so hard she'll have marks. Nate shakes his head.

"Are you mad?" I ask, unable to keep my voice calm. "You could have killed yourself."

"Accidents don't happen often—"

"You can only die once, anyway." My throat constricts with worry. I wish the rest of the group would back me up, but the three of them are silent.

"Well, I won't be adding it to my list of offerings yet, clearly," Daniel says.

I purse my lips. Damn, I'm so angry I swear I'm half expecting steam to come out of my ears.

"From now on, you'll change your offerings to something safe." I poke my forefinger in Daniel's chest with every word. Normally, I would do this forcefully, so he could feel the sting, but he's in enough pain today, so I'm gentle. A good day in my family is one during which I don't want to kill anyone—for their own good, of course. Today is not one of those days.

"I am in the business of extreme adventures," Daniel retorts. "The opposite of safe. What would you have me offer, anyway?"

"Extreme knitting, or quilting," I spit. Blake and Nate chuckle. *Now* they decide to chime in. I have the sudden urge to poke them as well. It wouldn't be gentle at all.

"I'm sure people searching for adrenaline would line up," Daniel says dryly.

"Make them knit while they also have to balance a ball on their nose. That would get their blood spiking," I volley.

"Alice, relax!" Daniel insists.

"I can't."

Daniel gives me an exasperated look. "Why can't you be more like Summer? Hug me, pet me?"

Blake intervenes. "Oh, but one month from now when you get crazy ideas again, Alice's voice will still be in your head. Your ears will probably still be ringing. I know mine will."

"I'm so happy I amuse both of you. I just want you to be safe, Daniel."

"I am safe. It was just a scare."

I swallow, crossing my arms over my chest. "But what if next time it isn't just a scare?"

"Then it will serve as a lesson to someone, and they will offer quilting."

"Not funny," Summer says in a low voice. It dawns on me that she might have kept quiet all this time because she was still emotional from seeing Daniel. "Just promise you'll think about ways to make this safer, okay?"

"Sure."

"Promise," I insist.

"Fine, I promise."

I run a frustrated hand through my hair. He's just saying this to placate me. I have to let this go though. I'm far too stressed to come up with intelligent arguments instead of emotional ones, but I'll circle back to this topic later. We all have a stubborn streak in us, but even Daniel must know this isn't a game. It's flat-out dangerous.

"Did you have breakfast?" I ask him.

Daniel's expression relaxes, clearly relieved to be off the hook. "Nah, had them bring me right here to meet you guys."

"Nate here brought breakfast," Blake tells him. "He hooked up with Alice, thought we'd go easier on him if he brought food."

Daniel points at Nate. "You hurt her, you're a dead man."

Nate's jaw ticks. "Got it. It's the family tag line, apparently."

***

After breakfast, my siblings and I decide it's best if we head back to San Francisco. We were supposed to leave tomorrow, but between Daniel's ankle and the family worrying, we agree to cut the trip short. Nate will remain here the entire day, since he has plans with his team.

After we check out, Nate walks us to Blake's car. Blake and Summer lead the way. I'm right behind them, and Nate and Daniel are a few good feet behind me. Even so, I catch their conversation.

"I know a lot of people who're into extreme adventures. Some just for the camera, some behind it too. Accidents happen more often than you think," Nate says.

Daniel replies in a whisper too low for me to catch.

"It's a line of work that always keeps your family on edge," Nate continues. "I've seen wives of hotshot TV stars who made a living doing extreme stuff for the camera. They worry constantly, and it's not pretty."

"I can't change gears now or start over. I want to see this through," Daniel replies, and something clicks in my mind.

My siblings get in the car first, and I linger outside to say goodbye to Nate. Not wanting three curious stares on us, I pull Nate out of sight behind another car.

"Oy," Blake's voice comes through. "Don't overdo it with the kissing. We don't want to be late for dinner."

I roll my eyes, even though Blake can't see me. Mom asked us all to come by for dinner this evening.

"Pity you can't join us tonight," I tell him. "Even though you received enough threats from my brothers today."

"I'd rather spend the day with you and your crazy clan, but work calls. I still have to look over what the London office sent me too."

And cue the heartburn. *Shit, I have to stop reacting like this every time London is mentioned. He's here now, and that's all that matters.* Fisting Nate's shirt with both hands, I tug him toward me, giving him a hint. And he takes it. Tipping my chin up, he seals his lips over mine in a kiss that leaves me breathless and worked up.

"Great kiss," I say afterward.

"Has to last until next time. I'll see you. I'm coming in late tomorrow, but I'll call you."

"Okay. Oh, and thank you for talking to Daniel. Full confession? I was kind of mad that you didn't back me up in the lobby."

"You were doing a fine job by yourself. Told you, you're a force of nature."

"Didn't do much good." I shrug as Nate pushes two strands of hair behind my ears, and then his hands rest at the back of my head, the pads of his fingers pressing gently on my scalp.

"People don't like to be cornered, Alice, especially not in front of an audience. If you want to convince anyone of something, you must be calm and rational. Give solid arguments."

"Yeah, knitting and quilting weren't my brightest ideas."

"You were emotional. But you'll figure it out. You're smart."

He pulls me to him again, kissing me long and hard, and I have to remind myself where we are so I don't climb him. I want to memorize every sensation coursing through me, soak up all the goodness of this moment.

Is it normal to feel like you're wrapped in a cloud just because your man is kissing you? Is this what a real relationship is? To feel that you're a team with someone that you can talk about things, find solutions together?

Ever since last night—minus my morning freak-out—I feel like I'm dreaming. If it *is* a dream, I don't want to wake up. If it's real, I want to know how to make it last.

Chapter Seventeen

Alice

My siblings grill me about Nate for half the trip. The rest of the time, we grill Summer about Rome, making thinly veiled attempts to convince her to return to San Francisco sooner, although my attempts are less veiled than my brothers'.

During dinner at my parents' house, the entire family is too happy that Daniel's safe to admonish him. Remembering what Nate told me about cornering, I keep silent on the subject. But something Daniel told Nate keeps nagging at me—that he's started on this path and now he wants to see it through.

I also keep quiet because we're all enjoying Summer's visit, and the spotlight is on her the entire time. She's heading back to Rome all too soon, unfortunately. She leaves in three days, and who knows when she'll visit again.

After dinner, I ask Logan to come by one of my restaurants when he has time because I want to ask his advice about some financial issues, which is true. But I also want to ask for his help with Daniel.

Over the next week, Nate and I talk on the phone for hours every evening, but we have dinner and spend the night together only twice.

On Friday, Logan visits me at Blue Moon. We have lunch in my back office.

"This looks very promising." We're sitting at my desk, and he's inspecting the numbers on my laptop's screen. "I don't foresee any liquidity problems if you keep up like this."

I let out a breath of relief, resting my elbows on the desk. As the CFO of Bennett Enterprises, my brother is a whiz with numbers, and I like picking his brain whenever he has time.

"And if you do have problems, we can always bail you out," he continues.

"It's not what I want, you big oaf."

In the beginning, I tried to do everything on my own, then realized asking my brothers for counsel was a good thing because they're brilliant. Sure, they often accompany advice with an offer to bail me out should anything go wrong, but I've learned how to push against their alpha tendencies without biting their heads off.

They want the best for me and are sometimes overprotective. I want to be independent. We'll always clash and make up, but that's what family does.

Taking a spoonful of my tiramisu, I grip the plate possessively because my brother is eyeing it hopefully. He already finished his. While enjoying the exquisite sweetness, I become aware of the tightness in my neck.

"Is there something else on your mind, Alice?" my brother asks. "You look tense."

I haven't given him a heads-up that I want to talk about Daniel. He would've just worried needlessly.

"I do want to talk to you about Daniel."

Logan pinches his brows together. "What about him?"

"Well, ever since the incident, I've been worrying more than usual about the extreme adventures part of his business."

"Me too," Logan says, leaning back in the chair, lacing his fingers on top of his head. My stomach relaxes a tad at his response.

"Really?"

"Yeah. I spent those hours we were waiting for your call researching anything that can go wrong in a situation like Daniel's. Then I fell into the rabbit hole and read about all kinds of accidents during extreme adventures. It's a nightmare. Why are you laughing?"

"I did exactly the same thing."

"Well, we *are* related."

"Have you ever talked to Daniel about this?" I continue.

"Nah, I didn't bring it up. What good would it do? He never listens to what I say."

I'm silent for a few seconds, waiting for the punch line. Then I realize Logan is serious. Can he really be so far off base?

"I can't believe you actually believe what you say doesn't matter to Daniel."

My big brother actually looks disconcerted. I don't think I've ever seen this look on him.

"We have nearly thirty years of proof that whatever I say goes in one ear and right out the other."

I shake my head, searching for the best words to explain this to him. "Not true at all. He and Blake look up to you. They always have. I know it's hard to believe because they crack a joke whenever you say something, even when you're serious."

"Especially when I'm serious."

"Yeah, but look, when Daniel and Blake turned sixteen, I asked them what their aspirations were—basically what they wanted to be when they grew up. They both said they wanted to be like you."

Logan looks stunned for a brief second. "Were they drunk?"

"Duh! They turned sixteen and smuggled in tequila, and I covered for them."

"Of course you did."

"Hey! They were covering my ass every time I asked, so I owed them. We had our survival methods. But that's not the point. Besides, haven't you heard the saying that drunk people and kids always tell the truth?"

"Yeah. They actually said they want to be like me?"

"They worshipped you as kids, even more than Sebastian."

"But they brush me off every time I give them advice."

"It's a pride thing. Ego. You should understand, you have enough of it for the entire family. They want to prove they can succeed on their own."

Logan opens his mouth but I hold up a hand to stop him. I need him to hear me out first.

"I know what you're gonna say, that they spent a lot of time living the big life, just spending what they got off the dividends, but put yourself in their shoes for a second. All throughout their teen years and college, they saw Bennett Enterprises become one of the most successful companies in this country. The press practically idolized you and Sebastian. Everyone from friends to teachers were expecting the rest of us to do something extraordinary too. The weight of all those expectations can be so paralyzing that you choose to put off the moment when you try something just because you know you can't match your siblings' success. And you don't want to disappoint anyone."

A moment of silence follows as I draw my breath because, sweet Jesus, that felt like giving an entire speech.

"Alice, are you talking just about Blake and Daniel, or also about you?"

I cringe, but I should have seen this coming. Of course Logan would read between the lines. "About me too, but that's not the point."

"It is, because it's obviously important to you. I never—Jesus, neither Sebastian nor I ever wanted to put pressure on you."

"You didn't," I reassure him. "We put it on ourselves, but I guess we couldn't help it."

"When we set up Bennett Enterprises, we worked a lot, but we also had luck on our side. Anyone who thinks success only takes hard work is deluding themselves. I hate all those articles painting Sebastian and me like some kind of…." He frowns, obviously searching for the right word.

"Superhumans?" I offer helpfully with a grin. "Geniuses? Don't sell yourself short—you are."

"The point is, if hard work was all it took for success, there wouldn't be so many hardworking people struggling."

"I know." I always appreciated that my oldest brothers never turned snobbish, believing they're above others because they built a bona fide empire.

"Whatever any of you chose to do, you'd never disappoint us. I was just riding Blake's and Daniel's asses for so many years because I didn't want them to waste their entire life going from party to party."

I grab my brother's hands over the table, needing to make him understand. The last thing I want is for him to feel guilty over this.

"I know, and Blake and Daniel do too. As I said, the pressure comes from the inside. I think some part of Daniel wants to change gears with his business, but the other part thinks he'll disappoint everyone if he doesn't pull through."

"Nonsense," Logan affirms, then in a softer voice adds, "Really?"

"Yeah. Just talk to him about this, see where it gets you. Maybe I'm wrong, but I don't think so. I get heartburn just remembering the accident."

"Me too. I'll talk to him. And Alice, just so you don't have any doubts, I'm proud of you."

"Thank you." My voice is uncharacteristically emotional, but Logan is kind enough not to point it out.

"You don't have to prove anything to anyone," he adds sternly.

"I know that now," I assure him with a smile. "I struggled before, but turning thirty-one had its perks. I gained some wisdom in addition to a few pounds and developing a case of acute sweet tooth—although it was chronic before anyway."

Logan chuckles, stretching his hand out to grab my plate. I slap it playfully.

"Hey! Doesn't mean you can have my tiramisu."

Logan lifts his hands in mock defense. "Was just trying to be of assistance. I personally believe you're in perfect shape, but if you fear the sweet tooth, I can help. I'm a practical man."

"You're an opportunist." Quickly I gulp down the last bite of tiramisu, unwilling to risk tempting Logan too much. "Besides, I'm the one who steals everyone's food. It's a documented fact."

"True. By the way, I've heard a rumor that things escalated between you and Nate during the trip."

"No rumor. It's true, and you're not getting any details."

"How about I just ask him for details?"

"Don't meddle."

"It's the family hobby." His expression grows more serious. "I just want to look out for you."

"How about this? If you ever need to punch him, I'll tell you."

"Deal."

"Not that it matters, but who chirped?"

"Summer."

"Little traitor." Out of the sisters, Summer is the one who most fiercely guards the boys' secrets. Apparently, she doesn't extend the courtesy to me. At least Blake and Daniel are on my side.

The corners of my mouth lift of their own volition in a smile as I think about this past week. I can't wait to see Nate again. It's a little nutty to miss him already, but when it comes to him, I'm greedy.

"So Blake's and Daniel's sixteen-year-old birthday wishes were to be like me, huh?" Logan asks, jolting me out of my thoughts.

"Shouldn't have told you. Would you like an extra chair for your ego?"

Logan flashes a grin. "Make that a couch."

Chapter Eighteen

Nate

I'm one of those people who's always proudly claimed I went into my line of work because I loved it, not because of the paycheck. I chose to work in television because I always liked good stories. As executive producer, my job often revolves around things like financing and operations—anything but the story—but I don't mind. Usually. But over the next two weeks, I become increasingly frustrated that ninety percent of my time is spent reining in the financial and operative chaos. Turns out old man Teller was excellent on the creative part, but not much else. The workdays are even longer than I'm used to. When Friday rolls around, it's dark outside when I finally leave work.

My go-to activities to put a trying day behind me are going for a long run or hitting the gym. Usually I choose the run, as I prefer to be alone when I recharge. I could also throw myself into more work, this time doing something I actually enjoy. The London studio keeps asking me for help, clearly barely keeping afloat under Abbott's rule. But right now, I'm not in the mood for any of that. Instead, I want to check on a certain brunette who's taken over my life recently, hear her voice, ask how her day has been.

On the way to my car, I take out my phone, intending to call Alice, when I notice she sent me a text message a few hours ago, right after I messaged her telling her all about what a joy my day was. Didn't have time to check my phone afterward.

Alice: Oh no, I was hoping you were having a better evening than me. A customer just sent their order back to the kitchen for the third time.

She sent me the next message ten minutes later.

Alice: God, she sent it back a fourth time!!! I know the customer is king, but I really want to kick her out.

And yet another one almost an hour later.

Alice: Last message, I promise.... I couldn't help it, I snapped at her. This day can't be over soon enough. The only good thing was my trip to the senior center to bring them treats. Ms. Williams was asking about you. Wish I could see you today.

The second I finish reading, I decide to change my plans. We'd originally decided to meet tomorrow, but her wish is my command. Putting my own trying day on the back burner, I focus on what could light her up, turn this around for her. True, my mad seduction skills would take her mind off everything, but tonight I want to go the extra mile.

When I finally get to my car, an idea strikes me. Gunning the engine, I call her. She answers immediately.

"Hey," she greets, and the background noise blares so loudly that my ear is ringing.

"You're still at the restaurant?"

"Guilty. Since the day was such shit, I thought I'd stay here until closing time."

"I'm kidnapping you," I announce, hitting the gas pedal.

"What?" She laughs softly. Damn, that laughter could bring me to my knees.

That's precisely when I realize I'd do absolutely anything to make this woman laugh, to make sure she's safe and happy.

"I'm kidnapping you," I repeat. "I'll be there in fifteen minutes. You need to be whisked away."

"Do I now? On a white horse? Will you be my knight?"

"Do I qualify as a knight if I drive a car?"

"I don't know, I have pretty specific requirements for a knight."

"Will spoiling you do? Followed by burying myself inside you? To the hilt?"

At that thought, I increase my speed, visions of Alice under me filling my mind.

"You're counting your chickens before they hatch, Becker."

She's trying to tease me, but I hear the longing in every syllable.

"I haven't even agreed to be kidnapped," she adds. Now she's just digging herself a hole.

"You don't have to. If you don't come with me willingly, I'll throw you over my shoulder and carry you out through the front door for anyone to see."

"Caveman."

"Absolutely."

"You can't carry me on your shoulder. The skirt I'm wearing is short enough that everyone is going to see my panties. They're red, and the fabric is see-through."

I nearly crash into the car in front of me. "Keep talking like that and I'll remove those panties in no time."

"Threat or promise?"

"Both."

When I pull up in front of the restaurant, Alice is already waiting for me outside, holding a take-out box in her hand. And she's wearing a shirt and black pants.

Climbing out, I round the car and open the door for her.

"What a gentleman!"

"Where's that short dress you mentioned?"

She hovers in front of the open door. "Thought you needed an incentive to drive faster."

"Someone missed me."

"Just your kissing skills."

"I see. You have no shame using me, do you?"

"None," Alice exclaims decisively.

Taking the box out of her hands, I place it on her seat, then concentrate on her.

"So, are you going to kiss me or what?"

Part of me is tempted to tease her some more, but my need for her overpowers it. I swipe my tongue once over her plump and pink lower lip before crushing my mouth against hers.

I'm addicted to this woman, to the way her body responds to mine. She pushes herself against me, and when I feel her soft, full breasts against my chest, I lower one hand down her back. Only the knowledge that we're not ten feet away from her restaurant keeps me from palming her fine ass.

When I pull away, we both breathe raggedly.

"I've daydreamed all day about you kissing me like that," she says in a low, throaty voice. She fists the hem of my shirt with both hands, licking her lips and clearly wanting a repeat. I kiss her forehead instead and she pouts. I love her playful side.

"You deserve to be teased for misleading me."

"I only partly misled you." Kissing the hollow of my neck, she whispers, "My panties are red and see-through."

Then the little vixen winks and climbs in the passenger seat, keeping the take-out box in her lap. I fight the vision of her underwear while I walk to the driver seat, but once inside, with her scent filling the space, the vision changes into me lowering those panties with my teeth and burying myself between her legs.

Needing a distraction, I focus on her take-out box while gunning the engine and driving away.

"What's in there?" I ask.

"I made you lemon tarts. Started them when you messaged me. Thought I'd surprise you by showing up at your place tonight."

Hell, this woman is downright perfect. I love lemon tarts.

"Thanks."

"I like taking care of you," she says softly. In fact, she sounds almost shy, which is very unlike Alice. Glancing at her, I notice she's fidgeting in her seat, casting her eyes downward as if she just shared a secret.

It strikes me that I'm not the only one who isn't used to this kind of intimacy, to sharing my daily life with someone else. Alice has always been close to her family, but not to people outside of it. Still, she just went out on a limb with her confession, and even though I've no clue how to do this, going out on a limb with her feels natural.

"And I like taking care of you." Taking her hand, I turn it palm up and kiss it. I swear she exhales so sharply, I wonder if she was holding her breath, waiting for my answer. "Hence the kidnapping."

"Where are you taking me?"

"You'll see. Now open the box so I can eat those tarts."

***

A little while later, we arrive at our destination. It's a mom-and-pop shop with the best ice cream in San Francisco. I remembered Alice telling me a while ago how she hasn't found ice cream as good as in Rome.

"Oh my God, this is delicious," she exclaims after taking her first mouthful of the creamy treat. "Why didn't I know about this place? It's my duty to know who's making the best treats. I'm going to tell Summer that Americans do it just as good as the Italians."

She licks her overfilled cone with gusto and speed. She requested five scoops, and the server warned her four would be better or she'd have to eat quickly to keep it from melting. Alice assured him she was up to the task. This is Alice. She doesn't do anything in halves. Since I'm already full of lemon tarts, I just bought one scoop, in a cup not a cone.

"Hate to break it to you, but the guy who owns the shop is Italian."

"Damn. It's on my list to hire an Italian chef anyway. Our dessert selection needs to step up the game. I'll ask Summer to approve him. She's constantly sending me pictures of the desserts she's eating in Rome."

We walk to the small park opposite the ice cream shop and sit on a bench. Even at this time of night, the park is buzzing with people: teenagers with skateboards, couples, street artists.

We're silent for a few long minutes while we eat, and there's something very relaxing about not needing to fill the silence, just being with each other. Predictably, I finish my one scoop before Alice has eaten even half of her top scoop.

I toss away my empty cup and then focus one hundred percent on her. A gust of wind blows and Alice snuggles against me on the bench, which was exactly what I was aiming for. It might be the end of July, but you can always count on wind or fog in San Francisco, even in summer. *Thank you, Mother Nature, for siding with me.*

She smells like a sinful dream, her sweet and seductive perfume enticing me to kiss her neck and shoulders and other parts of her. I want to savor her.

Pushing her hair to one side, I lazily run my thumb up and down her neck, watching with satisfaction as she trembles slightly. It surprises me every time that she's so responsive to me.

The temptation to pull her to me and kiss her, lose myself in her like I've wanted to all day, is strong. It would be only too easy to distract her. But like the good guy I am, I let her enjoy her dessert first.

"How is Summer? Didn't get to talk to her much at Joshua Tree."

"She loves Rome. I mean, you can hardly not love that city. I visited her there a couple of times. It's breathtaking. It's like living history. For an art lover and an artist like her, it's the perfect place. She's very happy there."

"But?" Judging by the wistful note in her tone, there must be a big downside.

Alice gasps, looking at me. "How did you pick up on the 'but'?"

"Something in your voice tipped me off." I move my thumb from her neck to her jaw, tracing the contour. Alice and I have always been in sync in some ways, but I wasn't able to pick up stuff so quickly before. Or maybe now I'm paying more attention than before. After all, for years, whenever I thought about her, my brain supplied the warning that I should keep my distance.

"I'm afraid she'll like it so much she'll stay there. I'm terribly selfish, but I can't help it."

"You're not selfish." Kissing the side of her head, I add, "You really miss Summer, don't you?"

She nods with a sigh. "I do. She's the baby, and I got so used to hovering over her that I feel like a limb is missing now. And yes, I'm aware of how dramatic I sound." She attacks her cone with renewed focus while I wonder how many ways this woman will surprise me.

Yes, I've always known the siblings are very close, but Alice never showed this soft side of herself to me before. I like discovering this new trait, learning her. The realization that I've earned more of her trust hits me, along with the reminder that I'd better not mess this up.

"You sure you don't want more?" She holds her cone out to me.

"Since when do you share your food? If I remember correctly, you're the one stealing everyone's food all the time."

"I make exceptions from time to time. And I can't believe you ate just one scoop. And it was vanilla."

"What's wrong with vanilla?"

"It's just so safe. And there were so many interesting flavors to choose from."

"Like apple?" I tease, pointing to her cone. "Why would you choose that? It smells like soap."

She slashes the air with her forefinger. "Watch it, Becker, or I'll start thinking we're not compatible. Your list of negative traits is already making me doubtful."

I grip her wrist midair, bringing it close to me, and kiss her sensitive skin. "What negative traits?"

"You sometimes snore, and…." Her voice trails off as I touch her skin with the tip of my tongue.

"And?" I press.

She whisks her hand away. "And you use your seductive powers to derail my thoughts. That is the lowest of low."

"Completely unforgivable," I agree, not bothering to hide my amusement. "So, nothing tips the scales in my favor?"

"I didn't say that." With a wink, she takes another mouthful of ice cream. "You're funny, you have no issues with being used as a pillow, and your shirts make for fantastic robes."

"Your priorities are fascinating."

"Why do I have the suspicion that by 'fascinating' you mean 'weird'?"

"Your words, not mine."

Scoffing, she licks her frozen treat again. "Eating something delicious is hands-down the best way to end my day."

"Where do I fit in the equation?"

She peeks at me sideways, as if weighing her words carefully. "You're the bonus."

She says nothing at all afterward, focusing on her ice cream. She's down to the last third of it, and I swear she's savoring it like her life depends on it. To my dismay, she starts making little noises at the back of her throat. They remind me of those she makes when we're tangled in the sheets and I'm driving inside her.

"Alice, I don't like those sounds you're making." It's my duty to warn her, give her a heads-up that I might pounce on her.

"Why not?"

Putting my lips to her ear, I whisper, "Because it turns me on."

She gasps lightly, which doesn't help the situation in my jeans in the slightest.

"I'm trying to be on my best behavior right now."

She tilts her head. "I like you more when you're on your worst behavior."

Damn, this woman keeps me on my toes. Her eyes hold a challenge, as they always do, but I have a lot of aces up my sleeve.

"You've just earned yourself a night full of teasing," I inform her.

"A bit optimistic, aren't you? About spending the night with me?"

"I'm always optimistic, and you didn't protest that I picked you up—"

"Because my car is at the mechanic's. Again."

Well, well, and here I took her lack of protest as a sign that she wanted to spend the night with me and I'd drive her back in the morning. I don't let that deter me.

"I'm not just optimistic but also relentless. I don't give up until I get what I want. And lately, I want you all the time." Bringing my lips to her ear again, I tug gently at her earlobe with my teeth. "Here's a secret. I like persuading you."

"I have a secret too. I want to be romanced and seduced over and over again. You're just so good at it, I can't help wanting more."

I pull back triumphantly. "It's a done deal, then. You'll be romanced properly and repeatedly."

"Really?"

"Yeah."

"Why?"

"Because you deserve it, and look at you. Just by saying it, I've made you smile. Anything that makes you smile goes."

She hunches her shoulders, a thinly veiled surprise crossing her face. It's there only for a fraction of a second, but I don't miss it, and it causes all my protective instincts to spring to life.

"What just went through your head?" I ask, because I haven't yet mastered the art of reading her so well.

"No one's ever said that to me. Well, no one who doesn't share my last name."

Instinctively I want to wipe from her memory every asshole she dated who didn't put forth the effort to find out what makes her smile.

"Well, I'll make sure to repeat it often, and make good on my words."

"It's a dangerous thing to say around me. I might take advantage."

"I'm counting on it."

She eats the last bit of her cone, and I wait until she swallows before finally pulling her into a kiss, losing myself in her sweet taste. She parts her lips, welcoming me. Our tongues clash in an unexpected desperation to taste and explore.

When we pull apart for air, I rest my forehead against hers.

"I want to learn you, Alice. I used to think I knew all there is about you, but you keep surprising me. I'm beginning to see there are sides to you I've never seen before. I want to discover them all."

"That's a lot of work." She breathes heavily, and I become aware that she's fisting my shirt.

"I'm up to the challenge."

"So am I," she says softly. "I want to discover everything about you too. I want to make you happy."

"You already do," I say right before I lower my mouth on hers again.

Chapter Nineteen

Alice

We leave the park shortly after I finish eating, and I snuggle against him on the way to the car because it's gotten really windy. Nate seems pleased, draping his arm around me. He'd parked right in front of the shop, which is now closing.

"Hey, can we buy some more to go? I want a second serving tonight. If you behave, I'll let you have some too."

Nate flashes me a grin. "Whatever you wish." He's a little too excited considering he's not a fan, but I'm not about to look a gift horse in the mouth.

We buy a to-go container filled to the brim. Afterward, Nate and I chitchat with the vendor while he closes the shop, and after he leaves, Nate and I head to the car.

It makes me giddy that Nate brought me here.

It feels a little silly to be so excited about something so small, but my mother's words from a few years ago come back to me. She said love is in the little day-to-day things. That when she thinks about the love she has for my father, the first things popping in her mind aren't their wedding, or the proposal, but the way they look after each other each day. The way they share the joys and encourage each other in the difficult moments.

"Why so silent?" Nate asks, snapping me out of my thoughts. We're in front of the passenger door, but instead of unlocking it, he traps me against the car, his hands on the roof at each side of my head.

"Just enjoying being together."

Nate tips my head up, sealing his mouth over mine, and I nearly melt in his arms. This kiss feels different than the ones before, though I can't say why. He threads his fingers through my hair, deepening the kiss, and I figure out what is different.

This feels a lot like love, no matter how much I'm telling myself not to get ahead of myself, not to project things.

"I need you," he whispers when we pull apart. "Tonight. Every night."

"I need you too."

***

The next half hour passes in a blur. I don't remember when we got in the car, or when we decided to spend the night at his apartment, but even though Nate is speeding through the streets of San Francisco, I still feel like he's not driving fast enough.

We make a conscious effort not to touch each other until we're inside the apartment. Once inside, I toe off my shoes, barely managing to place the box on the table in the living room before Nate places one hand on my waist, spinning me around so I'm facing him.

He brushes away a rebel strand of hair that has caught at the corner of my lip. Then he slides his thumb across my upper lip, then my lower lip, pressing gently in the center. I open my mouth a little and he heeds my invitation, sliding his thumb in my mouth. I run my tongue across the tip.

"Jesus, Alice."

In one swift move, he pulls me flush against him. Splaying my hands on his chest, I swear I can feel his heart hammering against his ribcage, just as I can feel how hard he is for me already. He tips his head down, kissing me deeply, the kind of kiss that wipes away every thought, filling every cell with warmth and love, and hunger for more. When we finally come up for air, we're both gasping.

"You have too many clothes on, Alice." His lips part in a grin.

"Then start taking them off."

Without another word, he proceeds to rid me of them, first my shirt, then my pants and shoes. I do the same with his clothes, pure need and desperation driving our hands.

"This is not very gentlemanly of you," I tease. "I was going to have some more ice cream first."

Tilting his head to one side, he studies me, and I can practically see the wheels spinning in his brain. *Uh-oh.* I might have woken a monster.

Without taking his eyes off me, he removes the lid of the cup.

"Here you go." The challenge in his tone matches the heat in his gaze, and their combined force has my skin buzzing with awareness *everywhere.*

"Are you going to eat too?"

"Oh, I'll eat, just like I'll eat you. In fact, why don't I do it at the same time?"

His words prompt a wave of heat to wash over me, concentrating low in my body. He dips his thumb in the cup, then smears it around the tips of my breasts. Before

I have a chance to recover, his hot tongue licks across the same spot, and I grip the counter behind me to steady myself.

"Nate, what are you doing?" I whisper.

"Taking what's mine. You're mine, Alice. Every single part of you. Your laughter, your moans. All mine."

"All yours."

He repeatedly smears cold ice cream on my skin, then covers the spot with his mouth. The succession of hot and cold is excruciating, like going from high to low again and again until I don't know which is the high and which is the low. I only know I need this man desperately.

"I need you. Now. Please."

His blessed mouth, which is teasing one of my breasts, travels up to my neck until he reaches my ear. Biting my earlobe, he says, "Look at you, all hot and bothered and dirty. Why don't we go in the shower to clean you up?"

Best proposition ever.

Taking my hand, he leads me through his apartment and into the bathroom, which I love. My bathroom is an oasis, but his takes the cake. In the center is a tub large enough for two people; I've been imagining us in there with candles around us since I first saw it. But right now, we're heading to the shower. Turning on the water from above, he lets it run over us while pouring shower gel in his hands. He pushes me so my back is against the wall, spreading my legs open with his knee. His soapy hands travel over all the spots he kissed before, especially my breasts.

He touches and teases all my sweet spots, turning me to putty in his hands. This man knows how to work my body, exactly where to touch me to drive me crazy.

"I like having you like this," he murmurs.

"At your mercy?"

"Exactly."

"Clean enough, you think?" I ask when I can no longer stand the torture. I need him to take me right now. My God, he's so beautiful like this, with water running over him.

He kisses me so passionately he steals my breath. After pulling back, he still doesn't answer. I'm more hot and bothered than he is, so I set out to resolve that.

Dropping to my knees, I stroke his hard-on, licking him from the tip to the base, watching him inhale sharply.

"Alice…." He threads his fingers through my hair all the way to the roots, as if he desperately needs to hold on to me while my mouth explores him. He tightens his grip with every lash of my tongue, every lick across his crown. When he starts moving his hips back and forth slowly, as if making love to my mouth, I know I've brought him almost where I want him, but I'm not done.

Taking advantage of the fact that his eyes are trained on me, I slip my hand between my legs, touching myself intimately.

"Oh fuck. You're killing me, Alice."

He pulls out of my mouth, helps me to my feet, and flips me around so my ass is against his granite thighs.

"Grip the railing," he says in a low, commanding voice. "You'll need it."

Oh my. I love the promise in his voice. Knowing he'll make good on it, I grip the steel railing with both hands, licking my lips. I hate not being able to see what he's about to do, but I love it at the same time. When he drags the hot tip of his erection across one ass cheek and then the other, I shudder.

"Nate," I gasp. When he descends further, teasing the seam of my opening first with his tip, then with his hot length, my knees wobble.

"Don't push your delicious ass back," he whispers in my ear. "I want you to stand straight."

I don't quite understand what he means until he drives into me and *holy shit.* Because of the angle, he's so deep inside me that I gasp for air, hoping for some reprieve but only receiving more of *him.* He only stops when he's entered me completely.

Stilling inside me, he puts his mouth to my ear. "Alice, are you okay?"

"Yeah, I just didn't know it could feel like this. It's *so good.*"

Nate pulls out almost completely before slamming back into me. He grips the railing with one hand too, clasping it so tightly his knuckles turn white. He keeps the other arm protectively across my waist and pelvis, fingertips pressing against my clit.

A sea of sensations engulfs me, heat, pleasure, and pure joy coursing through my veins. I give myself to him with abandon. I'd trust this man to do anything he wants with me; he owns my pleasure, my body, and my heart.

Our sounds fill the space as we both succumb and lose ourselves in each other. The back of my head rests against his chest, and I turn slightly so my ear presses against his skin, catching his heartbeats. They're rapid and frantic, matching his strokes and my racing pulse. Our hearts beat in unison as we climb toward the cusp of pleasure together.

He loves me deep and desperate until he grunts out my name and my world spins on its axis. Nate holds me tightly to him until the haze of bliss clears, and then we play with soap and water again, cleaning each other.

Stepping out of the shower, we dry ourselves with the plush towels near the sink, and then Nate unexpectedly lifts me, slinging one arm around my back and the other under my knees. Instinctively, I rest an arm around his neck, grounding myself. Nate skims his lips against my temple in a gesture so full of tenderness that my heart nearly bursts. For some reason, I feel incredibly shy, which is ridiculous. I was naked when he ate off me, and in the shower. I've never been one to feel vulnerable after intimacy, but right now I am.

"What are you doing?" I ask when he exits the bathroom.

"Carrying you to bed."

"Oh my! You are a knight."

"Forgot my armor, I'm afraid."

Grinning, I lean closer to him. "You're naked. That's my kind of armor."

Chapter Twenty

Alice

There are two addictions I haven't been able to shake off my entire life: sweets and gossiping with my siblings (when I'm not the subject of said gossip). Nate is about to become my third. Ever since he surprised me with the ice cream trip two weeks ago, we've been spending a lot of time together, mostly evenings and nights and weekends. When the *Delicious Dining* team filmed their segment, Nate took the day off and was by my side. It was incredibly sweet.

Right now, we're in his apartment, but we've been in mine more often. So often, in fact, that I'm not sure I want to sleep in there alone again. This isn't crazy, right? I mean, who would want to go back to an empty, cold apartment when they've had a gorgeous, funny, and drop-dead sexy man in there with them? I swear every inch of my one-bedroom apartment smells like him.

As I check my appearance in Nate's mirror, I know I'm even more invested in this thing between us than I thought, and that's dangerous. We're having fun, and I'm having the time of my life with him even when we're doing nothing but talking, but I can't jump headfirst into something that's only a few weeks old. Even if I've known him for years, this is still fresh.

When I look over my shoulder in the mirror, I notice Nate is smiling. I've cataloged in my mind every smile of his over the years, but there's something different about this one.

"Nate Becker, what's up with your smile?"

He jerks his head back, obviously not having realized I was watching him in the mirror as he was studying me. By the time I turn around to face him, he schools his expression, shooting for a surprised, affronted one instead. Well, the joke's on him because, despite his efforts to hold back a smile, the corners of his mouth are lightly tilted.

"What do you mean? I smile all the time."

"Yeah, but this one's different."

I walk around the bed until I'm right in front of him. I love his 'I just got out of bed' look. His hair is mussed, his eyelids still a tiny bit heavy with sleep. Most of all, I like the five o'clock shadow on his face. It's a little coarse and makes kissing rougher, but there's something distinctly manly about that light beard. It goes wonderfully with his muscle-laced arms.

He tips his chin forward. "It's the Alice effect."

His answer warms me on the inside. I swear my toes curl. "Please explain yourself. I need more details."

He kisses the tip of my nose. "It's the smile I get when I wake up and you're next to me. Waking up next to your half-naked body is the best way to start my day, even though I wake up earlier than usual when you're with me, even on a rainy Saturday like this one. Actually, I wake up earlier *because* you're with me."

"Because you want to spend more time with me?" The eagerness in my tone borders on childish, but I love it when he speaks about me like this.

"No, because you're nearly choking me by sleeping on top of me."

Stepping back, I smirk and say in my defense, "You're a good pillow." Truth be told, I'm not a hugger when I sleep. I usually don't even hug my pillow. But I can't believe this is my life now, and that Nate is in it. I want to soak in as much of him as possible when I'm awake, so it must be my subconscious wanting more of him even while I'm asleep. "Go back to telling me how waking up next to me is the best way to start your day. I liked that part a lot more."

He steps in front of me again, effectively pushing me against the wall. Talk about being between a rock and a hard place. Well, I'll gladly take this hardship every single day. "So? You'd better lay it on thick, Becker. You just accused me of hogging you."

Honestly, I was just fishing for compliments, but Nate takes my words to mean something else—foreplay. He drags his knuckles down my cheek, then caresses my neck with the pads of his fingers. Instinctively, I tilt my head to the side, giving him access. He takes advantage immediately, placing his mouth where my neck meets my shoulder. It's my sweet spot, and *oh my*. My body's reaction is instantaneous. My skin simmers and my back arches. I feel Nate's lips curl in a smile against my skin as he kisses my neck and jawline before finally coming face-to-face with me.

"I still can't believe I'm lucky enough to wake up next to you," he says in a gruff voice, and I nearly melt on the spot. His caresses might have heated my body, but his words travel straight to my heart. The mere thought that he might want to wake up next to me for many more mornings fills me with so much hope it borders on elation.

It's the kind of hope that electrifies every cell and seeps into my bones. When it comes to work, I always strive to be a realist. When it comes to love, I'm allowed to hope and dream, right?

"I used to spend my weekends working," he says, pushing a strand of hair behind my ear with one hand. "Even if there wasn't anything pressing to do, I'd find ways to keep myself occupied: research for future projects, you name it. I needed to fill my time with something. But right now, all I want is to fill my time with you. The prospect of staying in with you all day—all weekend, in fact—sounds like the best idea I've ever had."

"It does, huh?" I feel ridiculously proud as I rest my hands on his chest. Knowing he's enjoying our time together as much as I am brings me pure joy.

"Yeah."

"I wonder what we could possibly do indoors all day."

Nate offers me a devilish smile in return, palming one breast. My nipple instantly responds. Without warning, he lowers his head to my chest, swiping his tongue over my other nipple once and then descending lower to my navel. He looks at me seductively while he moves lower still. I part my legs almost involuntarily and he smiles against my belly. I have an inkling I'm about to be teased, but I enjoy this too much to protest.

Nate skims his fingers down my bikini line, and the light touch sends a searing heat through the sensitive skin. He slicks his thumb across my opening once and my knees buckle. As if foreseeing this, he grabs one of my ass cheeks, his fingers pressing tightly against my skin. The thinly disguised desperation in his eyes has me trembling with anticipation. Tilting my pelvis slightly up toward him, he undoes me with the first lick across my sensitive spot, and when his lips suck gently at my clit, I'm about to break out of my skin.

Then he lets go of my ass, his mouth traveling upward on my belly again, and higher still as he rises. His fingers skim up my arms, turning my skin to gooseflesh.

"Why are you teasing me?" I complain. "Go back down there."

"Patience, Alice. I know what we'll be doing all day." His voice is like hot chocolate: rich, thick, and full of promise.

"You're shameless, but I'm completely on board with the plan." Especially because it means I'll get many chances to get my revenge, teasing him the way he did with me.

"Get dressed and let's have breakfast."

Ah, and so begins the first step of my revenge plan. Nate heads to the kitchen, leaving me alone to get dressed. I cover myself with a silk robe, fastening it around my waist with the belt but leaving the top open, showing plenty of cleavage. If I take large steps, one can clearly see I haven't put on panties. I intend to take large steps often.

I love Nate's apartment. It's rather small, like mine, just one bedroom, but his living room is enormous. The furniture is mostly white, the books and souvenirs from his trips lining the shelves and counters forming uneven splashes of color. It's beautiful.

Joining Nate in the living room, I help him set the table. As we prepare the breakfast, I can feel his gaze on me. Like the little devil I am, I shift my legs in such a way that he can clearly take a peek under the robe. I'm immensely satisfied when he sucks in a deep breath and immediately abandons his task of making fresh orange juice. He moves behind me, resting his hands on my shoulders and kissing the side of my neck.

"If you go on like this, we're going to eat in about a hundred years," I warn him.

"Maybe I'll just eat you, Alice. You taste so good."

His words travel straight between my thighs, and my cheeks burn. Licking my lips, I remind myself that I'm supposed to be the one driving him crazy, not the other way around. But I have a hunch that I don't stand much of a chance to win my own challenge. When Nate touches me, my body responds.

"Breakfast first," I find myself saying, and damn if I'm not proud for resisting him. "Don't forget the orange juice."

***

After we're done with breakfast, the sound of Nate's phone ringing reaches us from the foyer.

"Aren't you going to answer?"

"Nah, it's my work ringtone. It can wait until Monday. Today I'm all yours."

I flash him a grin, touching his feet under the table. But whoever is calling him doesn't give up. After the fourth time the phone starts ringing, I encourage him to answer it, as it could be urgent. Grudgingly, Nate leaves the table. He answers in the foyer, and I'm dismayed when he all but barks at the person on the other end. But as he returns to the living room, phone plastered to his ear, I hear his conversation partner barking too.

Not wanting to seem like I'm eavesdropping, I start clearing the table, bringing everything to the kitchen. While I put the dirty dishes in the washer, I try to block out his voice. If he wants to share the topic of the conversation with me later, then I'll gladly listen, but for now, I'm trying to offer him privacy. Unfortunately, Nate paces around the living room, and the person at the other end of the line talks so loudly I can't help overhearing, especially when Nate stops just two feet away from me. It's completely unintentional.

"They're sinking so fast in London, they'll beg you to take the job over in no time." The man at the other end of the line laughs wholeheartedly, as if he can't wait for the scenario to happen. Unease rises in my throat, constricting my breath. The fear that all this might be just temporary slices through me. Nate moves back on the couch and I hear nothing more, instead focusing on my tasks

My ears perk up when Nate finishes the call, which is exactly when I finish cleaning everything, and I raise my gaze to watch him. He's pacing around the living room. *Uh-oh*! I recognize this behavior. He's like a feline predator, ready to pounce. He's not just annoyed but downright mad.

"I can make more orange juice if you want," I offer from the kitchen island, breaking the silence.

Instead of returning to the table, Nate slumps on the couch, deep lines marring his forehead. "Lost my appetite."

Well, that won't do. I resolve to make his frown disappear by any means. Heading to the couch, I sit next to him, tucking my feet underneath me.

"Want to tell me what happened?" I ask, trailing my fingers up and down his forearm. He cocks his head in my direction, then turns to face me with his upper body too.

"Just so you know, my usual behavior when something doesn't go the way it should is to—"

"Be all serious and broody?" I finish for him.

"You can put it that way."

Seizing my window of opportunity, I climb into his lap. "Well, I won't deny that broody Nate is sexy, but I'd much rather see you smile."

Cuffing my wrist with his hand, he kisses my palm, smiling against my skin. "You make everything better just by being here."

I can't help swooning a little, over the moon that I'm already making him smile. The lines on his forehead are still visible though.

"So, how much trouble is there?"

"Nothing I can't handle, just not something I like to hear on a Saturday morning."

"What can I do to put you in a good mood?" I run my hand through his hair, ruffling it the way I do when he makes love to me. Tilting his head slightly back, I place a quick kiss on his chin.

"Well, since you mention it." He slips a hand under my robe, touching my inner thigh. He wiggles his eyebrows, but I vehemently shake my head.

"No, I'm still punishing you for teasing me this morning."

"Ah, so this is the game we're playing?"

"Yeah. You were so mean, you've earned yourself at least two more hours of punishment."

"I'll wear you down." Bringing me closer to him, he whispers in my ear, "You never can resist me for long, Alice. Remember your five-date rule?"

Ah, this cocky bastard. I'd contradict him if what he said wasn't actually true. Being so close to him is actually problematic because he can unleash his full seductive power on me.

While I climb out of his lap, I notice the TV remote wedged between the cushions and an idea strikes me. I once read that an effective way to take someone's mind off their problems is to do or say something ridiculous. Now, I usually avoid any situations in which there is even the slightest possibility that I might make a fool of myself, but right now I decide to do something I've only ever done in front of my family.

Grabbing the remote, I turn on the TV, searching for a music channel. Finally I settle on one playing a track I'm familiar with.

As the song blares in the living room, I start singing along, gesturing to Nate to join me. The poor man seems too stricken for words. I can't blame him; my voice is atrocious.

"How come I never knew you were an awful singer?"

I shrug, continuing to sing. When an instrumental part comes on, I explain, "I keep my dirty secrets well hidden. Come on, sing along. You can't be worse than me. And by the way, I never do this except around my family."

"Should I be offended or honored?"

"Definitely honored. It means I'm comfortable enough around you to show you my dopey side."

This has the unexpected effect of making Nate chuckle. He springs to his feet when the chorus comes on, singing along, and holy heavens. He's not worse than me, but he's not any better either.

We might be terrible singers, but we've got crazy dance skills. As the next song begins, Nate guides me through the moves in his own rhythm. Neither of us knows the lyrics, so we just dance our asses off.

"Bet you can't do a *Dirty Dancing* lift," I challenge. I always wanted to try that with a guy, but I never trusted anyone enough to ask. Plus, a man would require strong arms for such a move, and Nate is the perfect candidate.

"Why does everyone concentrate on that part of the movie? It's the most—"

"Stop right there before your soul mate potential drops even more."

"Tell me what to do. I blocked the scene from my memory."

As I explain to him what he has to do, he nods eagerly. A little too eagerly. I barely have time to analyze his facial expression—he's definitely planning something—when we start the operation. I pad back until there's considerable distance between us, and then, bracing myself, I run in his direction. When I'm right in front of him, Nate fastens his hands around my waist and lifts me expertly. I stretch out my arms above him, closing my eyes.

"We did it!" I exclaim. Nate twirls me around once, and when it's time for me to get back on the ground, I finally learn what his *plan* was. Instead of just placing me back down, he lowers me slowly until my pelvis is level with his face, swiping his tongue over my exposed center and luring a moan from me that is equal parts pleasure and embarrassment. Damn, I was so caught in the moment I didn't realize I was flashing him. But he foresaw this from the second I explained what the lift entailed.

"You're too cunning," I tell him, fastening my robe once my feet are firmly back on the ground.

"You just wanted your pussy on my face, admit it." He licks his lips. My intimate spot pulses in anticipation. "Knew you couldn't resist me."

"Well, you certainly put dirty in the dancing."

Unable to hold back any longer, I guffaw. He joins me seconds later, laughing in earnest, his troubles forgotten, which is exactly what I was going for.

Chapter Twenty-One

Nate

"I live for moments like this," Clara says Wednesday two weeks later during our lunch break. We decided to head out of the studio today, and we're sitting in a Mexican restaurant, wolfing down our food. Well, I'm wolfing down my food. Clara is clutching a magazine to her chest. She just finished reading out loud a review of a segment we did about six months ago, which was broadcast last week. "All those long hours, lack of sleep, and frantic pace. It's all for this."

"It's definitely motivating to have our work acknowledged," I agree, taking a huge bite from my burrito.

"Do you want to keep this?" She nods toward the magazine.

"Nah, I'll buy one for myself. You keep it. You're going to read it about half a dozen more times today."

She smirks. "Make it a dozen."

"Do you plan to do any work in between?"

"Don't be an ass."

I shrug, pointing to the to-do list on my phone. "That's waiting for us."

Clara finally sets the magazine next to her plate, concentrating on her food.

"I'll get to it right after I read the review a couple more times. By the way, are you going to take the weekend off again? Not to be nosy, but I need to know if I can relax again or if I'm going to receive frantic e-mails from you at unholy hours."

"You make me sound like an ass."

"No, I make you sound like someone who didn't want to have a private life, which you now do. I wholly approve of it, by the way. I'm learning to have a private life too. It's glorious. So, can I expect more free time?"

"So this has nothing to do with you wanting to know what I'm doing on my weekends?"

"Well, if you volunteer that information, I'll gladly listen, but it's not why I'm asking."

I'd believe her if Clara wasn't the most curious person in the world. In fact, she deserves a prize for not questioning me about Alice until now, especially since she seems to have become very close to Pippa. I've overheard them talking on the phone a few times, making plans.

"So?" she asks, almost bouncing off her chair.

"Eat, Clara, or we'll never finish lunch."

"Okay, how about this? I eat, you talk."

"Deal. First of all, you don't have to answer my e-mails on weekends. I just send them to you so you can get started on them Monday morning."

Clara swallows her mouthful of food, then says, "Yeah, but if I wait until Monday, you're grumpy. You tend to bite people's heads off when you're grumpy."

"I'm taking the weekend off," I assure her.

"Hallelujah! I've been telling you to do that for years. Can you tell me who finally convinced you?"

"Who? What if I took up a hobby?"

"Just a wild guess."

"And you're still not being nosy?"

She shakes her head vehemently. "No, just asking so I know how long the miracle lasts."

I barely hold back a smile at her transparent efforts.

"So? Is it Alice Bennett?" she presses.

"Yes."

Clara flashes me a megawatt grin. "I knew it. So you two are getting along well?"

I nod, but by Clara's reaction, you'd think I'd just announced my wedding. She claps her hands excitedly, then puts them together as if in a prayer.

"Thank you, God, for listening to my prayers. I knew only a good-hearted but wild woman could make an honest man out of him."

"What was I before?" I ask with fake horror.

She presses her lips together, her hands falling by her sides. "I can't insult you. You're my boss."

"I already feel insulted, so you might as well go on and say what you were going to."

"I'll just say this: I very much prefer this version of you."

To be honest, I prefer this version of myself too. Something's changed since Alice became a constant presence in my life. I've always liked solitude, having my own space. But now I like that I can feel her presence in my apartment even when she's not there, even though I sure as hell like it more when she is there. This is so different to the way I used to do things, to the way I used to *like* them, that I almost don't recognize myself.

Alice has taken over my entire place. My room smells like lavender, my pillow smells like her, and I have more dirty laundry than usual because Alice has the habit of wearing my best shirts inside the house. I don't really mind it because the woman looks sexy as sin wearing nothing but my shirts.

"Earth to Nate." Clara's voice snaps me out of my thoughts.

"What?"

"I'll be damned. I've never seen you like this, lost in thought, smiling to yourself like a goof."

I groan. "I really should set more professional boundaries between us. You calling me a goof means we just reached rock bottom."

Clara shrugs, eying the last bite of food on her plate as if undecided whether she should eat it or not.

"No, it means you're finally letting someone in. Now, take care of Alice, or I'm going to kick your ass."

"You've been hanging out with Pippa, right?"

Clara shrugs. "That doesn't have anything to do with this."

"So whatever I'm telling you stays between us?"

"Only if you insist."

"You work for me! You should be on my side."

"No. It's called female solidarity. A paycheck can't come in between." She shoves her spoon in her mouth, pointing to her now-empty plate, and I tell the waiter we're ready to pay.

"Good to know."

"By the way, have you read Horowitz's e-mail about the London studio's reaction to the proposals? The only parts they actually liked were the ones you brought to the table."

"I read it. Abbott will eventually get a grip on things."

"Or he'll be fired. Horowitz was saying the other day that he doesn't think Abbott will last one more month. He thinks they'll come begging you to take over after."

"I don't like to spend my time talking about what-ifs." My tone is sharper than it needs to be, but I have no desire for this conversation. For the longest time, I've carefully separated my personal and professional lives, but lately, every time someone mentions how Abbott might break under the pressure, I immediately think about Alice and what that would mean for us.

The waiter arrives with the tab. The second he's gone, Clara leans over the table. "So, if I take back what I said and swear anything you tell me stays between us, would your answer change?"

"Nice try, Clara. Nice try."

Chapter Twenty-Two

Alice

"These are fabulous." I'm in a fancy jewelry store downtown, trying on amethyst earrings from Pippa's newest collection, and they are just beautiful. I like to reward myself when I seal a new deal, and today I managed to convince one of the most popular San Francisco bands to play in Blue Moon twice a month. I've been after them for years; persistence pays off. Amethyst earrings are a totally acceptable reward. As the designer at Bennett Enterprises, Pippa will probably kill me when she sees me wearing them, insisting I don't have to buy anything she creates because she can just gift them to me. She doesn't understand. Buying them feels like I worked for them, and deserve them. "I'll take them."

Watching the vendor pack them, I fight to stifle a yawn, and it's not even seven o'clock in the evening. Running three restaurants is very different to owning one, or even two. It's not only more work, but different work. Nowadays I'm more often on the phone with potential partners and advertisers than in the kitchen or talking to customers. Some days I've even taken to working from home in the mornings since all I do is talk on the phone.

Dividing my time between three locations seems to be counterproductive, and I have to do something about it. I don't have the energy to plan that course of action though, so I just put it off and continue on the hamster wheel like I've been doing for months now.

"Thank you for stopping by today." The vendor hands me the small bag, and then I'm out the door. Despite being bone-tired, I smile, taking in the commotion around me in Union Square. It's buzzing with people of all ages, taking leisurely strolls or striding with purpose, and I'm soaking in the beautiful August evening.

There's also another reason behind my smile—I'm meeting Nate in about half an hour. It's been almost two months since he first asked me out that night in Blake's bar. He's cooking for me tonight, and I'm over the moon. He's been spoiling me until now too with quick dinners or breakfast, and I love being pampered almost as much as I love spoiling him.

But when I arrive at Nate's apartment later, he's in a bad mood. He prepared a delicious dinner, pork chops with Gouda cheese and salad, and I try to make small talk, but he's been replying with monosyllabic answers to most of my questions. I don't like it, and I like the scowl on his face even less.

After we're done eating, we clean up, returning to the table to finish our wine. I'm waiting patiently for him to share with me what's bothering him, but my patience expires after exactly one hour of scowls and one-word answers.

"Why are you so pissed off?" I ask.

Nate's scowl deepens. "Just issues."

Uh, if you think I'm gonna be satisfied by that, the joke's on you, buddy.

Crossing my arms, I face him with my chin held high. "Nuh-uh, nope. This isn't going to work."

Alarm flits on his face, replacing the scowl. "What?"

"You not sharing things. If you're in a bad mood, I want to know why. If something I did is bothering you, tell me. If—"

"It has nothing to do with you."

I nod as the small knot of tension at the back of my neck melts.

"Well, whatever it is, you can tell me."

"I'd just ruin your mood too."

"Your bad mood is ruining mine anyway, so spill it."

The corners of his lips lift in a small smile. *Now we're talking*. I swear I'd dance naked on tables if it would make him happy. I'm in such deep trouble.

He leans back in his chair, playing with the glass of wine in his hand. "Remember what I told you about Mom? About her troubles with her mortgage?"

"Yeah."

"I still can't convince her to let me help her. Talked to her today, didn't get anywhere. She's unbelievably stubborn."

My chest warms, as if I've just hugged a puppy. I love that he wants to take care of his mom. "She passed the trait on to you."

He sips from his wine absent-mindedly. Then he focuses, as if an idea suddenly struck him.

"Would you mind talking to her?"

His question shocks the hell out of me because Nate never asks for help. For as long as I've known him, he's never reached out to ask for anything, not of me or any of my siblings.

"Sure. I'll talk to her."

"Thank you, Alice. I thought maybe having someone who isn't *me* talking to her might change her mind."

"Should I call her?"

"How about paying her a visit?"

"I'd love to. I haven't seen her in years." My mind is already reeling with arguments I could use to convince her, and my throat prickles with unease. When it comes to family matters, I've always been better at delegating such issues. For example, Pippa is the best person to calm Sebastian's and Logan's fears of becoming fathers. Logan is the best person to convince Daniel it's okay to change gears when your initial plan isn't working out. But this is important to Nate, and I'll do my best. It's a good thing we're heading out to visit her in person; I'll have the opportunity to take in her body language as I feel out the situation. I swear my heart grew in size because my man asked me for help.

Since we're both done with dinner, I rise from my chair, heading to Nate and straddling him. He runs his thumb over my mouth, splaying his hand wide on my neck and jaw. When he looks at me, something in his expression tips me off that he realizes this is a big step for him, and for us. That this requires another level of trust. I lean into his touch like I'm starved for affection, even though goodness knows I shouldn't be. He showers me with attention and caresses every chance he gets—and I make sure he gets lots of chances— but the more I receive, the more I want.

"Talked to my mom today too. She and Dad are planning a big picnic two weeks from now, on Saturday. You're invited, of course."

Nate grins. "Ah, and I assume everyone will be there?"

I nod. "You're not going to escape the questioning rounds, I'm afraid."

"They like me already."

"Aha! That line of thinking will get you into trouble, mister."

"I can take whatever they throw at me. Or fire at me. It's gonna be a firing squad out there, but I can handle them. I know your family, and I won't disappoint them. Their approval is important to me too."

"I'll talk you up, tell them all about this lovely dinner and how you take care of me and make me smile."

"Interesting how now you withhold all those negative traits you always tease me with."

I huff, kissing his forehead before patting his shoulder. *Clueless man.* "I want my family to approve of you, not cut your balls off."

"I know them—"

"Shit!"

I've no idea how I managed it, but I've knocked Nate's glass of wine off. Its content spilled right onto me, and I'm soaked. Great! Red wine doesn't wash off.

"I can throw this shirt away," I mutter. "Do you mind if I shower now?"

"Only if I can't join you in that shower."

"Always with the dirty mind."

"Always," he confirms.

"No, you can't join me." Leaning in, I whisper, "You wait for me in the bedroom."

***

Nate

Standing in the doorway of the bedroom with a towel wrapped around her fifteen minutes later, Alice is every man's dream come true. I smile, remembering the way she pushed earlier, determined to get me to talk. In the past, I felt the need to permanently keep my guard up, not let anyone in. With Alice, opening up felt surprisingly easy. In fact, what I want to do now is tear down any walls she might have.

A few drops of water drip down her legs. She's not tall, but there's enough of Alice to feast on for hours at a time, which is exactly what I intend to do.

"Lose the towel."

"Giving me orders again?" she asks with sass in her voice.

"Yeah. I am."

Cocking a brow, she turns around, and just when I think she's about to flip me the bird, she lowers her towel slowly, revealing just a morsel of skin at a time. Damn this woman; she'll make me explode in my pants. She lowers it just enough to give me a peek at the crack of her ass. Fuck, she'll be the death of me.

"Come here."

She drops her towel completely, and I take one good eyeful of that round and perfect ass before she swoops around, heading in my direction. She stops right in front of me and I grab her ass with one hand, turning her around so her back is to me. Then I stand up from the bed, push her hair to one side, and start kissing her neck and shoulder, trailing down her spine as I lower onto the bed again. My mouth descends further and I press my hand on her back, pushing her forward. She immediately understands and bends forward. The motion brings her ass up, which is just what I wanted. Parting her cheeks, I lick her crack once.

"Oh fuck." She shudders and I grip her hips with my hands, steadying her. I want to discover her limit so I can take her over the edge every time. Alice straightens up and I turn her around yet again, needing to see her face. Then I pull her between my open thighs. Now we're talking. I run my other hand along her thigh until she shudders and rubs her inner thighs together almost involuntarily—a sign that wet heat rushed down between her legs. I want to worship this woman for the rest of my life. I'll never get enough of her.

"Open your legs for me, Alice."

She does what I say. She's between my open thighs, my cock right between us, begging for attention. I press my thumb on her clit while sliding two fingers inside her opening.

"Nate."

My name on her lips is such a powerful trigger that I barely resist pulling her in my lap right now. No, first I'll take care of her. While kissing her torso, her taut waist, and the underside of her breasts, I curl my fingers inside her, searching for the tender place that will undo her. The G-spot isn't a myth; it just takes patience and dedication to find it, and I have both. When she arches her hips slightly forward, dropping her head back, I know I found it. I press with my thumb on her clit at the same time my fingers work the tender spot inside, and my woman begins to unravel in front of me. The first sign is when she grasps my shoulders, and it's not just for support. How do I know? Because she digs her nails into my skin, showing me she likes it.

"I want you."

Unhitching my lips from her skin, I pull back. I want to see her expression when she explodes, which should be just about now. "I want you to come once before I'm inside you."

"Nate, I—"

Moans replace her words and my hard-on twitches as I rub its head against her inner thigh. Just imagining her wet heat squeezing my cock nearly has me losing control, but I hang in there, watching her, drinking in her beauty and sensuality. She shatters beautifully, spasming around my fingers. With my free arm, I secure her just as her knees buckle. Her entire body rides the wave of the orgasm, arching and shuddering against me. Her cries of pleasure are music to my ears. I wait until she regains some of her composure.

"Now ride me, Alice."

Breathing in and out, she manages a weak smile. "Give a girl some reprieve, will you?"

"No, you're tight now. You'll like it. Trust me."

When I'm certain her knees are strong enough to support her, I let go, lying on the bed instead. Licking her lower lip, Alice straddles me, resting her knees at my side. When she slides over me, I damn near black out.

"Alice. Fuck. You're so tight, babe."

"Oh my God!" She stills with me inside her, opening and closing her fists, breathing frantically.

She's so tight I'm about to come right now, but damn if I will. My golden rule is that my woman has to come first, but if I can give her seconds, so much better.

Alice slides with careful moves, and if I died now, I'd go a happy man. Her breasts bob up and down every time she rises and lowers herself. I cup one in my hand, kneading it, then tease the nipple with my palm. In response, she squeezes me good with her inner walls. My self-control hangs on a thread. I breathe in through my nose, staving off the orgasm, doubling my efforts when Alice whispers, "So close. I'm so close."

When my balls tighten, I push myself into a sitting position, gripping her hips and guiding her in my own rhythm. A white-hot flash licks up my spine when she tightens around me even more. I lick between her breasts, taking one peak in my mouth, then moving on to the other. Alice slips a hand between us down to her clit.

She knows what she likes and isn't shy about it. My hands are everywhere, cradling her head, guiding her hips, slamming her against me hot and wild. I'm a desperate man now, searching for the beautiful oblivion and ecstasy only an orgasm can offer. My entire body craves the release, even as I enjoy the pure torture from being buried to the hilt in this beautiful woman. She makes gorgeous sounds I want to eat up. I meet almost every moan of hers with a groan, trying to contain myself until she's there.

When she is, she explodes beautifully for a second time, writhing and calling my name again and again. My own orgasm hits me seconds later in a violent rush, radiating from the tip of my crown down to every cell. It's the kind of pleasure that goes bone-deep and doesn't let go, demanding everything I have.

Only when we're both completely spent do we collapse on the bed, Alice still on top of me, resting her nose in the crook of my neck.

"You are a goddess. And I'm going to remind you every day."

Chapter Twenty-Three

Alice

"Alice, for the love of God, drive faster or there will be no food left when we get there," Blake says. He's in the passenger seat and has been nagging me to drive faster since we hit the road.

We're meeting the entire clan for the picnic at my parents' house and it made no sense for everyone to go with their own car, so I got saddled with Blake and Daniel. Nate had to oversee some reshoots today and said he wasn't sure when they'd be over, so he'll stop by later. It's going to be a glorious day; I can feel it in the tips of my fingers. I so needed an outing with the family, and I'm happy everyone is coming. It's also going to be the first time Nate joins a family event as my guy. It feels like an important milestone.

"I don't think the car can take it. Whenever I go over sixty, it starts making scary noises," I explain.

"Here's a thought: buy another car," Daniel supplies from the back seat.

"But I like this one," I insist. "It's got personality."

In the rearview mirror, I see Daniel dragging his hands down his face, staring at me like I grew a second head.

"Always knew you were nutty," he says under his breath.

"Heard you."

"I meant for you to hear me."

Blake groans, then abruptly straightens in his seat, as if an idea just occurred to him. "Let's bet."

"On how long it'll take us to get there?" Daniel asks, looking equally animated. Whenever we're together, the children in us surface. That's a universal truth, at least in our clan.

I'd forgotten how much fun the twins like to have at my expense. I can't deny I like it though. It's our thing, and it has been for as long as I remember. Funny thing is I've never allowed any of my other siblings to tease me the way I've allowed Blake and Daniel. I suppose all of us have our soft spots.

Ah, I don't foresee much good for me in the near future. My nieces and nephews will have me wrapped around their little fingers.

"That too," Blake says. "I was thinking about which one of our oldest brothers will be the first to give Nate the talk, Sebastian or Logan."

"They'll corner him at the same time," Daniel says immediately.

"Agreed. They like to work together when it comes to intimidating someone," I explain.

The twins fall into an almost eerie silence.

"You're not worried?" Blake asks cautiously.

I shrug, focusing on the road again. As the sun comes out from behind clouds, I have to squint at the blinding light. Well, if there's a time for blinding light, it's mid-August.

"Nate can handle it. I have full confidence in him."

Another silence follows, right before Blake bursts out laughing.

"You have love blinders on, sister. But I'm neutral. I can assess everyone's potential better."

"Me too," Daniel adds helpfully.

"It's a good thing we're bringing ice." Blake whistles, lowering in his seat.

"Ice?" I ask, not following.

"In case anyone gets a black eye."

"Don't be an idiot. No one will."

"The beauty is in the uncertainty." Daniel earns himself a stink eye from me in the rearview mirror. "But I'm with Alice. Our oldest brothers will behave, even Logan."

Blake considers this. "True, Logan's acting strange. We've been getting along too well lately. He never rides my ass anymore. It's weird."

I grin, shaking my head. Knowing Blake, he'll provoke Logan over any tiny thing just to rile him up. It's always fun to watch. That reminds me, I should thank Logan. He must have spoken to Daniel and gotten through to him, because Daniel shared with me that he's thinking of focusing more on expanding his range of sport-related activities and dropping the extreme adventures part.

We talk about a soccer game for the rest of the trip, and I'm so engrossed in the conversation that I barely hear my phone when it chirps with an incoming message.

"What was that sound?" Blake asks. "The car begging you to drive faster?"

"You buffoon. It was my phone. Daniel, can you please take it out of my purse and read the message out loud? I don't like to look at my phone while driving."

Daniel rummages through my bag for a while until he finds my phone.

"It's from Nate," he informs me.

"What does it say?"

"Are you sure it's safe to open it?" he asks.

"Huh?"

"He's afraid he might stumble onto dirty talk," Blake explains with a shit-eating grin. That actually makes me pause, because… um… well, Nate and I are fond of sexting. But he should be at work now, so we're safe.

"We might be more laid-back than our older brothers," Blake continues, "but we still don't like to know about our sisters doing the nasty. It's a brother thing."

"I get it. The caveman gene is alive and well. Go ahead and read it, Daniel. If you're squeamish, cover your eyes and look through your fingers. Pass the phone to Blake at the first sight of a dirty word."

"Okay," Daniel says. "Here's what is says. 'Hey, shooting finished earlier, so I'm already here. So is everyone else, except for you, Blake, and Daniel.'"

"He's already there?" My throat dries up.

"Yes, not everyone drives like you," Daniel deadpans.

Blake chuckles, muttering something that sounds like "Let the cornering begin."

Sweat breaks out on my palms, despite my previous claims about having full faith in Nate. My oldest brothers have been known to scare off my dates before. Sure, I was young and those dates were wimps, but history is history.

Praying that my car doesn't leave me in the lurch, I hit the gas pedal.

"Look who's driving faster now," Blake remarks.

***

Nate

The picnic with the Bennetts reminds me of the old days. The clan is as loud and nutty as I remember it, only now it's even bigger. Having the picnic at their house was a great idea because their yard is huge, complete with a gazebo. It's warm and sunny now, but in case the weather turns unpleasant, we can take the party inside.

"This is a lot of food. It'll take a long time to grill everything." I survey the mountains of meat and vegetables. Jenna Bennett surveys it too. I have the utmost respect for her and her husband, Richard. They always had an open door for me, and for any of their kids' friends.

"Big group." Jenna gives me precise instructions on how long to grill each type of vegetable. I listen even though I know this stuff backward, remembering Alice saying that sometimes she lets her mom give advice she'll never use because it makes Jenna feel useful, and mothers need to be needed.

She only stops when one of Pippa's girls is tugging at her skirt. Pippa stands a few feet behind, clapping her hands and cheering her daughter. Bending down, Jenna lifts her granddaughter in her arms.

"I'll start with the grilling right away, Jenna. Clearly, Mia wants more of your attention." It was a wild guess, and by the way Jenna chuckles, the wrong one.

"This is Elena." She pushes Elena's hair away from her face and the toddler laughs, grabbing Jenna's sweater in her tiny fists and then a strand of Jenna's hair, tugging with surprising force for such a little thing. "Let's take you back to your mom and sister, shall we?"

"You're getting a kick out of being a grandmother, aren't you?"

"Absolutely. It's even more fun than being a mom. I do all the spoiling while their parents worry about pesky things such as educating them."

With that, she leaves me to get on with the food.

***

It's a good thing they have three enormous grills; otherwise, the process would take hours. I've barely poured the coals onto the first one when Sebastian and Logan join me.

"We're on grilling duty too," Sebastian announces.

Logan nods, extending a hand. "Pass the coal."

Two minutes later, I realize they plan to grill more than veggies and meat. They're also here to grill me, which I expected.

"So, what exactly is going on with you and Alice?" Sebastian asks, cutting right to the chase, looking straight at me while prodding with the coal fork around the coal.

"I was wondering when you'd start with this."

"You still haven't answered," Logan supplies, looking far less laid-back than Sebastian. Then again, I've known these guys for almost twenty years. Sebastian is the cool-headed and analytical one, while Logan is more impulsive.

"Alice and I are dating, and it's going great. I respect her, and I'm going to take care of her."

"We've known you for a long time," Sebastian says, and I hold my hand up.

"I know my track record. But what Alice and I have is the real deal."

Sebastian relaxes visibly at this, but Logan holds up a finger. "If you hurt her—"

"Let me guess, you'll kill me?"

Logan lifts a brow. "We're watching you. Closely."

"I'd be surprised if you didn't."

The sound of a car approaching makes the three of us turn around. Alice's battered old Ford comes into view.

"Sorry for being late, everyone," Blake explains once he, Alice, and Daniel are out of the car. "Alice here wanted to win the trophy for slowest driver of the year."

Alice elbows him but doesn't lecture him for making fun of her. Interesting. I get another treatment altogether when I tease her about her old car. Double standard if I've ever seen one.

"Uh-oh," Alice exclaims, heading toward me and pointing to her brothers at my side. Blake tails behind her while Daniel joins the rest of the group on the other side of the yard.

"Did you give Nate a hard time?" she inquires once she's in front of us.

"No idea what you're talking about," Sebastian says.

"So it's a coincidence that you and Logan are flanking him?"

I just smile, watching their interaction.

"There are three grills. Three guys are needed," Logan explains, knowing as well as I do that's shit. One person is more than enough to man the grills. Blake is snickering from behind his sister.

"Everything's fine," I say.

Alice folds her arms, surveying the three of us. "So they haven't flexed their big brother muscles on my behalf? I feel discriminated against."

That actually catches me off guard. She wanted them to corner me? This calls for a thorough revenge plan on my part.

Logan grins. "Nah, we did. But we decided he seems honest, so we're just going to keep an eye on him."

"Told you Logan's lost his touch." Blake steps right next to Alice. "Look at Nate. He doesn't look intimidated or pissed."

"Oy," Logan exclaims.

"Just so you know," Blake replies, "I'll pick a fight with you sometime today. Things need shaking up."

"Sometimes I can't believe the conversations in this family," Sebastian mutters.

Alice shakes her head at her brothers' shenanigans. I hold up my hand. "All right, show's over. I need to talk to Alice alone. Watch the grill until I'm back."

Without waiting for anyone's answer, I take Alice's hand, leading her toward the house. Once inside, I turn to face her, holding her against me.

"First things first." I kiss her thoroughly, needing to get my fill of her. I haven't seen her in three days, and that's about three days too long. Her sweet mouth welcomes me, her lips parting with ease. I lose myself in her warmth. We're both insatiable.

"Mmmm, I'll ask my brothers to corner you more often if it means I'll get kissed like that," she says when we pull apart.

"You don't deserve to be kissed like that after practically cheering them on. I remember you saying you'd talk me up."

"I did a while ago." Alice shrugs, laying her palms on my chest. "I was torn between wanting them to give you a hard time and defending you."

"This is supposed to make me feel better?"

She nods with conviction. "Yes. And when you wrote to say you were already here, I even panicked a bit and drove fast. Well, as fast as she'd go."

"That car—"

"Watch it. Make fun of it and you won't get laid."

"I'm confident enough in my seduction skills." I rub my thumbs against her bare shoulders in small circles and her cheeks redden. "See?"

"You're not playing fair." She fidgets in her spot, and some of that playful glint in her eyes has faded. She looks concerned now.

"Alice, everything okay?"

"Yeah." She fidgets even more, drumming her fingers on my chest. "So my brothers haven't scared you off, huh?"

"Of course not. That's how little you think of me?"

"No, but I thought it would be a good test." She swallows, glancing at me apologetically, as if she just let slip something she wasn't supposed to.

"What are you talking about?"

"Well, if you got scared about their big brother talk, it would've been a red flag."

There are times when I think I have her all figured out, and then she surprises me by showing me just how vulnerable she can be.

"This thing between us is important to me. You're important to me."

"Yeah?" She smiles, and everything feels right again.

"Yes."

"So I'm forgiven for secretly wishing my brothers would corner you?"

I kiss her forehead. "You, Alice Bennett, will never cease to blindside me. Now let's get back outside before someone interrupts us. Accidentally, of course."

We spend the rest of the day catching up with everyone, and I seem to get a variation of the talk from every member in the family. It gets annoying at some point, but I'm also glad that even as adults, they still have each other's backs.

***

“That went well,” Alice exclaims toward the end of the day, when most of the group is preparing to leave.

“Yeah, I got far fewer death threats than I was expecting.”

“Am I being childish to be nervous about tomorrow?”

We’re visiting my mother tomorrow. She was very excited when I told her we’re going over. Being surrounded by this loud and boisterous clan, I can’t help feeling guilty for not visiting her more often, even if she lives three hours away.

“I can guarantee my mother will not issue any threats. Unless she tries to feed us marshmallows.”

“Oh, crap. I remember her marshmallows. They’re hard as stones. A threat on their own.”

Chapter Twenty-Four

Alice

Next morning, we leave at the crack of dawn, or so it seems. I love sleeping in on Sundays, and though I doze off, Nate wakes me when we arrive and I scramble to put myself together, jumping out of the car and following him blindly as he leads me inside Babette's property. I'm so out of sorts I'm not even taking in my surroundings.

Calm down, Alice. This will go just fine.

When Babette meets us on the doorstep, she pulls me in a very tight hug, acting like she's never seen me before.

"Mom, you already know Alice," Nate says.

"Nah, I knew a teenage girl with a sharp tongue. Let me look at you. My, my, you've grown up beautifully."

"Thank you. I still have a sharp tongue, I'm afraid."

"Tsk, tsk! Never apologize for that. Best weapon to get you through life."

"You look great!"

"Add ten years and subtract ten pounds, a second divorce, and a pug, and you got a brand-new Babette."

Last time I saw Babette, she looked completely different. Her hair was dyed jet-black, for one. Now it's chocolate brown, and this color suits her much better. The black was too strong, painting her delicate features in a sharp light. She seemed to have a permanent scowl on her face back then, her mouth always set in a grim line.

Now she's beaming, holding her overweight and totally adorable pug, Felicia, in her arms.

"So good of the two of you to come visit me. Want to see the house, Alice?"

"Sure."

She gives us a quick tour of the bungalow, which is small but very quaint. It's clear Babette is very proud of it.

"I made lunch," she announces once we're out on the back patio. "You kids hungry?"

"Starving," I reply, elbowing Nate, who inspects the food with skepticism. Babette never was a great cook, and still isn't, if the dry-as-bone chicken we're eating is anything to go by. At least there are no marshmallows.

Over lunch, we chat about Nate's job, my restaurants, and her life here in the town.

"I'm so glad I decided to move here," she says. "Small towns have a charm all of their own."

"I imagine they do," I reply, and Nate and I exchange accomplice glances. We're both such city junkies that the mere thought of living in a town with a population of only three thousand makes us feel claustrophobic.

"Of course, it also has downsides," Babette says, glancing at the pug, which is in her arms again. She only put it down while she ate lunch. "The president of the pageant organizing committee, Clarissa Lawson, is out to get me, I swear. Felicia didn't win anything in any of the pageant competitions."

Nate told me all about his mom's new hobby—dog pageants—on the way, but part of me thought he was pulling my leg. It appears not.

"No one has anything against you or your pug, Mom. But the dog is overweight."

Babette covers the pug's ears. "Don't talk about Felicia like that."

"It's true though," I add.

"Letting her walk on her own now and again would help," Nate continues. "It would be great exercise."

"But she likes it in my arms, don't you, darling?"

In response, Felicia licks Babette's neck.

Nate doesn't insist on the topic, and after he finishes his chicken, he asks, "Mom, do you need me to fix anything around the house?"

Nate explained that he likes to fix things for her, and she usually has a long to-do list for him when he stops by. I'm to use that time to talk Babette into allowing Nate to help her with the mortgage payments.

His first task is to look at some of the wiring in the kitchen, so he heads inside the house, leaving Babette and me alone on the patio. Well, with Felicia, who is now sniffing Babette's plate tentatively.

"I'm so happy you two stopped by today," Babette says, scratching her dog's head. "I'd hoped Nate would bring you around every time he mentioned you."

"He's talked to you about me?"

She nods, beaming brighter. "I was so happy when he said you two were… well, whatever you kids are naming it these days. I was afraid I'd damaged him for good."

"What do you mean?" I ask.

Babette slices me with a glance that seems to say 'We both know what I'm talking about.' But I'm genuinely confused.

"Let's not pretend, Alice. I wasn't a good mother, just like I wasn't a good wife to either of my husbands."

"Babette," I say in a low voice, clueless as to what to add. I wasn't expecting this.

"It is what it is. Regrets don't repair the past, but it's good to acknowledge the things one has done wrong. It should help not repeating the same mistakes."

"You shouldn't blame yourself. It takes two people to make a marriage work."

"Honey, don't worry. I blame both my ex-husbands plenty." She chuckles, but her eyes grow sad. "But no man likes to come home to a hysterical woman. I wasn't working on my marriage, just driving the people I loved away. Do you think I don't know that my boy was so often at your parents' house because he couldn't stand my shouting?"

It takes a great deal of strength to admit one's mistakes and faults, and I respect her even more than I did before.

"You've changed a lot, Babette. You're so much calmer now."

She shrugs, holding her pug even tighter. "My second divorce really put things in perspective for me. Went to therapy too, and it helped a lot, but I was afraid my boy would choose to always have passing *liaisons* with women because I never painted a pretty picture when it comes to family. Even now I can't stop bitching about his father."

I press my lips to hold back a chuckle, wondering if she really thinks 'kids these days' use the word 'liaisons.' But I also ache for her, this strong woman with so many regrets.

"Babette, you did your best. And really, that's all any of us can hope to do."

"Doesn't mean I don't get to feel guilty about it."

Oh damn. Here's my best chance to convince Babette to accept Nate's help. I can guilt her into doing it. For the record, I was not planning to use this tactic.

I was going to talk her into it the clean way, by using logical arguments, and my own parents as an example. Using people's guilt against them is a tactic I only resort to when I need to make my brothers pay for something, but this is almost like a sign, really. I have to act on it.

"Nate worries about you."

Her head snaps up. "He told you about my troubles with the house."

I nod. "It's a beautiful house, and Nate earns more than enough. You'd be doing him a huge favor by allowing him to buy it for you."

"I'd be doing him a *favor*?"

"Yes. He wouldn't worry about you working two jobs and so on. You owe him some peace of mind."

I'll burn in hell for this but it might all be worth it, because by the pensive look on her face, she's considering this. Then she narrows her eyes at me.

"Alice Bennett, you trying to guilt me into accepting my son's help?"

Damn it. I wasn't expecting her to catch on so quickly. Am I really such an open book? At least if I confess, I might stay out of hell.

"Yes, ma'am."

To my surprise, Babette bursts out laughing. "Girl, you've got a sharp mind to go with that sharp tongue."

"I do what I can."

Shaking her head, she dials down the laughter to a chuckle, then frowns. "He really worries about me?"

"Yeah. A lot."

"But I don't want him to worry."

"Which is why letting him help you is a good idea. Look, my brother Sebastian also bought my parents a house."

Her fingers slash the air, pointing toward me.

"I know the whole story. Your parents sold the ranch to give him capital to start Bennett Enterprises. Not the same."

"Babette? Don't be so stubborn. It's good to know when to give in. And allowing your son to do something nice for you doesn't in any way mean you're less hardworking or that you don't deserve what you have."

Well, well, well, listen to me, morphing into Logan. Just a few years ago, I cringed when he was saying those things to me, but in the meantime, I agree with him. The wisdom of age. Maybe I should listen to my older siblings more often.

Babette winks at me. "You sure as hell have a way with words."

We put the topic to rest afterward, talking about everything else under the sun, but I've planted the seed and she's seriously considering it. That was my goal for today, because I know one thing about stubborn people: it takes time for them to change their mind.

After what seems like forever, Nate joins us again, announcing that he's finished fixing everything. We stay with Babette a while longer, then head out.

Babette's house is in a clearing surrounded by a small patch of forest, and we had to leave the car at the edge of the land. I'm trying to be careful where I step because the tree roots are thick, protruding from the earth. Nate's arm is around my waist, firm and dependable. He usually keeps his hand entwined with mine, or at the small of my back when we're walking. It's endearing because it always seems like he's doing it to protect me, and I love his protective side. I usually don't need it, but by God, I'm glad he's with me right now. Twice his strong grip keeps me from twisting my ankle when my heel catches on a root.

Once the road evens out and surviving doesn't require our utmost concentration, he asks, "Did you manage to talk to her about the house?"

"Yes, and she's considering it."

"Impressive. Every time I talked to her, the only thing she was considering was slapping me through the phone."

"I have my ways," I say with a shrug. "And I might or might not burn in hell for them."

"Am I supposed to know what that means?"

"It means I play dirty to get what I want sometimes."

Nate tucks me into his side as we head to the car, which is still a few minutes away. But I'm glad we get to walk a little more around here. There's something peaceful and serene about this sleepy town. I can almost understand why Babette moved here. After a tumultuous life, she probably needed this calm and silence. Hard as I strain my ears, there are no sounds reaching me beyond the chirping of birds. The other houses are miles away, so there's only the occasional sound of a car in the distance.

"Ah, but I already knew that about you, *darling*."

"So, what are the plans for the evening? Do I get you all to myself, or do you have to work?"

"I have to finish some stuff for the London studio, but it won't take me too long."

Ah, there it is, the elephant in the room. Until now, I've avoided questioning him about this directly, but I feel it's time I did.

"Do you think they'll ask you to take over the position there?"

Nate's grip on me tightens, as if he wasn't expecting the question. "Horowitz keeps saying Abbott will break under the pressure, but I give the guy more credit. He's going to learn the ropes."

That isn't much of an answer, but I'm a coward and don't press for more. I couldn't handle a straight answer.

"Thank you for bringing me with you today. Can I ask you something?"

"Sure."

"Babette said something about how she thinks you didn't have a happy family life and it might have impacted you. She thinks it was why you chose to have 'meaningless liaisons'—her words, not mine—with women."

"Funny, Clara said something similar once."

"Do you think it's true?"

Nate is quiet for a long while, and I wait with my stomach in knots.

"All experiences mark us in some way. But I think everything comes down to choices. For a long time, I chose not to get attached because it was easier."

"And now?"

My heart is in my throat as I wait for him to reply. We're right in front of the car but we stop before we reach it, under the shade of a tree with a beautiful crown full of blooms in shades of pink and white.

Nate is half turned to me, holding my gaze captive with his.

"Now I choose us." Stepping closer to me, he kisses one corner of my mouth, then the other. Suddenly I feel like someone lit a match inside me, joy spreading throughout me to the very tips of my fingers. He keeps teasing me, his mouth moving from the corner of my lips to my cheek and then heading to my ear. His proximity makes me shiver and want more of him. I yearn to hear him say more sweet nothings.

"Say it again," I whisper.

"I choose us, Alice, and I'll say it as many times as you want."

The shiver intensifies and he wraps his arms around me, his lips still to my ear. I want to feel closer to him still, climb inside him, as it were. I don't remember fisting his shirt but here I am, tugging at it with one hand. My other hand has slipped under it, feeling him up shamelessly.

"Someone's having dirty thoughts," he whispers.

"I need to feel closer to you."

"I aim to please."

Before I can react, he hauls me into his arms, pushing me backward until he has me against the car. Then he lowers his head, kissing me like a man determined to get me to melt at his feet… or at least get me so turned on that I forget where we are. Nate swipes his tongue over my lips, then dips it inside my mouth, exploring me, driving me crazy. My blood spikes with adrenaline and desire within seconds, and for the hundredth time, I wonder how this man can awaken my craving for him so quickly.

A low growl reverberates deep in his throat just as he unhitches his lips from mine.

"Alice, what are you doing to me?"

"Nothing you're not doing to me as well."

When he pulls back enough that I can look at him properly, the glint of desire in his eyes is so overpowering it takes my breath away. He exudes masculinity and power, and the expression on his face is feral. He pushes his hips flush against me, and I lick my lips when I feel his hard-on against my belly, heat pooling between my thighs. I'm so turned on I'd let him take me any way he wants right now. It scares me that I'm giving him such power over me.

"Sweet and wild Alice," he murmurs. "I need to be inside you."

I lick my lips. "Now? Here?"

In response, he cocks a brow. We're in a small forest with thick trees surrounding us. The chances of anyone seeing us, or even passing by, are close to zero.

"Anything against that?" He opens the door to the back seat, then guides me backward until I feel the soft cushion of the seat against my ass.

"No."

"Good. Climb inside."

A delicious shudder licks up my spine as I crawl onto the back seat, lying on my back. Luckily, Nate's car is spacious and I'm wearing a dress, which he pushes up my thighs as he joins me in the car, shutting the door behind him.

He spreads my legs, running his hand along my inner thighs before rubbing his fingers against my wet panties. Need zaps through me. He pushes the fabric covering my entrance to one side, bending over and swiping his tongue over my folds, his nose gently touching my clit.

"Oh God."

"Fuck! I want to lick you, but I also need to be inside you right now." He comes up to me until our faces are level. His arms are at my side, caging me and sustaining his weight. On a whim, I kiss his jaw, licking down his neck while I undo his zipper, freeing his erection. "How do you want this? Hard and fast? Sweet and tender? Either way, I'll be inside you in about five seconds."

Next thing I know he's teasing my tender spot with the thick head of his erection. *Fuck, fuck, fuck.*

"Any way. All the ways."

Breath rushes out of me when Nate slams into me, entering me to the hilt. I wasn't prepared to take him all at once, and the pleasure of him stretching me is so intense, I nearly break out of my skin. I widen my thighs even more, allowing him room to move, to drive into me hard and wild. He feasts on my neck and lips, and my moans fill the car. When his teeth graze the skin on my neck lightly, the pleasure burns through me. Pulling back, he looks between us, and I push myself up on one elbow. The sight of him sliding in and out of me is exquisite. Drops of sweat dot his forehead, one of them falling right onto my chest. It's incredibly erotic and intimate.

"Make yourself come, Alice. Touch your clit."

"I like it when you go all bossy on me."

I was meaning to tease him, but he drives inside me hard, stopping the rest of the words in my throat. God, he's so deep inside me, I feel like he's about to split me in half. I lower my hand to my clit and stroke it. An orgasm ravages through me within seconds, coiling through my body with lightning speed.

"Oh fuck, Alice." Nate cries out his own release, cradling me in his arms, holding me tightly to him.

We cling to one another for long minutes, both spent.

"You're a wild thing, Alice."

"Hey! You're the one who bossed me into climbing in the back seat and opening my legs."

"So it's my fault?" He chuckles, his voice soft.

"Of course. You and your irresistible charm. You're just as wild as I am."

"It's a good thing we found each other, then." Nate kisses my forehead, then pulls back, looking at me with warmth and something more… something that fills my stomach with butterflies. The moment feels raw and full of emotion as one thing becomes clear: I'm falling hard for this man, and there's nothing I can do to stop it.

Chapter Twenty-Five

Alice

"You're amazing," Nate informs me two days later, scaring the hell out of me because he snuck up behind me. We're at Blue Moon. It's the first corporate event we're hosting here, and I want it to run without a hitch. Blake is overseeing the bar, and I'm in charge of the restaurant and the kitchen. Nate is here as eye candy. "Just talked to Mom on the phone. She's letting me help her with this month's payment."

"Wow! I'm really glad." One of the waitresses comes to tell me about a customer complaint. "Sorry, Nate. I have to take care of this."

"Go ahead. I'll be at the bar."

I put out fire after fire the entire evening. Blake helps me out too when everyone's eating and the bar is less crowded. After dinner's over, I switch to the bar because my brother can use all the help he can get. To my surprise, Nate hops behind the counter too, lending a hand. We're so busy that we don't have time to exchange a single word.

"A gin and tonic, please," a familiar voice says in a thick British accent. Snapping my head up, I notice Colin in front of the bar. This is surprising. I haven't seen him since that last time he asked me out, months ago. I didn't know he had ties with the company who booked the event.

"Right away," I tell him with a smile. I was hoping not to see him again, but since he's here, I have to treat him like a customer. "Elegant choice. Very British."

"Someone who likes to be kissed at her workplace like a cheap whore isn't much of an authority on elegance."

His words feel like a slap. The woman to his right turns abruptly, gasping.

"That's no way to speak to a lady, young man," she chastises.

"This one's no lady, trust me." He looks at me with disdain, and a vein twitches in my temple.

"Enough," I cut in, barely keeping my rising temper in check. "I was fair to you. Don't be a dick."

The woman's jaw drops. Yeah, there goes her theory about me being a lady. Crap, I don't want to cause a scene.

"I'm sorry you were disappointed—"

"Oh, I was. Not because I necessarily wanted in your pants, but I hoped I might get an introduction to Sebastian Bennett."

I blink. "Let's move this conversation outside."

Catching Blake's attention, I gesture that I need a five-minute break, and he merely nods. Colin is lucky that Nate and my brother are too busy tending to customers to see him, or he'd be missing a few teeth already.

I step with him onto the terrace outside, leading him into a less crowded corner.

"What did you just say?"

"You thought it was a coincidence that I was in the same industry as your brother? Christ, you're not just naive, you're downright stupid. I got where I wanted without you or your brothers' help anyway. Imagine my surprise when I received the invitation for tonight's event and saw the name of the restaurant."

I curl my hands into fists, not wanting to cause a scene in front of all these people. It's been a few years since someone other than a reporter tried to get to my siblings through me. My instincts told me right from the start that something was off with Colin, and now I know why. Still, his words don't hurt any less just because he's a jerk.

"Get out of my sight, Colin." Keeping my voice low is a monumental effort, and I fight against every instinct that wants nothing more than to slap him.

"Or what? Humor me."

"Or I will forcibly remove you from here," Nate's voice booms. I hadn't seen him approaching, but judging from the tightness in his features, he heard what Colin told me. "Apologize to her, or you won't be able to talk at all tomorrow."

Nate's voice is loud enough to catch the attention of several guests. Now I'm not just angry but also mortified.

I touch Nate's arm, hoping that will convey my message that I need him to calm down. It doesn't. Nate yanks his arm away, glaring at Colin. The idiot smirks, looking between me and Nate.

"Ah, you're the TV guy who almost shagged her while I was watching. She must be a hell of a good lay if you stuck around for so long. It's sure not her brains. Dumb as they come, this one."

Nate grips Colin by his suit jacket before I even have time to blink.

"Nate!" I say in a low voice, but that's not helping much. We're attracting stares already.

"You piece of shit," Nate says. "Apologize to her."

"Nate, let him go," I say sharply. Instead, he just intensifies his grip.

Finally, Colin starts looking frightened, possibly realizing Nate isn't someone you mess with.

"I'm sorry," he squeaks.

"Now say it like you mean it," Nate says through gritted teeth.

"I apologize, Alice. I completely stepped out of line."

"Apology accepted. Nate, let him go."

Nate stares at Colin menacingly before releasing him with such force that Colin stumbles backward. Nate points at him. "You so much as look the wrong way at Alice and I'll knock your teeth out."

Colin scurries away inside without another glance, like the coward he is. The guests on the terrace are eyeing Nate and me skeptically, and I want to dig a hole in the ground and disappear inside it.

"You okay?" Nate asks, visibly calmer.

"Don't talk to me right now," I reply, once again fighting to keep my voice down. Realizing I need some fresh air—and by fresh, I mean someplace where there aren't a dozen people watching us—I head to the staircase leading down to the terrace and into the small garden surrounding the building. Nate is right behind me. I stop once I reach the bottom of the staircase, turning to Nate.

"Alice?"

"Why did you cause a scene? The guests were watching."

Nate cocks an eyebrow. "He was being a jerk to you, and he needed to apologize. I don't give a fuck about the others."

I swallow, trying to calm down. He was just defending me. "But I do. I own this restaurant, Nate. I need to make a good impression on the guests."

"So I was just supposed to hear him talk to you like that and do nothing?"

"I was handling it."

"By the smug look on his face when I joined you, you were in for another string of insults."

"I was trying to handle it diplomatically."

Nate smiles. "Not your strong suit, eh?"

"Well, no. I'm much better at being rude and straightforward, but as I said, I was trying not to cause a scene. I would've gotten rid of him eventually."

"Let me do the dirty work from time to time. You're mine, Alice. That means I'll protect you from anyone, even if you don't want me to. I'll protect you especially when you don't want me to because it's when you need it most." Before I can reply, he steps right in front of me. "You understand? You are *mine*."

I shake my head. "You're stubborn and possessive."

"Sounds like I'm a catch."

"I didn't mean those as compliments," I inform him, crossing my arms over my chest.

"That's how they sounded to me."

"How do you figure?"

"You can easily rephrase that to determined and protective. Both positive traits."

Despite my annoyance, my lips twitch with a hint of a smile.

"I won't apologize for wanting to protect you."

"I wasn't really expecting you to," I reply, disarmed by his passion and honesty. "But I'm warning you, I'm still mad at you."

"I'm counting on it, darling. In fact, hold on to the anger until we get home. Unless you want to leave now?"

"No, the event isn't over." I'm a little suspicious of his sudden good mood. "Why do you want me to hold on to the anger?"

"Because there's a kind of sex I'm dying to try with you."

"What kind is that?"

He wiggles his eyebrows, leaning in. "Make-up sex."

***

Nate

We arrive at Alice's apartment hours later, but she's still fuming. That moron stuck around for the entire event, and even though he didn't so much as go near her again, I can tell he annoyed her. It sure as hell annoyed the fuck out of me. If I had my way, I would have thrown him out of the building. With a punch, so he'd know better than to disrespect Alice again. Just remembering how he talked to her makes my blood boil. But right now, I have to set that anger aside and focus on Alice. She's my priority.

"Nate," she says once we step inside her living room, "Maybe it's best if you don't spend the night here. I'm still mad, and I'm not good company when I'm mad."

Her face is tight with suppressed anger and she keeps smoothing her hands down her dress, her fingers twitching every now and then.

"I disagree. You're great company no matter what. You've got to let all the anger out or it will eat you up."

"Nate!"

A red hue's spreading on her neck. By now, I know her enough to understand exactly what that means.

Here's the thing. Alice's skin becomes so gorgeously flushed on two occasions: when she's embarrassed and when she's pissed. Right now she's pissed, and maybe it makes me a jerk, but it's a good look on her. Alice always has fire simmering just beneath the surface, but she only unleashes it when we're in bed, or when she's mad. And it's a turn-on. I fantasize about riling her up some more, coaxing all the fire out of her, then wrestling her to bed, but it would be selfish. She needs me in other ways right now.

"If you're waiting for me to leave, you'll be disappointed."

Her eyes widen, like she was caught in the act. I've learned to read Alice's expressions like an open book.

"I have to learn to school my expression better around you," she murmurs.

"Or you can tell me what's bothering you so we can fix it."

"I don't know if there's anything to fix."

"Then we can talk about it and see where it gets us."

"I'm just mad at myself for not seeing through him right from the beginning. That I'm so *naive*."

Instantly I know what has her out of sorts, and it makes me see red. "No, you're not."

Closing the distance to her, I wrap my arms around her, hoisting her up against me, needing to make her understand.

"There will be assholes trying to take advantage of you, but you've got me to take care of them."

She frowns, looking adorable. "You want to be my personal protector?"

"Lover, protector, whatever you need."

"Okay."

Right now, she looks at me with a hopeful expression, as if she's convinced I can do no wrong, and that makes me want to be worthy of her trust forever. She has a way of making me feel like I'm a better man when I'm with her. She's mellower now, calmer, but there's more I want to tell her. "You're kind and generous, and the smartest woman I know."

Pushing her against the nearest wall, I tip her chin up, running my thumb over her lower lip before I slant my mouth against hers. She presses her delicious soft curves against me instantly, giving herself to me without restraint. This is one of the things I love most about Alice; she doesn't give her trust easily, but when she does, there's no holding back. Her soft and low sounds of pleasure reverberate in my mouth, deepening my desire for her. I want to be the one to give her pleasure for all times. I want to be the one who gives her everything she needs, who makes her smile every day.

She deserves to be happy every single day. I'd die a happy man if I have the chance to worship this woman for the rest of my days. The thought barrels into my mind so abruptly that I nearly buckle under its weight.

Of course, Alice picks up on it, pulling back a bit. "What are you thinking?" she whispers.

"Too many things."

She's only inches away from me, close enough for me to hear and feel her sharp intake of air. Her hands, which were resting on my forearms, grip me almost involuntarily.

"Good things," I reassure her, and she releases my arms. "Very good."

The corners of her lips lift up and she places them on the hollow on my neck, whispering, "I'll let you get back to them, then."

I swear the more I have of this woman, the more I want. I want it all: her fire, her sweetness. I thread my fingers in her soft hair, tugging at it as I lower my head to her neck, kissing down her collarbone and then back up until I reach her ear.

Bringing her closer to me, I bury my head in her hair. She rests her head on my chest, feeling small in my arms. And the thought of anyone making her feel small has all my protective instincts spring to life.

"You know when to kick ass and, unlike me, also when to be diplomatic," I continue.

"Thank you. When did you get so good with words?"

"It's easy with you, Alice, and I took a page out of your own book."

She pulls away, inspecting me. "What do you mean?"

"You said it's important to share things, and that if I'm mad, you want to know why. It's a two-way street, and if you push, I push back harder. What we have is beautiful and solid."

I have no idea where this is coming from, but I need to say it and she needs to hear it, so I don't hold back at all. She's everything, and all that was before her was nothing.

***

Alice

He cradles my neck, peppering my face with kisses: my forehead, my temples, each of my cheeks, then the tip of my nose. "You and me. This right here is real. So damn real."

Everything in my field of vision blurs but him. I can see him clearly.

"You have no idea how much you mean to me, Alice. No idea."

"Then tell me," I whisper, and his breath catches. I clasp his wrists with my hands while he's still touching my neck. Intertwined like this, I look him straight in the eyes. The walls have come down, the last wisps of wariness gone, and he's laying himself bare in front of me.

"I'm in love with you."

"That's a good thing because I've been falling for you for a while now."

A long while, if I'm honest, but it's only become clear to me tonight how much I love this man. I love him with an intensity that scares me and fuels me at the same time.

The corners of his mouth lift in a heartfelt smile. "I love you, and I can't believe I'm lucky enough to have you, my Alice."

My Alice. The words fill me with warmth and emotion. Rising on the tips of my toes, I plant my lips over his, desperately needing to kiss him. When he slips his tongue in my mouth, loving and exploring, I grow even greedier. I want to become one with him. I want to climb inside him and live there. Heat spears me, concentrating low in my body. It's as if his words lit a fuse and his kiss brought wildfire. I ache for him to touch me intimately, to kiss and love me.

"I need you inside me," I murmur between kisses.

"You read my mind."

In a tangle of limbs, we rid each other of clothes. I'm shaking slightly, and with surprise, I notice that he is too. When we're both buck naked, he lifts me in his arms, carrying me like we're newlyweds. Once we're in my bedroom, he carefully places me on the bed, parting my thighs. Instead of climbing over me right away, he peppers my entire body with kisses. He starts with my neck, paying special attention to the sweet spot at the base, then descends to one of my shoulders, kissing his way over my chest to the other.

He touches my breast, moving his palm in a circular stroke over my nipple until it turns so tight it's almost painful. Heavens, this man knows what he's doing. His mouth moves to my stomach, stopping at my navel, kissing it once before continuing the descent. Naively, I thought he'd go down in a straight line, directly to the prize. Instead, he veers off to one side, nibbling my hip. My fingers tug at his hair, gentle but desperate enough to show him I'm ready for more. That I *need* more.

When he hooks one of my knees over his arm, lowering his head, my sex clenches. Nate licks me where the cheek of my ass meets my upper thigh and my hips buck off the bed. Needing to grasp something more firmly, I move my hand from his hair to the bedsheet. Nate lifts his mouth, and for a few excruciating seconds, I only feel his hot exhales caressing my skin. I'm holding my breath, anticipating his next move. Leaning forward, he runs his lips over my clit.

"Nate!" I fist the sheets, all the muscles in my body contracting. I'm so wound up I might explode from foreplay alone. He teases my skin with one hand, moving in small circles on the outside of my thighs before shifting to the sensitive skin on the inside.

"You're so beautiful, my Alice."

Licking my lips, I draw a deep breath. "I like how that sounds."

"Then I'll keep saying it until it sounds silly."

"I don't think it ever will," I admit. My next words are unintelligible because Nate parts my folds with his fingers, blowing a breath on my heated flesh. I feel so very exposed right now, but I also don't feel the need to shield myself. Tonight is more raw and real than ever before.

With the first stroke of his tongue across the opening of my sex, my body turns to putty. I feel every lash of his tongue everywhere, as if every nerve in my body is wired to my core. I explode in an orgasm so powerful my entire body arches, and even my fingers and toes curl.

"Fuck, I'll never tire of making you come apart like this," Nate says.

Raising my head, I notice he's stroking his erection, and the realization that he was touching himself while pleasuring me with his mouth turns me on to no end. Though desperate to have him inside me, I move onto my knees, pushing him on his back, and say, "My turn. Keep your hands to yourself."

Instantly Nate drops his hand and I take over, stroking him with long and measured moves, dipping my head to swipe my tongue across his crown in between. His breath becomes increasingly shallower, his chest rising and falling in rapid succession. When I take his balls in one hand, licking him from the base right to the tip, he lets out a loud, almost primal grunt that vibrates through me.

"Alice! I need to be inside you. Right now."

I decide to tease him some more, right until he grips my hair, his fingers pressing on my scalp, showing me how desperate he is. The next seconds are a blur in which Nate pulls out of me, then hooks a muscle-laced arm around my stomach, flipping me on my back. His pupils are dark and dilated, desire glinting in them as his gaze rakes over me, searching.

"Take whatever you need, Nate. I'm yours."

He climbs over me, pushing my thighs together and placing his on the outside, caging them in. When he finally slides inside me, the sensation is new and powerful: tighter and somehow more intimate. My hands are at the side of my head, palms up, and Nate interlaces his fingers with mine as he begins to move inside me, slowly and lovingly.

"I love being inside you. It's all I need," he murmurs. "All I'll ever need."

His strokes become more desperate, and when he pulls out, flipping me on my stomach before grasping my hips and pulling me up on all fours, I don't complain. I relish this display of control and desperate need. He slams against me passionately and relentlessly, and I move in his rhythm, desperate for release myself. When I feel him grow inside me, his nails digging into my hips, my orgasm unfurls, traveling through me like a shock wave. It's sweet, electrifying, and all-consuming.

When we're both spent, I collapse on the bed on my stomach, feeling Nate's chest on my back, his warm breath in my ear.

"My Alice."

Chapter Twenty-Six

Nate

"Guest of honor, huh?" Clara exclaims, inspecting my invitation next Friday morning. There will be a gala tonight, and everyone working at the San Francisco branch is invited. Horowitz told me about it days ago but forgot to mention that I'm a guest of honor. I only found out when the invitation was delivered.

"Yeah, which means I have a speech to write." Which is why I'm sitting at my desk at the studio, staring at a blank document on my laptop instead of doing my job. The only good part about being a guest of honor is that I can invite one person to join me. Alice was ecstatic about it.

"And no time for it."

"Thank you, Captain Obvious."

"Well, this day can't get any crazier." As Horowitz's laughter resounds through the open door of my office, Clara jerks her head back. "I spoke too soon. What is he doing here?"

"No idea." Horowitz doesn't come down to the studios unless shit hits the fan.

Seconds later, the man himself steps inside, holding a stack of papers in his hands. "Hello, Clara. Can you give me a few minutes with Nate?"

"Sure."

She casts a worried glance my way before leaving. The moment the door closes behind her, Horowitz places the stack of papers on my desk, then claps his hands.

"Abbott quit. The London team is desperate for you to take over the job. Here's the contract. They want you to start right away."

***

Alice

The gala is in full swing by the time I arrive. I'm glad I took the extra time to let Pippa do my hair and makeup because I would've stuck out like a sore thumb if I had taken my usual low-maintenance approach. As it is, my fancy hairdo with the bright red flower that matches the red shoes do make me stand out, but in all the right ways. The venue is clearly old luxury with high ceilings and low-hanging crystal chandeliers. Round tables with exquisite tablecloths are scattered throughout the room. The centerpiece is the stage at the back for speeches.

With careful steps, I wander around, looking for Nate. The venue is packed with men wearing suits, which makes it even more difficult to identify my man.

Yeah, I'm going to repeat that a few more times in my mind because it sounds too good. *My man.*

"Well, well, if I don't have the honor to be the date of the most beautiful woman around," Nate says from behind me.

I swirl around, grinning from ear to ear. "I was desperately trying to find you, but with so many suits…."

"You, on the other hand, are very easy to notice. And very beautiful. You—"

"Nate, the man of the hour," one such suit exclaims, stepping right between us and shaking Nate's hand. "Congratulations on the London offer. Horowitz told me this morning, right after he brought you the contract. I knew Abbott wouldn't last a year. Bastard gave up less than three months into the job. You'll do great."

Nate tenses instantly. My mouth goes dry, the words feeling like whiplash. Someone calls the suit, and he takes off with a curt nod at me. I need a few seconds to gather my wits, and to steel myself.

I blink at Nate, waiting to hear what he has to say. Why didn't he tell me all of this? Granted, I just saw him, but according to the suit, he's known since this morning. He had all day. Unless he decided already and didn't know how to tell me. My stomach constricts, and I taste bile at the back of my throat just as a wave of nausea hits me. I feel so silly now in my ridiculously high shoes and with the stupid flower in my hair. No one needs to dress up to have their heart broken.

"Congratulations," I say softly, looking at my hands.

"I meant to tell you today, but I didn't want to tell you over the phone."

"Of course."

"I haven't accepted the job yet, Alice."

The key word being *yet*. Snapping my head up, I see a multitude of emotions warring on his face. Hope, fear, uncertainty. I know how much he wants this, and how much he worked for it. If there's one thing I understand, it's hard work and chasing dreams.

"But you will," I say when I finally find my voice again. "Because it's a once-in-a-lifetime opportunity, isn't it? To be at the helm of the show you idolize."

"Alice—"

"I'll watch every single episode," I promise. "You'll be great."

"Listen to me." Desperation tinges his voice, and it makes my eyes burn. "Maybe there will be other opportunities that don't require me to move an ocean away from you."

I nearly choke up. "Do you honestly believe there will be other opportunities for exactly what you want?"

His silence is my answer, and I know deep down that I can't let him give this up just to be here with me. It wouldn't be fair. Maybe he would say no anyway, but it wouldn't be right to ask. It would be selfish and inconsiderate. Even if he said yes, years from now he could resent me for it.

My mind scrambles with a solution, a way to make this work, but I come up blank. To be honest, the effort to not cry takes all my concentration—not enough neurons left to be smart. So I do the only thing that seems logical. Taking a step toward him, I rise on my tiptoes—even in heels, I'm shorter than him—and kiss his cheek once.

"You'll love London," I whisper. "And you'll do a great show. I'll watch every episode, and—" My voice cracks on the last word, but I'm persistent. "And I'll think about our time together. About how much it meant to me. To us. You'll do great, you'll see."

Nate hooks a forceful arm around my waist. "Alice, stop. Don't—"

"I need to leave now, okay?" My voice is unsteady. Nate's grip on my waist tightens. "I need you to let me go so I can do that."

"Stay."

"I don't think I can," I whisper, inhaling deeply. His scent, both earthy and fresh, fills my nostrils. When he touches my forehead with his lips, it feels like a stamp on the letter that was our love story.

"Becker," someone calls in the distance. I use it as my chance to leave. Pulling out of his grasp is easy because he doesn't resist anymore.

"I'll go with you."

"You're the guest of honor," I whisper. "You can't bail. Call me tomorrow, if you want. Or don't. It's better if you don't call. Easier."

As the suit who was calling Nate's name steps into view, I paste a plastic smile on my face, say goodbye, and then twirl around. As if through a haze, I walk toward the entrance door. My heart is pounding so hard it's making me nauseous, and my eyes are burning.

I just need to make it out of here, that's all.

Chapter Twenty-Seven

Alice

The next morning I wake up with a stiff neck and no feeling in my legs. With a groan, I press my fingers on the aching spot at the back of my neck.

I feel like a bus ran me over. Serves me right for sleeping in an armchair with my legs curled under me. My head has probably been bobbing around searching for a pillow the entire night.

When I returned home last evening, I plopped into my favorite armchair and threw my own pity party. At some point, I fell asleep, and now I have a stiff neck to show for it. God, I'm a mess. When I regain the feeling in my legs somewhat, I climb out of the armchair, heading to the bathroom.

Holy bejeezus. The reflection in the mirror belongs in a horror movie. Mascara is nice and sexy when freshly applied, but not so much after you cry yourself to sleep with it on. With a sigh and a heavy heart, I pour makeup remover on a cotton pad and clean my face, losing some eyelashes in the process. Next I shower, scrubbing my entire body before carefully shampooing and rinsing my hair twice.

When I step out of the bathroom, I might be clean, but I don't feel any less miserable. Heartbreak can't be washed away. My heart seems to have doubled in weight overnight. It hangs so heavy in my chest that I don't know what to do with myself. I swear every breath hurts.

Normally, I would call Pippa because my sister always makes everything better, but she has two babies constantly glued to her and a family who needs her. As much as I need her, it would be selfish of me to call her. Briefly I consider calling Summer, but I don't feel like relaying everything over the phone. Pep talks or commiseration only work in person. Besides, I need someone to give me a tight hug and tell me everything will be okay. You can't hug over the phone.

Resigned with having only my blanket to snuggle, I curl up in my bed, sighing. It's Saturday, which means I should be at Blue Moon, but I can't bring myself to dress up and head out in the world. The mere thought of smiling at patrons and making chitchat gives me a headache. Besides, somehow I'm sure people would take one look at me and see right through my facade. Hugging my pillow tightly, I bring my blanket to my chin and wallow.

It's early afternoon when my door buzzes, forcing me out of bed. Reluctantly, I head to the front door, wondering who it might be. Peeking through the peephole, I'm startled. It's Pippa.

What's she doing here? Did I actually call her and forget? I'm not so far gone, am I?

Gulping, I open the front door.

"Why aren't you answering your phone? I was worried."

"I was asleep, didn't hear it. Why are you worried?"

She tilts her head to one side, her hands on her hips. "I heard what happened with Nate."

"How?"

"I have my ways."

"Clara?"

"Yep."

"Then by all means, come inside and join my pity party." Leading her to my living room, I relay everything that happened last night, from Horowitz's proposal to my parting words to Nate. I thought replaying those moments in my mind would crush me further, but instead it brings a wave of relief, as if by saying them out loud I took a weight off my shoulders.

By the time I'm done, I notice I'm curled on one side on the couch. My head is in Pippa's lap, and she's stroking my hair in a soothing gesture.

"Pippa?" I ask quietly. "Why aren't you saying anything?"

"You love Nate, don't you?"

"Yes." I have the distinct feeling that my heart is crawling up my throat, obstructing my breath.

"And the man loves you. I mean, there's no denying that. I've seen the two of you together."

"Not the point." Pushing myself into a sitting position, I glance at my sister suspiciously.

"How is this not the point?"

"The point is I don't want him to think he has to choose between his dream and me."

"So you made the choice for him."

"Isn't it easier that way?" I want to call Nate because I don't like how I left things between us, but I haven't been able to muster the energy or the courage yet.

Pippa shifts closer to me, putting her delicate hand on top of mine. "Alice, you're the most determined person I know. You never choose the easy way. You always find a way to make things work. Who are you, and what have you done to my sister?"

"I could ask you the same thing. I need sugar and a lot of love. Not tough love, Pippa." My voice is almost pleading.

"I digress," she says firmly, but not unkindly. "When you find the man who makes you feel loved and cherished every day, you fight. You find solutions. He adores you. You honestly think he'll be happy without you?"

"No? Yes? I don't know? Please be my sweet, non-ass-kicking sister again. I can't think. My brain got fried sometime last night. Heartbreak sends the neurons into a coma. Why isn't there some research on this?"

"Cupcakes or donuts?"

I breathe out with relief. "Cupcakes."

"I'll be right back."

She hurries out of my apartment, her silky blonde hair bouncing around her shoulders, and returns about fifteen minutes later with bags of goodies.

"Ended up buying donuts too. They looked too delicious to just leave them there."

"That's my sister," I exclaim with a half-hearted fist pump.

For the next few hours, we stuff ourselves with carbs and sugar, talk about everything under the sun except Nate, and my sister allows me to wallow. I'm almost convinced my sweet-natured sister has kicked her tough-love tendency to the curb for the day. Oh, how deluded I was.

When the last of the donuts and cupcakes are gone, Pippa claps her hands once. I almost expect someone to pull up a curtain behind her and announce, "Showtime."

"Okay, before we go into a sugar and carb coma, we need to make a plan," she explains.

I'm sitting on the floor, in front of my couch with my knees pulled to my chest. Groaning, I watch Pippa pace around my living room, full of energy.

"Have you considered moving with him to London?"

A knot locks in my throat as I rest my chin on my knees. "Yes, but that would mean being so far away from all of you."

"You can always visit, Alice," she says gently. "Like Summer does."

"Did you consider moving with Eric to Boston?"

When Pippa met Eric, he was in San Francisco for a few months only, expanding his business on the East Coast. His life and the headquarters of his company were in Boston. In the end, he decided to remain in San Francisco.

My sister sighs, stopping her maddening pace. Just as well, because I was starting to get a headache just from watching her.

"Initially I dismissed the idea because I didn't want to be so far away from the family. But in the end, if he hadn't stayed in San Francisco, I would have moved to Boston," she says with utmost certainty.

"I have three restaurants in San Francisco though. It's not some online business I can run from anywhere. I worked hard for all of this."

Pippa is not to be deterred. She points to the ceiling, as if saying *I have an idea.*

"Where's your laptop?" she asks.

"In my room."

With a nod, she disappears into my room, returning with my laptop. She sits next to me on the floor, opening the lid. "Let's go through your daily tasks."

Licking my lips, I nod. This feels good, productive. I pull up my weekly calendar on the screen. Pippa scans through it.

"So you spend roughly half your time in telephone conferences with various marketing partners. Tourism agencies, hotels, magazines…."

"That's right. I have contracts with some, but with others it's a matter of being on friendly terms so they recommend my restaurants."

"And you do this every day?"

"Yeah, mostly in the mornings but also in the downtime between lunch and dinner. I have designated hours every day for this. The people I speak to rotate, obviously, but I like having a dedicated time to talk to them. I like my plans."

"I wish I were more like you, more organized. Instead, my plan is to put out the fire burning the brightest."

"Hey, whatever works for you is best."

"Okay, but you could do this from anywhere, right? Calling, I mean. You'll have to work around the time zone difference, but it's doable. How often do you meet in person with these people?"

"Once every few months."

"See? You could fly in."

"Yeah, but as you said, it's just half of what I do."

Pippa scrunches her nose. Oh crap, I know this reaction. She employed it rigorously when she was checking my homework way back when and found mistakes.

"Yeah, the other half needs some streamlining."

"What?" I ask defensively.

"Alice, you're a control freak."

"Gee, finally caught up to that, didn't you, Sherlock?"

She points to my screen where my weekly schedule stares back at us. I have tasks assigned for every hour.

"Let's start with the most obvious part. Why do you spend lunch and dinner in the restaurant *greeting patrons*?" She points to those two words on the screen as if they're an offense of the highest order.

"People like the personal touch. They like knowing the owner is there and really cares about them having a good time, not just about the money they spend there."

Pippa nods patiently but scrunches her nose again. "Except you have three restaurants now. Which means you have to rotate between them, so at any given time, you have customers who never see you anyway. What's the point to keep doing that?"

I run a frustrated hand through my hair, wishing we had more cupcakes. "When I expanded, I just wanted to keep the personal touch somehow."

"Alice, I love you, but from a purely business perspective, it's insanity. You're micromanaging everything. Once you expand, the personal touch goes away. It has to, or you'll kill yourself running around. You can't be in three places at the same time. Just taking away that task from your list would free up a considerable amount of time. You can't work twelve hours a day forever."

"I know," I admit in defeat.

"So after removing that, the last thing requiring your presence in the restaurants is supervising your managers. You seem to double-check everything they do. Do you not trust them?"

"I do, but I trust myself more."

"Listen, in the early days of Bennett Enterprises, I did everything in the design area from drawing to prototyping. When we grew, I obviously had to let some of my duties go. I focused on design, others on prototypes. And guess what? They messed up. Once someone cut a twelve-carat diamond in half by mistake. Once—"

"Holy crap! How the hell do you cut a diamond by mistake?"

"I still have no idea to this day. The point is people make mistakes, and they learn. Then they mess up again. It's normal. But if you don't trust them to do their job, what's the point?"

Biting the inside of my cheek, I feel a tad embarrassed. The worst one of my managers can do is order the wrong type of ingredients, or not enough, or forget to pay the bills on time, which compared to messing up a freaking diamond sounds like a fluke.

Sighing, I say, "I suppose I could have the managers hand me a daily report."

"You should at any rate. We introduced a very handy reporting tool in Bennett Enterprises last year. Christopher could tell you about it, he knows the ins and outs. You probably don't need half the options it has, but it'll be very helpful."

"I'll talk to him."

"You co-own and run one of the locations with Blake. Ask him to do some of the tasks you don't feel comfortable leaving to your location managers yet." Shoving the laptop in my lap, she adds, "Imagine you're living in London starting tomorrow. Make your daily plan based on that. Factor in spending one week every two months here. Monthly in the beginning if you need to. And don't say the airfare will cost a fortune."

"It is a point though."

"Not when Bennett Enterprises owns a private jet. Using it won't make you any less of an independent, ass-kicking woman."

"Yeah, but I don't work at Bennett Enterprises."

Pippa smirks. "You're a shareholder. If you fight me on this, I'll tell Sebastian to give you a piece of his mind."

I wince, remembering my brother's stricken expression when he realized I'm donating all the income I get from the company. For the next hundred years or so, I'm going to make sure I only give him reasons to smile. He's a great brother.

"I don't always play dirty, but when I do, it's for a good cause. Now make that plan."

Frowning, I flip the calendar to a week sometime in the future. My mind freezes for a split second upon seeing the blank screen. Chewing the inside of my cheek, I try to visualize how a typical day would look.

My fingers almost fly over the keyboard as I fill in the calendar. My pulse quickens, and for the first time since last evening, my heart feels light. Maybe we can make this work. If he wants it to.

"This looks plausible," I say once I'm done.

Pippa nods thoughtfully. "It wasn't so hard. I knew once you had a plan you'd see things differently."

"I can't decide if it's annoying or endearing that you know me so well."

Pippa bats her eyelashes, kissing my cheek. It's amazing how we change from grown-ass women to our ten-year-old selves when we're alone together. "Just looking after my sister. Now how about calling Nate and telling him everything?"

Panic coils inside of me. "What if he doesn't want me to go with him though? What if he pushes me away?"

This is possibly my greatest fear, and why I haven't called him until now.

"Ah, now we're getting to the real crux of the issue. You were the one who pushed him away, right? Were you trying to beat him to the punch or something?"

"I think so," I admit. "But maybe he agrees with me. He's not exactly banging down my door, is he?"

Pippa snorts, pushing herself off the floor and stretching her legs. I have the feeling my sister is about to kick my ass again.

"Men's egos sometimes stand in their way. You should know it—we have six brothers. That's all the research we need. After what you told him, he's probably trying to make sense of everything, licking his wounds and so on."

"Right."

"Call him."

"What if he doesn't want me to?"

"You'll have to put yourself out there and see what happens."

Chapter Twenty-Eight

Nate

"This isn't the quality it should be, Dylan," I bark, analyzing the footage he brought me. I made him re-edit it twice, but it's still not where it should be. "The last twenty seconds need more work. I want the new version in fifteen minutes."

He walks out of my office muttering expletives but I don't give a damn. I've been at the studio by myself the entire weekend working. Dylan should be grateful I didn't call him in too. The least he can do is hand me a goddamn decent edit.

I need another coffee, or ten. I haven't slept more than a handful of hours since Friday. I went through the motions after Alice left the party, but I couldn't bolt since I was a guest of honor. Then I went home and spent hours staring at the ceiling, trying to make sense of everything. I need to talk to her, damn it, but I need to wrap my head around what happened first. On Saturday morning, I came to the studio, doing the one thing I knew would take my mind off Alice—work. I repeated the whole cycle on Sunday, but I just can't sleep. The damn bed smells like her. It feels like her.

When the team showed up today at work at eight, I'd already been here since five.

"Mondays are usually shitty, but today takes the cake." Clara steps inside, hands on her hips. "What's with the barking? Half the staff looks like they're gonna cry, the other half like they're about to murder you. Should I have napkins on hand? Or a gun?"

"Jesus, Clara. Slow down."

She crosses her arms over her chest, surveying me. "Have you had breakfast?"

"Just coffee."

"Let's get out of here and get some food into you. And more coffee."

"I don't—"

"Do it for the team. They need a break from you."

"Shit. Am I that bad?"

"Yes, you are. And I never lie to you."

True. I've been taking out my anger on all of them, and they don't deserve it.

"Fine, let's go."

I swear the room sighs in unison as Clara and I cross the studio, heading toward the exit.

"Hot dogs?" she asks. "A bit hardcore in the morning."

"I don't care."

"Hot dogs it is."

We walk side by side down the stairs and out of the building, crossing the street to our usual hot dog stand. After buying two, we head to the small park behind the truck, walking around aimlessly.

"Want to tell me what's wrong?"

"You were at the gala. You know what's wrong."

"Well, I saw Alice leave, looking upset. You'll have to fill in the blanks."

The last thing I want is to talk about it, but Clara watches me like a hawk. She won't let it go, so in as few words as possible, I tell her what happened with Alice. The words come out fast, like ripping off a Band-Aid, but under it, the wound is still raw, blood gurgling out.

"Did you talk to her since?" Clara asks, her voice softer now.

"No."

Clara cocks a brow. "Why not?"

"What part of 'don't call me' wasn't clear to you? Was clear as day to me." I opened myself up to Alice in a way I haven't done with anyone before, and clearly it was a mistake. Even so, I can't deny I want to talk to her. We have a great thing, and I don't want to give up on us.

"This might come as a surprise to you, but people sometimes don't say out loud the things they really want to say."

"What's that supposed to mean?"

"I bet what Alice really meant was 'please call me as soon as possible, declare your undying love and grow old next to me.'"

A young woman pushing a stroller passes us, throwing us a startled look. Yeah, I'm about as confused as she is.

I stare at Clara, my head spinning. "Are you pulling my leg right now?"

She shakes her head, muttering under her breath something that sounds a lot like "Men are so clueless."

"I'm being serious."

"What part of the things she told me led you to that conclusion?"

"Look, you and Alice have known each other for years."

"How is this relevant?"

"Because during that time she saw you chase around the world for opportunities. She knew how much you wanted this."

"Still not following."

We come to a halt in front of a small clearing where a group is practicing yoga, or whatever requires them to put their legs around their necks.

"She knew this was your dream, and she thought you'd choose the job over her. Maybe she was just afraid of getting hurt."

"But I told her I hadn't accepted the job yet."

Clara smiles tightly. "She probably thought you'd eventually resent her if you gave up on your dream for her."

"How do women manage to have entire conversations in their head in the time it takes me to decide if I'll drink a whiskey or a gin tonic?"

"We're fast thinkers. Get with the program, Nate. Anyway, saying 'yet' is not exactly reassuring. I've known you for three years, but even I'd bet that 'yet' changes into 'I'm moving tomorrow.' Maybe she just wanted a graceful, dignified exit."

"What if she just wanted an exit?" I push. "She didn't even consider a solution, like long-distance or moving with me."

"That just tells me she has great self-preservation skills. Get out before there's a chance of being turned down or pushed away."

"Women are complicated creatures," I say in frustration.

Clara flashes me a grin. "I'll simplify it for you. What do you want?"

"I want Alice in my life. I don't care how. And yes, as improbable as it might seem to you, I actually did think about turning down the job."

Clara opens her mouth, then closes it again. This might be the first time she doesn't have any comeback.

"I mean, I get paid a truckload of money for what I do now here. What's the point of always chasing the next thing? The people I care about are here—"

"Who are you, and what have you done with Nate Becker? Alice has been an excellent influence on you. Talk to her."

"What if you're wrong," I insist, "and she just doesn't want any of this?"

"You'll have to man up and accept it." Pressing her palms together and lacing her fingers, she adds, "Go out on a limb and take a chance, Nate. Call her. Where's your phone?"

"At the office. Turned it off on Saturday. Horowitz was starting to annoy me with his calls."

"Ah yes, he's pretty desperate for you to take the job."

I feel more alert than I have in hours. "I have no plan."

Looking behind me, Clara presses her lips together. "Then think fast, or improvise. As your assistant, it's my duty to tell you that improvisation isn't your strongest skill unless you're trying to entertain a crowd, so think fast."

"Why?"

"Two of the Bennett brothers are hurrying toward us. They look pissed."

"Took them no time at all."

"Don't worry, they have no guns. Just very pointy pitchforks."

Glancing behind me, I see no sign of any Bennett brothers.

"I was just messing with you," Clara says when I turn to her again. "You work best under pressure. Figured you'd come up with a plan in no time then."

"You're unbelievable."

She shrugs. "Was worth a shot. Though I *am* surprised that none of the Bennett brothers are here kicking your ass."

"I'm completely innocent here."

"You don't understand how the brother rule works. Sister meets man. Sister is brokenhearted. The conclusion is man must be beaten to a pulp."

"I did always love your knack for simplifying things. My bet is Alice didn't tell them. She's one who prefers to fight her own battles. Or in this case… bolt."

"Do you love her?"

"Damn right, I do."

"Then you'll figure it out. Now, not to toot my own horn, but my improvisation skills are great. If you were, say, to need to take the rest of your day off, I could step in and convince everyone you had a legitimate reason for leaving. You could stay and wrap the day, of course, but I'd hate to see you bite someone's head off. I have a hunch that aggressive streak rearing its ugly head today won't subside until you talk to Alice. Take the day off. It's for the good of the team."

"You know what your special skill is? Talking so much that you confuse anyone to the point they agree with you just so you stop. But I do want to take the day off. Are you sure you can handle things here?"

"I owe you for many things. Go! I'll take care of everything here."

Chapter Twenty-Nine

Alice

"You're going to cut your fingers." Tim, my Blue Moon chef and all around savior, hovers around me as I'm dicing chili peppers for a marinade. Tim has been feeding me delicious things all day. Delicious and healthy things, which makes him a superhero in my book. It's like he could see the heartbreak written all over me since I stepped into Blue Moon today. "No one wants marinade with a side of fingers."

"Ew, I didn't need the visual."

"Neither do the customers, so let someone else do the dicing."

I contemplate arguing, but the truth is my mind has been wandering every ten seconds. Nate has taken over my thoughts. I called him on Saturday, but it went straight to voice mail, and I haven't tried calling him since. I figured he'd contact me when he sees it. No sign from him yet, so he still hasn't turned on his phone, or—I refuse to consider another option. Yeah, I'm stubborn.

I'm giving him two more hours. If I don't hear from him, I'm taking matters into my own hands and will seek him out.

"Alice, there's someone asking for you," one of the servers says, poking his head inside the kitchen. My heart leaps in my throat. It could be anyone from a delivery person to a patron, but I can't keep myself from hoping.

"I'll be right out."

First I wash my hands; there's no worse way to doom a conversation—professional or romantic—than by accidentally rubbing your eyes after cutting chili peppers.

My palms become clammy as I walk into the dining area. Drawing in a deep breath, I berate myself for being downright ridiculous. But when I spot Nate pacing in front of the entrance, my breath catches. Tall and steady, his delicious gaze rakes over me immediately. I close the distance to him with quick steps, smiling at the customers on the way. When I come to a halt in front of him, my pulse is frantic.

"Hi."

"Hi back. Sorry, I turned off my phone over the weekend, so I only saw your call today. Thought about calling back, then decided to do this in person."

"You came here. It's all that matters. Let's go outside." Some of the customers are watching us curiously, and I want this talk to be private. Outside on the deck, the air is more biting than crisp, and I shudder involuntarily.

"Here." Nate shrugs out of his jacket, draping it around my shoulders.

"No, I'm okay. You—"

"Don't start fighting me, Alice."

"Fine." Drawing in a deep breath, I add, "I'm sorry I left on Friday."

"I'm sorry I didn't stop you."

I open my mouth but Nate brings his hand to my face, placing his thumb against my lips. "I'll speak first."

"Always so bossy," I mutter around his thumb, then press my lips together because I'm dying to hear him out.

"I'll talk to Horowitz and turn down the job in London. I don't want to be away from you, Alice. What you and I have is special, and I won't let this go. I'll figure everything out, I promise."

My heart drums frantically in my chest, the pounding echoing in my ears. "So, can I talk now, or are you going to boss me around some more?"

He tilts his head to one side, as if this decision requires all his concentration power. "I'm tempted to boss you around some more, just because I love seeing your reaction. But what you were going to say?"

Clearing my throat, I suddenly feel anxious again. The skin at the back of my head prickles, and my mouth has dried up.

"I don't want you to give up on your dream. I can manage my restaurants even from London. I'd have to fly in a week every two months or so, maybe more in the beginning because I'll miss my family like crazy, but—"

Nate jerks his head back, clearly not having expected this. "Are you serious?"

I nod eagerly. "I made a plan, simulating how my workdays could look. There are some details to streamline, but it looks possible."

The corners of his mouth twitch, his eyes glinting. "You made a plan?"

"Yeah."

"When?"

"Over the weekend."

He stares at me thoughtfully for a few seconds before shaking his head. "You are incredible. I've barely processed what happened on Friday over the weekend. Clara was right. Women think at a different speed than men."

"Clara is a smart girl. In the interest of honesty, Pippa came by my house on Saturday and encouraged me to do it. Once I had it all in front of me, I realized I could make it work. I'll *make* it work, because I want you to live your dream, and I want to be next to you when that happens."

Bringing his other hand up, he splays his fingers on my jaw and my cheek, squeezing lightly. "Do you mean this?"

"Every word."

We're standing near the edge of the deck. The water in front of us is glinting beautifully, reflecting the weak sunrays.

Dropping my voice, I whisper, "I'm going to tell you a secret."

He flashes me a cocky smirk. "You can't imagine your life without me?"

"With the risk of my admission going to your head, yes. But also, I even considered up and leaving, with no plan, just to be with you."

"I'd take care of you, always. I love you, Alice."

"Can you say that again?"

"I love you. For years, I wasn't feeling at home anywhere. Now I feel at home whenever you're with me. You're my home, Alice."

He lowers his hand from my face to my waist, pulling me to him. Goose bumps form on my arms instantly. Sighing, I cocoon against him, inhaling his delicious scent. I don't think I'll ever get my fill of him. Then he wraps both arms around my waist, bringing me closer still. Dipping his head, he buries his nose in my hair, right below my ear. And then he takes in a breath so deep it makes my knees weak. It's like he hasn't taken a deep breath in days. When his lips touch my neck lightly, I warm all over.

"My family is going to go berserk when I tell them I'm moving to London," I whisper. "After they calm down, they'll be happy for us."

"Hmm, I know something that might soften the news."

"Do tell."

"I'll ask them for your hand."

I gasp in surprise, pulling back so I can look straight at him.

"What?"

"Marry me, Alice."

My mind doesn't process his words right away, but when it does, my entire body reacts. Butterflies roam in my belly and a bolt of energy zips down my spine, extending to my limbs until my toes curl and the tips of my fingers prickle with excitement.

"Is there a question mark anywhere?" I tease.

"Nah, not my style." Pushing a rebel strand of hair behind my ear, he lingers with his fingers at my earlobe. "I want you to be my fiancée when we move to London."

"When's the job starting?"

"Theoretically right away, but I can negotiate to start next week."

My jaw drops. "That's gonna require a lot of planning."

"Luckily you're a planning genius."

Tilting his head forward, he brings his mouth to mine, swiping his tongue once over my lips before sealing his lips over my mouth. The kiss is explosive and all-consuming, taking my breath away. Fisting the lower hem of his shirt with both hands, I pull him to me, flattening myself against his chest. I become greedier by the second, wishing I could feel his skin against mine, wishing we could disappear under blankets and only resurface in a few days, or weeks.

"So that's a yes?" he whispers when we pull apart. The door of the restaurant swings open and a couple steps out. They nod at us politely before stepping onto the narrow path leading to the outer gate.

Once they're out of earshot, I eye Nate.

"No question, no answer." I shrug one shoulder playfully before crossing my arms over my chest. "Everyone will think we're hurrying because you knocked me up."

He kisses my forehead and then my temple, feathering his lips down my cheek all the way to the tip of my nose. I barely restrain myself from smothering him with kisses. If I kiss him again, I won't be able to stop.

"No problem. We can start with that project right after I put a ring on your finger."

Pushing myself away from his grasp, I shake my head, hoping to clear it. I firmly believe this man can get me to agree to anything if he focuses his smoldering gaze on me long enough.

"By the way, about the engagement ring—"

"I'll buy it from Bennett Enterprises. Didn't even occur to me to go to the competition."

"Would be a pretty serious incentive to say no when you pop the question."

He sighs. "You won't let me off the hook, will you?"

"Of course not. You have to drop on one knee, open the lid, pop the question."

"You just moved from closet romantic to full-on romantic."

I flash a grin. "I know. I'm not even sorry."

"Any other requests?"

“I want an epic bachelorette party. But the girls will see to that.”

Epilogue

Alice

One year later

"This is epic," I exclaim, my eyes glued to my laptop screen.

"You'll have to close that for takeoff. And you've seen it half a dozen times."

"I think a dozen comes closer." After mine and Blake's episode on *Delicious Dining* aired months ago, the network decided it was so good, they'll do another one. Blake did it, and it *finally* aired last week. I loved it. I've been rewatching it quite a few times. We're taking off toward San Francisco, and the flight attendant has already told me to close my laptop once. "I'll just watch this bit, and then I'll put it away."

Nate kisses my temple but doesn't argue. Smart man. Our life in London is hectic but beautiful. Our apartment is lovely. I fly out to San Francisco about every six weeks, not only for work purposes but also because I have withdrawals if I don't see my family often. Sometimes, like now, Nate joins me and we have a full program, visiting both my family and his mom. No matter if we're in San Francisco or in London, when we're together, everything feels right, balanced. Sometimes to find your balance, you have to put yourself out there, not hold back at all, no matter how scary that might seem.

Managing the restaurants from afar is a challenge, but I've learned to love it. It keeps me on my toes, drives me to focus on the essential parts. Besides, I took Pippa's advice and asked Blake if he'd mind helping me manage all the locations, and he immediately agreed. We're equal partners in the business now, and my little brother does me proud. Which doesn't mean I can't tease him when he makes an ass of himself on TV. There is a particular moment in the episode that I keep rewatching and laughing at every time.

When I finally put my laptop away, Nate says, "You're not going to let Blake live it down, will you?"

"Of course not. It's my duty as a sister to tease him."

Nate takes my hand, kissing my knuckles and then the back of my hand, lighting up my nerve endings. Thank heavens this is a twin seat, because if we had a neighbor I'd be afraid he could feel me heating up. When Nate catches me eyeing the engagement ring on my finger, I smile sheepishly.

"Admiring the ring again?" he asks.

"It's a great ring." One month after moving to London, Nate surprised me by officially asking me to marry him. Got on one knee, popped the question, and gave me the most beautiful ring—a classic princess cut in white gold, but with a green sapphire instead of a diamond. I absolutely love it.

"Can't wait to put another one on your finger."

"We have to wait until after the twins' weddings." Christopher and Victoria announced they want to get married this year. Shortly after, Max and Emilia set the date too, also for this year. That means we'll wait a while, because three weddings in one year is too much, even for my family.

"Or I could use my persuasion skills." He wiggles his eyebrows, holding my gaze captive with his.

"No, you can't use your *bedroom stare* when we're in public. Absolutely not. We agreed."

"You don't make the rules, fiancée."

His voice sends tendrils of heat all over my body, and I'm starting to understand the benefits of a private jet. Despite my siblings' insistences, I refused to use the company's jet because it still doesn't feel right, no matter what they say. So here I am, captive to his charms, *in public.*

Unable to form a witty comeback, I resort to elbowing him slightly. Just then a flight attendant passes us, asking if there's anything we need and reminding us to shut off our phones. Before I do, I send my mother a quick message, letting her know we're taking off on time. We're heading straight to their house from the airport, where she's hosting a family dinner.

"Oh, that reminds me. Clara is going to be at dinner too," Nate states. "She's slowly becoming an adopted Bennett."

Clara has become very close to my family indeed. It's endearing to watch her with them. After having lost her parents so young and spending most of her childhood in group homes, I think she's a little overwhelmed by the size of the family, not to mention our shenanigans. And I'd agree with Nate, except I have my doubts. Adopted Bennett is a moniker my family came up with years ago for close friends—*platonic* friends. The last few times Clara attended family events, I caught Blake giving her some very non-platonic looks. They were downright hot.

Now, I don't want to get ahead of myself, but I'm fairly certain my dearest brother is the next to fall. If not, Pippa and I are more than happy to give him a push.

Other Books by Layla Hagen

The Bennett Family Series

Book 1: Your Irresistible Love

Sebastian Bennett is a determined man. It's the secret behind the business empire he built from scratch. Under his rule, Bennett Enterprises dominates the jewelry industry. Despite being ruthless in his work, family comes first for him, and he'd do anything for his parents and eight siblings—even if they drive him crazy sometimes. . . like when they keep nagging him to get married already.

Sebastian doesn't believe in love, until he brings in external marketing consultant Ava to oversee the next collection launch. She's beautiful, funny, and just as stubborn as he is. Not only is he obsessed with her delicious curves, but he also finds himself willing to do anything to make her smile.
He's determined to have Ava, even if she's completely off limits.

Ava Lindt has one job to do at Bennett Enterprises: make the next collection launch unforgettable. Daydreaming about the hot CEO is definitely not on her to-do list. Neither is doing said CEO. The consultancy she works for has a strict policy—no fraternizing with clients. She won't risk her job. Besides, Ava knows better than to trust men with her heart.

But their sizzling chemistry spirals into a deep connection that takes both of them by surprise. Sebastian blows through her defenses one sweet kiss and sinful touch at a time. When Ava's time as a consultant in his company comes to an end, will Sebastian fight for the woman he loves or will he end up losing her?

Book 2: Your Captivating Love

Logan Bennett knows his priorities. He is loyal to his family and his company. He has no time for love, and no desire for it. Not after a disastrous engagement left him brokenhearted. When Nadine enters his life, she turns everything upside down.

She's sexy, funny, and utterly captivating. She's also more stubborn than anyone he's met…including himself.

Nadine Hawthorne is finally pursuing her dream: opening her own clothing shop. After working so hard to get here, she needs to concentrate on her new business, and can't afford distractions. Not even if they come in the form of Logan Bennett.

He's handsome, charming, and doesn't take no for an answer. After bitter disappointments, Nadine doesn't believe in love. But being around Logan is addicting. It doesn't help that Logan's family is scheming to bring them together at every turn.

Their attraction is sizzling, their connection undeniable. Slowly, Logan wins her over. What starts out as a fling, soon spirals into much more than they are prepared for.

When a mistake threatens to tear them apart, will they have the strength to hold on to each other?

AVAILABLE ON ALL RETAILERS.

Book 3: Your Forever Love

Eric Callahan is a powerful man, and his sharp business sense has earned him the nickname 'the shark.' Yet under the strict façade is a man who loves his daughter and would do anything for her. When he and his daughter move to San Francisco for three months, he has one thing in mind: expanding his business on the West Coast. As a widower, Eric is not looking for love. He focuses on his company, and his daughter.

Until he meets Pippa Bennett. She captivates him from the moment he sets eyes on her, and what starts as unintentional flirting soon spirals into something neither of them can control.

Pippa Bennett knows she should stay away from Eric Callahan. After going through a rough divorce, she doesn't trust men anymore. But something about Eric just draws her in. He has a body made for sin and a sense of humor that matches hers. Not to mention that seeing how adorable he is with his daughter melts Pippa's walls one by one.

The chemistry between them is undeniable, but the connection that grows deeper every day that has both of them wondering if love might be within their reach.

When it's time for Eric and his daughter to head back home, will he give up on the woman who has captured his heart, or will he do everything in his power to remain by her side?

AVAILABLE ON ALL RETAILERS.

Book 4: Your Inescapable Love

Max Bennett is a successful man. His analytical mind has taken his family's company to the next level. Outside the office, Max transforms from the serious business man into someone who is carefree and fun. Max is happy with his life and doesn't intend to change it, even though his mother keeps asking for more grandchildren. Max loves being an uncle, and plans to spoil his nieces rotten.

But when a chance encounter reunites him with Emilia, his childhood best friend, he starts questioning everything. The girl he last saw years ago has grown into a sensual woman with a smile he can't get out of his mind.

Emilia Campbell has a lot on her plate, taking care of her sick grandmother. Still, she faces everything with a positive attitude. When the childhood friend she hero-worshipped steps into her physical therapy clinic, she is over the moon. Max is every bit the troublemaker she remembers, only now he has a body to drool over and a smile to melt her panties. Not that she intends to do the former, or let the latter happen.

They are both determined not to cross the boundaries of friendship…at first. But as they spend more time together, they form an undeniable bond and their flirty banter spirals out of control.

Max knows Emilia is off-limits, but that only makes her all the more tempting. Besides, Max was never one to back away from a challenge.

When their chemistry becomes too much to resist and they inevitably give in to temptation, will they risk losing their friendship or will Max and Emilia find true love?

AVAILABLE ON ALL RETAILERS.

Book 5: Your Tempting Love

Christopher Bennett is a persuasive man. With his magnetic charm and undeniable wit, he plays a key role in the international success of his family's company.

Christopher adores his family, even if they can be too meddling sometimes… like when attempt to set him up with Victoria, by recommending him to employ her decorating services. Christopher isn't looking to settle down, but meeting Victoria turns his world upside down. Her laughter is contagious, and her beautiful lips and curves are too tempting.

Victoria Hensley is determined not to fall under Christopher's spell, even though the man is hotter than sin, and his flirty banter makes her toes curl. But as her client, Christopher is off limits. After her parents' death, Victoria is focusing on raising her much younger siblings, and she can't afford any mistakes. . .

But Victoria and Christopher's chemistry is not just the sparks-flying kind. . .It's the downright explosive kind. Before she knows it, Christopher is training her brother Lucas for soccer tryouts and reading bedtime stories to her sister Chloe.

Victoria wants to resist him, but Christopher is determined, stubborn, and oh-so-persuasive.

When their attraction and connection both spiral out of control, will they be able to risk it all for a love that is far too tempting?

AVAILABLE ON ALL RETAILERS.

The Lost Series

***

Lost in Us: The story of James and Serena

There are three reasons tequila is my new favorite drink.

• One: my ex-boyfriend hates it.

• Two: downing a shot looks way sexier than sipping my usual Sprite.

• Three: it might give me the courage to do something my ex-boyfriend would hate even more than tequila—getting myself a rebound

The night I swap my usual Sprite with tequila, I meet James Cohen. The encounter is breathtaking. Electrifying. And best not repeated.

James is a rich entrepreneur. He likes risks and adrenaline and is used to living the high life. He's everything I'm not.

But opposites attract. Some say opposites destroy each other. Some say opposites are perfect for each other. I don't know what will James and I do to each other, but I can't stay away from him. Even though I should.

AVAILABLE ON ALL RETAILERS.

***

Found in Us: The story of Jessica and Parker

Jessica Haydn wants to leave her past behind. Hurt by one too many heartbreaks, she vows not to fall in love again. Especially not with a man like Parker, whose electrifying pull and smile bruised her ego once before. But his sexy British accent makes her crave his touch, and his blue eyes strip Jessica of all her defenses.

Parker Blakesley has no place for love in his life. He learned the hard way not to trust. He built his business empire by avoiding distractions, and using sheer determination and control. But something about Jessica makes him question everything. Not only has she a body made for sin, but her laughter fills a void inside of him.

The desire igniting between them spirals into an unstoppable passion, and so much more. Soon, neither can fight their growing emotional connection. But can two scarred souls learn to trust again? And when a mistake threatens to tear them apart, will their love be strong enough?

AVAILABLE ON ALL RETAILERS.

***

Caught in Us: The story of Dani and Damon

Damon Cooper has all the markings of a bad boy:

- A tattoo
- A bike
- An attitude to go with point one and two

In the beginning I hated him, but now I'm falling in love with him. My parents forbid us to be together, but Damon's not one to obey rules. And since I met him, neither am I.

AVAILABLE ON ALL RETAILERS.

***

Standalone USA TODAY BESTSELLER
Withering Hope

Aimee's wedding is supposed to turn out perfect. Her dress, her fiancé and the location—the idyllic holiday ranch in Brazil—are perfect.

But all Aimee's plans come crashing down when the private jet that's taking her from the U.S. to the ranch—where her fiancé awaits her—defects mid-flight and the pilot is forced to perform an emergency landing in the heart of the Amazon rainforest.

With no way to reach civilization, being rescued is Aimee and Tristan's—the pilot—only hope. A slim one that slowly withers away, desperation taking its place. Because death wanders in the jungle under many forms: starvation, diseases. Beasts.

As Aimee and Tristan fight to find ways to survive, they grow closer. Together they discover that facing old, inner agonies carved by painful pasts takes just as much courage, if not even more, than facing the rainforest.

Despite her devotion to her fiancé, Aimee can't hide her feelings for Tristan—the man for whom she's slowly becoming everything. You can hide many things in the rainforest. But not lies. Or love.

Withering Hope is the story of a man who desperately needs forgiveness and the woman who brings him hope. It is a story in which hope births wings and blooms into a love that is as beautiful and intense as it is forbidden.

AVAILABLE ON ALL RETAILERS.

***

Published: Layla Hagen 2017
Cover: http://designs.romanticbookaffairs.com/

***

Acknowledgements

There are so many people who helped me fulfil the dream of publishing, that I am utterly terrified I will forget to thank someone. If I do, please forgive me. Here it goes.

First, I'd like to thank my beta readers, Jessica, Dee, Andrea, Carrie, Jill, Kolleen and Rebecca. You made this story so much better!!

I want to thank every blogger and reader who took a chance with me as a new author and helped me spread the word. You have my most heartfelt gratitude. To my street team. . .you rock !!!

Last but not least, I would like to thank my family. I would never be here if not for their love and support. Mom, you taught me that books are important, and for that I will always be grateful. Dad, thank you for always being convinced that I should reach for the stars.

To my sister, whose numerous ahem. . .legendary replies will serve as an inspiration for many books to come, I say thank you for your support and I love you, kid.

To my husband, who always, no matter what, believed in me and supported me through all this whether by happily taking on every chore I overlooked or accepting being ignored for hours at a time, and most importantly encouraged me whenever I needed it: I love you and I could not have done this without you.

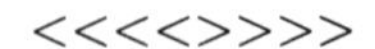

CPSIA information can be obtained
at www.ICGtesting.com
Printed in the USA
LVOW10s1528050517
533411LV00001B/56/P